# THE SÉANCE

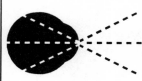

This Large Print Book carries the
Seal of Approval of N.A.V.H.

# THE SÉANCE

## HEATHER GRAHAM

**THORNDIKE PRESS**

*An imprint of Thomson Gale, a part of The Thomson Corporation*

**THOMSON**

**GALE**

Detroit • New York • San Francisco • New Haven, Conn. • Waterville, Maine • London

THOMSON

GALE™

**LIBRARY OF CONGRESS CATALOGING-IN-PUBLICATION DATA**

Graham, Heather.
    The Séance / by Heather Graham.
       p. cm. — (Thorndike Press large print basic)
    ISBN-13: 978-0-7862-9796-2 (alk. paper)
    ISBN-10: 0-7862-9796-4 (alk. paper)
    1. Spiritualism — Fiction. 2. Serial murders — Fiction. 3. Orlando (Fla.) —
Fiction. 4. Large type books. 5. Ghost stories. I. Title.
    PS3557.R198S38 2008
    813'.54—dc22                                                    2007038736

Published in 2008 by arrangement with Harlequin Books S.A.

Printed in the United States of America on permanent paper
10 9 8 7 6 5 4 3 2 1

For Mary Walkley, with many thanks
for many things,
and with very best wishes to
Leigh Collett

# PROLOGUE

Christie opened her eyes.

Everything seemed to be as it should be. The small porcelain clock on the mantel — Gran's favorite, brought over from Ireland — sat in its place, the seconds ticking away softly. A night-light burned in the bathroom, because she didn't like total darkness.

The air conditioner hummed.

The clock chimed softly.

It was midnight.

Then she realized what was wrong. Granda was in the room. He was watching her from the old white rocker that faced her bed. He was smoking his old pipe and rocking gently, and he smiled as she opened her eyes.

"Granda?" she murmured.

"Ah, girl, I woke you," he said. "I didna mean to do so."

"It's okay, Granda," she told him, curious. "Is anything wrong?"

"No, my girl, just the way it is," he said, and he leaned toward her. "I want you to be good to Gran, that's all, Christie. Be there for her."

She almost laughed aloud in protest. She was twelve years old, and she didn't even live near Gran, so she could hardly be much help to her. "I'm a kid, Granda," she reminded him. "I can't even go to the mall by myself."

She was rewarded with one of his deep and endearing smiles. "So y'are young, girl, so y'are. But children can give a lot of love."

She frowned, surprised suddenly that he looked so good, and that he was so calm, just sitting there, rocking, the pleasant odor of his pipe tobacco so strong. Gran had been on him about that pipe lately. And he had tried to stop smoking it to please her, which had been easy enough, since he'd been sick in bed so much lately. That was why she was there then, actually, when she should have been back home and going to school. They had come up to help Gran. Of course, Gran wasn't alone. Christie's uncle, her mother's brother, and his wife and two sons lived in the area, but Christie suspected that her grandmother needed her mother. Certainly her mother believed that daughters had more of a bond with their parents

8

— or maybe daughters were just more useful.

"She should know it, aye, she should, but you make sure she knows I love her, eh?" Granda said.

"Oh, Granda. She knows."

"And your mom, too. But she has your da, and he's a good man."

"Mom loves you, too, Granda," Christie said firmly, feeling it was important that he really understood that.

"Aye. And you love me, too, eh, moppet?"

"Of course!"

"Gran is the one who will miss me most."

"What are you going on about, Granda? You're not going anywhere!"

"Be there for her," he said, then rose and set his pipe on the mantel. He came to the bed, sat by her side and scooped her into his arms against his chest, and held her as he had often done when reading her a story — or making one up. She seldom knew what was true and what wasn't, because Granda had, so Gran told her, the gift of blarney. But she loved him and loved his stories, and all her friends loved him, too, because he had such a way with the tales he'd brought over from the old country.

He smoothed back her hair. "The Irish are special," he told her. "They have the gift of sight."

She remembered one time when Granda had said so in front of her father. He had remarked dryly, "Ummhmm. Special. Give 'em a fifth of whiskey and they've got the sight, all right."

Granda hadn't been angry; he'd laughed right along with her father. Her dad hadn't been born in Ireland, like her mom, but his parents had been born there. And even though she wasn't quite a teenager, she was very aware of what went on around her.

A lot of their Irish friends did have a habit of consuming whiskey.

"Guard your gift," Granda said softly to her.

"Oh, Granda, I'm too young to drink," she told him. "Honestly."

He laughed. "I mean the gift of sight, y'little sass," he told her playfully. "I have to go, Christie. But I'm all right. You let Gran know that, okay?"

"Where are you going?" she asked him.

"Somewhere beautiful," he said. "Where all wars cease, where God sees goodness, not religion. Where the grass is as ever green as that I knew in Eire."

The way he spoke was scaring her. She hated when anyone talked about death. She knew that her grandparents were older, that

10

things happened. But she always thought as long as she was cheerful and convinced them that they were still young, nothing could go very wrong. "A place that beautiful?" she teased. "We should go with you."

" 'Tis not to be, not now," he said. "All in time. Gran will meet me one day. Till then, you give her what she needs."

He smoothed her hair again. Then he frowned for a moment, looking around.

"What is it, Granda?" she asked.

He shook his head. "Ah, well, 'tis all new to me, but it seems . . . well, there are many doors. Indeed, I have opened a new door. No reason to worry, moppet." He held her close, smiling tenderly. "You just remember all I've said to ye, me little girl." Cradling her, he began to sing an old lullaby. Granda had a great voice. He'd never been a performer — except in pubs — but he could have been, she thought proudly. He didn't think a thing of his talent — all Irish men could be tenors, if they chose, in his opinion.

As he held her, singing, she drifted off to sleep.

In the morning she heard the soft sound of tears coming from the parlor. It was a parlor in this house, and not a living room, like she had in Miami. Her grandparents had

11

bought the place before so much of Orlando had been bought up by the Disney Company, then hotel and restaurant chains, and other mega-entertainment companies. It was one of the really old houses in the area, one of the very few that had been there before the Civil War — or the War of Northern Aggression, as some of Granda's friends liked to call it. It had been falling to ruin when they had found it, which was why they had been able to afford it. They called it a Victorian manor. Christie's two cousins — even though they were boys — found it creepy. She loved it — but then, she loved her grandparents, and they never insisted that she turn off all the lights.

Now it was daylight. But even from her upstairs bedroom, she could hear the soft sound of sobbing down in the parlor.

She stepped from the bed and hurried to the top of the stairs. She heard her father's voice first. "Mary, Seamus is at peace now. He's at peace."

"Hush now, Sean," her mother said to her father. "Mom knows that. We'll all be crying just because we miss him so."

Gran suddenly looked up the staircase, looking sad but strong. Gran always looked strong. She held out her arms. "Christie, girl."

12

Christie ran down the stairs to sit on her grandmother's lap, and hugged her, frowning. "Gran? What is it?"

"Granda. He — he's gone."

"Gone?" Christie said with a frown. Then her memories of the night washed over her like a wave. "Oh . . . he told me that he had to go."

There was a strange silence. "When you were at his bedside, Christie?" her father asked.

"No, Dad. Last night. He was in my room, smoking his pipe, sitting in the rocker. He told me that he had to go, and that you'd meet him in time, Gran. He said that I needed to be here for you. He said it would be green, like Eire. And . . ."

Again there was silence. Moments later there were people at the door. Her grandmother set her down as the paramedics and police entered. Christie frowned, wondering why the police were there, then found herself forgotten as the paramedics hurried up the stairs. She followed. Someone asked Gran what had happened; she explained that she had awakened to find him cold.

"He's been dead for hours, since at least midnight," someone else said. Then someone got on the phone with Granda's doctor, and Christie realized that since he had "passed" at home, they had to make sure Gran hadn't killed him.

Christie was appalled.

But it was only then that she realized the rock-bottom truth of it.

Granda had gone.

Granda was dead.

But he had been in her room!

After midnight.

Her mother saw her and took her hand. Her mother was sobbing, and Christie felt her pain, her own sense of loss, but somehow, hers wasn't as bad. Granda had been at peace, ready to live in a land that was as green as Eire again.

"Mom, it's all right, it's all right," she said urgently.

Her mother was distracted and didn't seem to really hear her. "He was ill," she whispered. "In pain. And now . . . he's not."

"I saw him, Mom. Last night. He loves you all so much. He said he's fine, and he wants you to be fine, too."

"Out of the mouths of babes," her father said gently. "Hey, it's cold today, young lady. You need slippers."

"I'll take her," her mother said.

Her mother walked with her to the room, still distracted, crying, quietly now, the tears sliding down her face.

When they reached Christie's room, her mother paused and stared at Christie, frowning. "I . . . I can almost smell his tobacco in here."

"He was here. With me. I told you that, Mom."

Her mother looked at her then as if hearing her for the first time. She forgot all about slippers as she paled and walked away.

That night, the Irish of the area came. First and foremost the family, of course, her uncle and aunt and her cousins, all in mourning, the boys, who were slightly older than Christie, looking very mature and somber, and being tender and even courteous to her.

Granda had left explicit instructions. He was not to be mourned. His life was to be celebrated in the old way. So his cronies also came, and they drank beer, and they lamented, but they celebrated, too, telling stories, drinking more beer. Granda's family did him proud, hosting all those who had loved him the way it was done in the old country.

Seamus Michael McDuff was buried three days later.

At the gravesite, everyone cried. He had been seventy, had had a full life. He'd come from Ireland to the United States with his wife, his daughter and his son, and he'd created a good home for them. He'd been a pastry chef, and he'd worked very hard and saved his money, and finally he'd opened his own restaurant, where he also employed his Irish knack for a ditty and blarney, entertaining as well as feeding many people. He'd loved God and his family; he'd been a good man.

It was while the ancient Irish bagpipes were emitting the mournful notes of a lament that Christie saw him again.

Most people were standing, but Gran was still seated when he went to her side, touched her hair and whispered into her ear.

Gran looked up, startled, frowning. Then it seemed to Christie that the hint of a wistful smile shone through her tears.

Granda turned, as if aware that Christie was watching, and winked. He looked so healthy. So much younger. His playful Gaelic self.

She couldn't help smiling, too.

The service was coming to an end, the bagpiper playing "Danny Boy."

It was then that she looked up, across the expanse of the cemetery.

There was another funeral going on, small in comparison to her grandfather's. There

16

were a man and a woman and a priest. Just
three people. The woman was crying her
heart out. The priest was speaking, obviously trying to comfort her. Strangely, it
seemed to Christie that they were in a
hurry, as if they didn't want to be seen by
anyone else.

There was something so terribly sad about
it.

She saw her grandfather again. He was
eyeing her with a touch of wistful humor.

"Love is all we can take with us to the
grave," he murmured. "It is the greatest part
of any existence, and in that, I have died so
rich."

She wanted to speak to him; she also
wanted to scream.

Because he couldn't really be there.

She heard him whisper. "If y'would, girl.
Kindness to others, in me honor."

She realized that his service had come to
an end, and somehow she was holding a
rose. She followed the others' lead and
dropped it down on the coffin. She turned
away and noticed that one rose had fallen
on the ground. She picked it up and, without thinking, started walking over to the
other funeral, which had ended. The priest
and the distraught couple were gone. Only
the caretakers were there now, getting ready

17

to lower the coffin into the ground.

"Do you know this man?" the caretaker asked as she drew nearer.

"No."

"Then . . . ?"

She set the rose she was holding on the coffin. "Go with God," she murmured.

"Christina!" She heard her mother's voice, calling. She turned away from the sadness of the grave where so few had mourned and hurried back to her family.

Later, thinking that it would make her grandmother feel better, she told Gran that she'd seen her grandfather. Gran stared at her, then said, "Aye, lovie, I sensed him there, that I did."

But that night, to her surprise, her mother seemed angry. "Christie, please, stop saying that you're seeing your grandfather. Stop it. It's hurtful, do you understand?"

She didn't understand. "I wasn't hurting anyone," Christie protested.

"And you wandered off . . . God, that was dreadful. To think that he was buried at the same time, on the same day, as my father."

"Mom, what are you talking about?"

Her mother shook her head. "Christina, I'm sorry. I love you so much, and I know you're hurting, too . . . but you're dreaming. Dreaming at night, daydreaming when

18

you're awake. You cannot see Granda. And you must stop saying that you do!"

Her mother was upset, of course; she had just lost her father. Christie understood that. But, it was almost as if her mother were . . .

Afraid.

If she really was seeing her grandfather, wasn't that a good thing?

To be honest, she wished that he would come again, closer, that he would speak to her, that he would explain.

Who had that other freshly dug grave belonged to?

Her mother hadn't answered her, but she heard other people talking. Everyone said it was terrible. There had been a murderer on the loose, but luckily he was dead. He'd been killed by the police, or he was the police, or something like that. She was irritated by the way people clammed up when she came near. She was nearly a teenager, after all, tall for her age, and she was actually developing a shape. It was insulting to be treated like a child. Then she realized that she had set a flower on a murderer's grave. That was disturbing. But she had seen Granda just before, and he had spoken about kindness. . . .

"What's going on?" she asked her friend

Ana, who lived down the street and was her own age. Ana had come to the funeral and then back to the house afterward, of course, along with her parents and her cousin Jedidiah, looking handsome in his military uniform. Her grandparents' next door neighbor was there, too, Tony, who was eighteen already. He and Jed were off talking, so she was able to talk to Ana alone.

"You didn't know?" Ana asked her. "They got that guy that was killing people. I guess maybe you didn't hear as much about him down south, but up here, people were paranoid. He was buried today, too."

And she had put a rose on his coffin.

Later, when she was alone with her grandmother, she was told again to stop talking about seeing her grandfather.

"You loved him, my girl. I know that. But you must stop saying you've seen him, though I know you are only trying to ease my heart."

"Am I hurting you, Gran?" she asked.

"No, it's not that."

"Then what?"

Gran looked at her very seriously. "It's dangerous. Very dangerous. So today you've said goodbye. Never, ever think of him as speaking to you . . . being near you . . . again."

"Granda would never hurt me."

"Not Granda."

"But —"

Gran was suddenly intense. "To see Granda . . . you have opened a door. And God alone knows who else might pass through that door."

Gran's words chilled her.

"Gran, was Ana telling me the truth? No one thinks twelve is old enough to understand anything, but it is. Tell me, please, was a murderer buried today?"

Her grandmother's face went white. "Never speak of it, never speak that name in connection with your grandfather!"

"What name?"

"Never you mind. It's over. An awful time is over. And your grandfather . . . well, he's in God's arms now. Where monsters go, I do not know."

Gran kissed her then, and held her. " 'Tis all right, my girl, 'tis all right. We have love. I have you, and I have your Mom, and my dear son and his lads. . . . 'Tis all right."

Christie looked at her. She wanted to scream, because it wasn't all right. They were always trying to shelter her from the world, but surely it was better to understand the world than hide from it.

But here in her grandparents' — her

grandmother's now — house, everyone was too upset.

Too lost.

She didn't know why, and it made her afraid. Not afraid of Granda, but just . . .

Afraid.

Afraid of the dead.

That night, she didn't sleep. She lay awake, praying silently in her soul that he wouldn't come.

And he didn't.

She had probably just been so upset that she was imagining things.

Granda, don't come again. Don't ever come again. If you love me at all, please, don't ever come again.

She told herself that all she felt was the whisper of a breeze, though there was none. A gentle touch, as if . . .

As if she had been heard and understood.

Her grandfather didn't appear.

In fact, she never saw him again, not even in dreams.

And as the years passed by, slowly, certainly, she forgot.

It had only been a dream, just as her mother had said.

She was able to believe that for nearly twelve years. And then one day she learned that her grandmother's words were true.

Seeing the dead . . .
Was dangerous.

# 1

An autopsy room always smelled like death, no matter how sterile it was.

And it was never dark, the way it was in so many movies. If anything, it was too bright. Everything about it rendered death matter-of-fact.

Facts, yes. It was the facts they were after. The victim's voice was forever silenced, and only the eloquent, hushed cry of the body was left to help those who sought to catch a killer.

Jed Braden could never figure out how the medical examiner and the cops got so blasé about the place that they managed not only to eat but to wolf down their food in the autopsy room.

Not that he wasn't familiar enough with autopsy rooms himself. He was, in fact, far more acquainted with his current surroundings than he had ever wanted to be. But eating here? Not him.

This morning, it was doughnuts for the rest of them, but he'd even refused coffee. He'd never passed out at an autopsy, even when he'd been a rookie in Homicide, and he didn't feel like starting now.

Even a fresh corpse smelled. The body — any body — released gases with death. And if it had taken a while for someone to discover the corpse, whether it was a victim of natural, self-inflicted or violent death, growing bacteria and the process of decay could really wreak havoc with the senses.

But sometimes he thought the worst smells of all were those that just accompanied the business of discovering evidence: formaldehyde and other tissue preservers and the heavy astringents used to whitewash death and decay. Some M.E.'s and their assistants wore masks or even re-breathers — since the nation had become litigation crazy, some jurisdictions even required them.

Not Doc Martin. He had always felt that the smells associated with death were an important tool. He was one of the fifty percent of people who could smell cyanide. He was also a stickler; he hated it when a corpse had to be disinterred because something had been done wrong or neglected the first time around.

There wasn't a better man to have on a case.

Whenever a death was suspicious, there had to be an autopsy, and it always felt like the last, the ultimate, invasion. Everything that had once been part and parcel of a living soul was not just spread out naked, but sliced and probed.

At least an autopsy had not been required for Margaritte. She had been pumped full of morphine, and at the end, her eyes had opened once, looked into his, then closed. A flutter had lifted her chest, and she had died in his arms, looking as if she were only sleeping, but truly at rest at last.

Doc Martin finished intoning the time and date into his recorder and shut off the device for a moment, staring at him.

He didn't speak straight to Jed, though. He spoke to Jerry Dwyer, at his side.

"Lieutenant. What's he doing here?"

Inwardly, Jed groaned.

"Doc . . ." Jerry murmured unhappily. "I think it's his . . . conscience."

The M.E. hiked a bushy gray eyebrow. "But he's not a cop anymore. He's a writer."

He managed to say the word *writer* as if it were a synonym for *scumbag.*

Why not? Jed thought. He was feeling a little bit like a scumbag this morning.

Doc Martin sniffed. "He used to be a cop. A good one, too," he admitted gruffly.

"Yeah, so give him a break," Jerry Dwyer told him. "And he's got his private investigator's license, too. He's still legit."

This time Martin made a skeptical sound at the back of his throat. "Yeah, he got that license so he could keep sticking his nose into other people's business — so he could write about it. He working for the dead girl? He know her folks? I don't think so."

"Maybe I want to see justice done," Jed said quietly. "Maybe the entire force was wrong twelve years ago."

"Maybe we've got a copycat," Martin said.

"And maybe we got the wrong guy," Jed said.

"Technically, we didn't get any guy, exactly," Jerry reminded them both uncomfortably.

"And you feel like shit for having written about it, as if the cop who was killed really did do it, huh?" Doc Martin asked Jed.

"Yeah, if that's the case, I feel like shit," Jed agreed.

Jerry came to his defense again. "Listen, the guy's own partner thought he was guilty. Hell, he was the one who shot him. And Robert Gessup, the A.D.A., compiled plenty of evidence for an arrest and an indictment." Jerry cleared his throat. "And so far, no one has been proved wrong about anything. We all know about copycats."

"Thing about copycats is, they always miss something, some little trick," Doc Martin said. "Unfortunately, I wasn't the M.E. on the earlier victims. Old Dr. Mackleby was, but he passed away last summer from a heart attack, and the younger fellow who was working the case, Dr. Austin, was killed in an automobile accident. But don't worry, if there's something off-kilter here, I'll find it. I'm good. Damned good."

"Yeah," Jerry Dwyer said, adding dryly, "Hell, Doc, we knew that before you told us."

Martin grunted and turned the tape recorder back on. Jerry gave Jed a glance, shrugging. He'd warned Jed that they might have trouble. He'd told him right out that if Martin said he had to leave, he had to leave.

An autopsy was a long, hard business, and Jed knew it. In his five years in Homicide, he'd learned too well just how much had to be done meticulously and tediously. And messily.

He'd never expected to attend one when his presence wasn't necessary in solving a case, but the truth was, he didn't have to be here today.

Except in his own mind.

The woman on the table was already out of her body bag. There had been no need to inspect her clothing. She hadn't been found with any.

The discovery of her body on the I-4 had been not just a tragedy but a shock to the police and anyone who had been in the area for the original killings twelve years ago. Her name was Sherri Mason; she had come to what the locals called Theme Park Central in the middle of the Florida peninsula because she'd wanted to be a star. The police knew her identity because her purse — holding not just her ID but fifty-five dollars and change and several credit cards — had been found discarded near her naked body.

She had been found not just lying there but carefully displayed, arranged, stretched out on her back as if she were sleeping, her arms crossed over her chest, mummy-style. They were assuming, an assumption to be verified during the autopsy, that she had been sexually assaulted.

Just like the other five victims — those who'd been slain twelve years ago.

The problem was, everyone had spent the past twelve years assuming that the killer of those five young women — found beside the same highway and left in the exact same position — had perished himself. He had been a cop named Beau Kidd, shot by his own partner, who had discovered him with the body of the fifth woman. Beau had drawn his own weapon, giving his partner no choice but to fire. He'd never gone to trial, since he'd been pronounced dead at the site, exhaling his last breath over the body of his final victim.

Assuming he really had been the killer. Certainly the remaining detectives working the case and the D.A.'s office had thought so, and there had been enough circumstantial evidence to make the case.

That evidence had been sound, Jed knew. He had investigated the case himself after he left the force. He had interviewed as many people who'd been involved as he could find. His first book, the one that had made his reputation as an author, had been about the case. A work of fiction, names changed, but it had been clearly based on the career of the Interstate Killer.

Like everyone else, he'd unquestioningly blamed the deaths on the man who had died, one of the detectives assigned to the case.

Jed put the past and all his doubts out of his mind as Doc Martin went on to make observations and take photographs. The body showed signs of rough handling, with abundant bruising. As expected, she had been sexually assaulted, but, as in the past, the killer had been careful. More testing would be necessary, but every one of them was glumly certain there would be no fluids found from which to extract DNA.

The majority of the bruising was around her neck. Like the original victims, she'd been strangled.

Occasionally the M.E. had a question for Jerry, who explained that Sherri had last been seen at a local mall, and that her car had been found in the parking lot there. She had met friends to see a movie, then left alone. When she hadn't shown up for work the following day, a co-worker had reported her missing and filed the report when the requisite twenty-four hours had passed. On the third day after her disappearance, she had been found alongside the highway.

Jed realized that Jerry was staring at him. "The same?" he inquired.

"I didn't attend any of the original autopsies, remember?" Jed replied.

"You did the research," Jerry reminded him.

Jed hesitated, shook his head grimly, and

spoke. "The previous victims disappeared and were discovered within a few days. They bore bruises, as if they'd fought with their captor. There were signs of force, but no slashes, no cigarette burns or anything like that. No DNA was ever pulled from beneath fingernails, and no DNA was acquired from the rape kits. That was one of the reasons for thinking the killer was a cop. Whoever killed those girls knew how to commit a murder without leaving evidence."

"None of you were on the case, or even near it?" Doc Martin asked, looking up.

Both men shook their heads.

"I wasn't here, either, at the time. I was working Broward County back then," Doc Martin murmured. "Hell, come to think of it, Jed, you weren't much more than a kid at the time."

"Eighteen, and in the service," Jed told him.

Doc Martin settled down to work then. After the back of the body had been inspected, it was bathed and any trace evidence collected in the drain. Tools clicked against the stainless steel of the autopsy table. Scrapings were taken from beneath Sherri's nails, but Jed was already certain that they would find nothing. Next came the scalpel, the Y incision, the removal of organs and fluids for testing. Everyone went quiet. Jed found himself thinking about Sherri's dreams. She had come to Orlando looking for a start. To create a résumé to take with her to New York or California. With all the theme parks in the area, she'd had a solid chance of finding work as a dancer or singer.

So who had she met, what had she done, that had changed the shimmering promise of life that had stretched before her?

"Well, Doc?" Jerry asked quietly. Jed gazed at his old friend. Jerry had been on the force for several years before he'd joined himself. He, too, had spent his fair share of time in the autopsy room. But today . . . This death had affected them all. She'd been so young. Death was part of living. But losing life at a time when dreams were at their strongest was especially poignant.

Doc Martin looked at them, shaking his head sadly. "The tox screens will take a little time, but I'm not expecting they'll turn up anything. The kid was clean. Dancer, I imagine, hoping to grow up to be a fairy princess. Cause of death? Strangulation. Was she tortured before death? Hell, yes — I'd sure call it torture to be continually assaulted, knowing that death is probably imminent. The bruising appears to be indicative of her having been forced and the fact that she fought. We'll analyze the nail scrapings, of course, but —"

"But if her murder was committed by the Interstate Killer," Jed said dully, "there won't be any DNA beneath the nails. And there won't be any semen in the vaginal canal."

"Just like twelve years ago, like a cop or an M.E. or a crime scene tech, someone who knew exactly what would nail him, did it," Jerry said.

"Or an avid student of forensics?" Jed said.

Doc Martin was thoughtful for a moment. "No way to know for sure, but it's certainly possible."

A few minutes later they were standing outside the morgue. The sun was high and hot, the sky the kind of crystal blue the state was known for. But the storm clouds were already brewing. Hell, it was summer. That meant a storm like nobody's business sometime during the day, around three or four, usually. Locals loved the phenomenon, though the tourists had a penchant for running from the theme parks when the rains started, not realizing they would be gone in an hour or so.

Then the night would be beautiful, crystal clear, even if humid and hot.

"Well?" Jerry demanded, staring at Jed.

"Well, either everyone involved fucked up entirely and Beau Kidd wasn't the killer, or we've got a copycat out there who studied the case and is imitating the original too damn well."

"Hell, I knew that."

"Jerry, I was in and out of town when it all went down," Jed reminded his friend. "And I wasn't on the force then, either. Who's your partner these days?"

"O'Donnell. Mal O'Donnell. And he wasn't around twelve years ago, either. Hey, you want to get some dinner?"

Dinner? Jed's stomach turned at the thought. Did that make him a wimp? he wondered. He could still smell death and disinfectant. Still, he started to agree, hoping, probably vainly, that Jerry might say something that would give him a clue to the truth about the murders. Did he feel guilty? Hell, yes — if he'd made a mistake. Not only had he made the perp in his novel the homicide cop, even though the man's name had been changed for legal reasons, but the case he had used was glaringly evident.

The real cop was dead.

Yeah, but his parents weren't. And they had to live every day with the world's belief in their son's guilt, a belief he had perpetuated in his novel.

Jed realized that he wanted the current killing to be the work of a copycat — he didn't want to be responsible for the continued life of a horrible mistake.

"Hey, you in there somewhere?" Jerry asked him.

"Yeah, sorry." Jed looked at his watch. "I can't join you for dinner. I have a commitment."

"Yeah?"

"My cousin Ana. One of her best friends when she was growing up just moved into her grandmother's house. I promised I'd show up for the housewarming."

"Cool. Where's the house?"

"Almost horse country. An old pre–Civil War place, one of the few still left in the area."

"Ah. A rich kid."

"No, not really. I grew up down the street, and Ana is still there, since she bought her parents' house. Christina's place is just older and bigger. Her grandparents were immigrants and bought the place way before the theme park explosion, when the countryside was nothing but groves."

"Must be worth a fortune now," Jerry noted.

"Yeah, I guess. But you know how neighborhoods build up. Christina has almost an acre, with a big sloping lawn, almost looks like the place is on a hill, but there's a modern ranch on her right, and a 1930s art deco–style bungalow on her left."

"Sounds cool," Jerry commented. "Better than the cookie-cutter housing developments that have gone up everywhere. Anyway, if you think of anything, give me a call. And stop by the precinct sometime. The guys will be happy to see you."

"Yeah, they like to torture me about my books."

"What? You a sissy now? Can't take the torture? I'm betting I'll see you soon enough," Jerry told him. He pointed a finger. "I know you, and you're not going to let this go. And that's cool with me," he added. "We've got the mayor and the governor breathing down our necks. The feds even have a squad on it."

"Then I'm sure the perp will be caught."

"Yeah?" Jerry said morosely. "We had about six counties' worth of detectives and the feds on the case the last time. Anyway, keep in touch. Have fun hobnobbing with the rich and famous."

"I told you, Christina's family wasn't rich," Jed said, laughing.

"If she sold that place, she'd be rich now."

"She won't sell it," Jed said flatly. But did he really know that? Christina had been his kid cousin's friend. He didn't actually know her all that well, though for some reason he felt as if he did. He had just seen her six months ago at her grandmother's funeral. The gangly kid she had once been had grown into a beautiful woman. Tall and slim, but shapely. Regal, and stoic in the face of grief. She'd been wearing black, a suit with one of those slim pencil skirts. Her hair had been a blaze of deep red against the black, something Jed remembered well. The sun had lit up the length of it as it swept down her back, and the color had been almost startling.

Irish red, he reckoned.

She hadn't cried at the service, but those enormous blue eyes of hers had been filled with a greater depth of emotion than any tears could have evoked. She'd loved her granny, the last of her family except for two cousins. He knew them, too, though they weren't the same age. Dan and Michael had graduated one after the other right behind him, but they'd had different interests and hung out with different friends. He'd gone for a basic BA, while Michael and Daniel McDuff had gone into the arts. Daniel was still struggling as a performer, while Michael did freelance production work for several of the local theme parks and planned to found his own company one day.

Jed knew through Ana that despite having grown up several hours away in South Florida, Christina had been the closest of the three grandchildren to her grandmother. According to Ana, Christina and her grandmother had shared a special bond.

He'd turned down tonight's invitation at first. He had never been a real part of the crowd. But oddly enough, it was the memory of Christina at her grandmother's funeral that had turned him around. She had grown up not just beautiful but intriguing. She'd acquired an air of sophistication that was best described as alluring. In addition, she'd lost her parents just five years earlier, and had worn a lost and weary look he knew all too well himself.

He wished that he could somehow ease things for her. It was so easy to become bitter after so much loss. He had certainly done so, but Christina didn't look as if she had.

He was surprised by how eager he felt to go, even if Ana's old friend had grown up very nicely and he felt that they shared a bond of grief.

He usually avoided any woman who might

be considered a friend. He didn't like sympathy, and he didn't like to talk. Margaritte had been dead for four years. He wasn't as dead inside himself as he had been, but he still wasn't certain that he even liked people in general, much less that he wanted to let himself get close to anyone. Best to veer far away from anything that might be an actual relationship. Barhopping and one-night stands were his preferred mode of existence.

Still, Ana had begged. And for a while, at least, he didn't want to think about the Interstate Killer, and whether the original was alive or dead.

Or the fact that he was very afraid the nightmare was starting all over again.

There were still boxes everywhere.

For the life of her, Christina couldn't figure out why she'd given in when Ana had insisted that she have a housewarming before she was fully moved in, but in Ana's mind, it was good luck. At least she'd said "small gathering" and meant it. Just Ana, maybe her cousin Jed, Tony and Ilona from next door, and her own two cousins, Mike and Dan. The menu was simple: sodas, beer and wine from the quick mart down on the highway and barbecue delivered by Shorty's.

41

That was easy enough, she supposed.

But still . . .

This was her first day. The first day when she was completely out of her condo in Miami, when her boxes were filling this house, when she would sleep here for the first time after inheriting the house and deciding to move in.

Ana arrived early, while Christina was still considering the piano question. The piano was a crucial part of her work. It was almost like a physical attachment.

The light in the parlor was best, but she didn't like having shelves piled with paper and drawers full of disks around, or all her office supplies cluttering up the small room. Still, her piano looked great right in front of the bay window.

It was staying, she decided. She would eventually find — and be able to afford — some good oak or maple office furniture that would suit the decor. And if not, the library was across the hall, a perfect place for office supplies and equipment. She could just walk across when she needed something. No big deal.

Why were there so many boxes? she wondered with dismay.

Because I'm incapable of parting with anything, she reminded herself.

She felt like the keeper of the family heritage or something. It was so hard to believe that everyone was gone except for Mike, Dan and herself. And neither Mike nor Dan felt the need to keep things like the cocktail napkin her mom had saved from her first date with her dad. Or all the hundreds of pictures from Ireland, or even the pictures of all of them as kids.

Her thoughts were interrupted by the clang of the old front door bell. She opened the door to let Ana in. Ana had a big box in her hand, with a plastic-wrapped cardboard tray on top. Christina quickly reached over to help her.

"No, no . . . if I just aim for a flat surface, I'll be fine," Ana told her cheerfully.

A flat surface sounded easy enough.

An empty flat surface involved deeper thought.

"The pass-through between the kitchen and dining room," Christina said quickly.

Ana cut a path through the hall and parlor to reach her destination. Except for the clutter of boxes, the house was clean. It was a large, airy place, the perfect family home, in Christina's mind. The hall worked as a breezeway, a traditional old time "shotgun" approach that allowed the house the best of whatever breeze was available. The stairway stood to the left of the hall and led to the second floor, a beautifully carved banister leading the way.

Ana knew her way around the house. She had been Christina's friend forever, and had spent plenty of time here whenever Christina was up visiting her grandparents.

"This really is a super place," Ana said, leading the way.

The house was wonderful. Christina had always loved it, and her grandmother, knowing how much she loved it and how well she would take care of it, had left it to her. But neither Mike nor Dan had been forgotten. They had received trust funds from the woman who had come to the U.S. to make her own way, and had done well simply by being hard-working, careful and smart.

"Okay," Ana said, setting down her burden. "Now I'll have a beer. Want one?"

"Sure."

Ana headed for the refrigerator and produced two icy bottles, which they clinked together in a toast. "To you living here full-time," Ana said.

"I always knew I would, but I really didn't want the day to come," Christina told her.

"She lived a good long life," Ana said.

A long life, but an often painful one, Christina thought. Gran had lost Granda too soon, and then, much too young, her daughter and son, and their spouses, but she had called on an inner reserve and been there for her three grandchildren. Maybe she had been tired. Ready to join those who had gone before her.

"Ah, that she did," Christina said softly, lifting her bottle again and offering her best imitation of her grandmother's heavy accent.

The doorbell rang again. The two of them hurried to answer it.

"Hey, is Jed coming?" Christina asked Ana.

"He said he was. But that won't be him. He said he was meeting a friend for something work-related this afternoon and he'd be late if he came at all."

"Who would have figured he'd become a bestselling writer, huh?" Christina asked.

"I thought he was going to be a football hero and get me lots of dates," Ana said with a sigh.

Christina rolled her eyes at her friend, shaking her head. Strange, she barely knew Jed anymore. He'd seemed like a god when they'd been kids. She'd seen him at her grandmother's funeral, where he'd been reserved but kind, but she'd felt so bereft that she'd barely noticed anyone. He'd said the right things, though. While everyone else had been telling her what a good and long life her grandmother had lived, he had simply said that he knew how she would miss her gran, and that losing someone hurt, no matter how old they'd been, even if knowing they'd had a long life and lived it well eventually helped with the healing process.

He would know, she thought, having lost his wife when she was only twenty-five.

"Hey, there, you two," she said, pleased, as she opened the door. Dan and Mike had come together. They were just a year apart and had often been taken for twins, they were so much alike. Dan had half an inch over his older brother's height of six two, but they both had the deep red hair that seemed to run with an unbridled strength in the family, and the warm hazel eyes that had been Gran's. Her own were blue — her father's eyes.

"Welcome home, little cutie," Dan said, stepping in and giving her a hug.

"Little? She's five ten, if she's an inch," Michael said, shaking his head as he followed his brother inside. They loved to tease her about her height. It had started when she reached her current max in eighth grade and never stopped.

"Ha, ha, love you, too," she said, accepting a hug from Michael in turn. They were both good-looking and always had been. She peered past them to the porch, then stared at them, puzzled.

"What, no dates?"

"Ana told us it was family night," Dan said, grinning.

"Hey, there's a real little bit," Michael said, catching hold of Ana and lifting her up for a hug. She really was tiny — five feet even — and they loved to tease her, too.

"Put me down," Ana commanded, then swung on Daniel. "And don't you even think about it."

"I'm innocent," Dan said.

"Like hell," Ana muttered, but she gave him a grin. Adulthood had taken them in different directions, but it didn't matter. A bond had been formed when they were young, when this house, and Gran, brought them together, and it had never been broken.

Only Jed Braden had been on the outside, Christina thought. A year older than Michael, two years older than Dan. And somehow different, set apart. Maybe it had been his determination to go into the service. Not because he longed to go to war, but because he wanted the benefits to get through college. He'd been gone a lot once he joined up, and then he'd gotten married in a beautiful ceremony to the gorgeous, gentle Margaritte. He'd drawn even further away from them after that, shouldering increasing responsibility by becoming a cop and then a detective.

And then a widower and famous but semi-reclusive writer.

She shook off thoughts of Jed. It felt slightly uncomfortable somehow, seeing him again.

Maybe because they seemed to meet all too frequently at funerals.

"Hey," she said cheerfully, realizing that her cousins were staring at her, waiting for her to speak. She offered a huge smile. "I admit I hadn't really planned to entertain strangers tonight, but you guys could have brought the current loves of your lives," Christina told them.

"I have no love in my life," Dan said with a feigned mourning note in his voice.

"I want no love in my life," Mike said, and his tone was sharper. He'd been married once, and his divorce hadn't been a pleasant one, though he had dated since.

"Well, Tony from next door is coming, and he's bringing Ilona, the girl we met at the funeral. They live together," Christina told them. "So come on. The menu's barbecue and beer. I'll get the plates out as soon as I get some of the boxes off the chairs so we can use the parlor."

"I'll help," Ana said as they all walked deeper into the house. Suddenly she let out an exclamation as she pulled something out of a box. "Look, it's a Ouija board."

"I never throw anything away," Christina admitted sheepishly.

"Why would you even consider throwing this away?" Ana demanded. Picking up the Ouija board, she walked over and sat in a wing chair and stared at it raptly. "Oh, my God, remember? We used to have so much fun with this thing."

Christina found herself feeling strangely irritated, wishing she'd thought to stick the damn thing somewhere out of sight, or, that she'd gotten rid of it altogether.

She groaned aloud. "We had fun because we were kids who knew the answers we wanted to hear, so we pushed it around to get them," she said.

"We've got to play with this sucker again," Ana said, entranced, and obviously unaware that Christina was nowhere near as anxious as she was to dredge up past fun and games. "Don't you remember? We had so much fun. Sometimes you'd wrap a towel around your head like a turban and call yourself Madame Zee, and we'd have a séance. It was so much fun. But this guy . . ." She patted the Ouija board affectionately. "We asked it so many questions. It was great. We have to play with it again."

"Why? I know what I'm going to be when I grow up," Christina said. "And we are all grown up, in case you haven't noticed."

"Supposedly," Mike threw in skeptically.

"Grown up — not dead," Ana said with mock impatience. "Let's ask it something."

"I don't want any answers to any questions — prophecies can be self-fulfilling," Christina said.

"Maybe you don't want any answers," Dan said. "But I want to know if I'm going to have to be a fluffy all my life."

"Fluffy?" Ana giggled. "Don't you mean 'fluffer'? And don't you have to be a girl for that? Or maybe not, these days."

"Cute, shorty, very cute," Dan said dryly.

"A lot of the entertainers at the parks call playing a character being a 'fluffy,' " Christina explained, unable to hide a smile. "Dan is in the running to play Zeus in a new show, but in the meantime . . ."

"In the meantime, I'm Raccoon Ralph," Dan said.

"Raccoon Ralph?" Ana said, and burst

into gales of laughter.

"If we were still kids, I'd be bopping you on the head right now," Dan said.

"Thank God we're not kids, then," Ana said.

"Enough of that," Mike said, suddenly serious. "You two need to be careful," he said.

"We're just teasing each other," Ana told him, frowning.

Mike shook his head impatiently. "I wasn't talking about you and Dan. I'm talking about you and Christie. I was watching the news earlier," he said. "They were warning women to be careful. There's been a murder."

"A murder?" Christina asked.

"Are you talking about the woman they found along the highway?" Ana asked.

Mike nodded. "You must have heard about it, even down in Miami," he said to Christina.

"I did. But it was just one woman, right?" Christina asked.

"Yeah, but it's got a lot of people around here worried. The killer is a copycat of the Interstate Killer," Mike told them.

"I saw it on the news earlier, too," Ana said. "It sounded like they don't know if they really got the right guy to begin with, right?"

"I don't think anyone is admitting that yet," Mike said.

"Can it be the same guy?" Christina asked. "I mean, I'm not an expert, but I always thought that a killer like that escalated until he was killed or caught and locked away. Would a serial killer take a break that long?" She felt vaguely uneasy. She knew that the so-called Interstate Killer had plagued the central part of the state a dozen years ago. She also knew that he had supposedly been killed.

And buried.

"Maybe he didn't take a break," Dan theorized aloud. "Maybe he was gone . . . traveling from state to state."

"Possibly. They say that killers often keep on the move. Thank God for computers. They've made a big difference," Mike said.

"Jed will know more about it," Ana said confidently.

"That's right. He wrote a book about the killings," Dan said.

"Jed wrote a novel," Ana said. "Based loosely on real events."

Michael was quiet, frowning at Christina.

"What?" she demanded.

He shook his head, then pointed a finger

at her. "Sherri Mason, the woman who was killed, was five feet eight inches tall, about one hundred and thirty pounds. She had blue eyes — and long red hair."

They all stood in silence for a long moment.

"Wow. Thanks a lot for that," Christina said at last.

Ana slipped a supportive arm around her friend's waist. "We can handle ourselves. It's the unwary who usually wind up in trouble."

"That's not the point," Michael said, and took a deep breath. "Christie, you have to be careful. The last victims, twelve years ago . . . they were all tall. And all had light eyes and —"

"And long red hair," Dan breathed softly.

"Just like Sherri Mason," Mike said. "Who was killed just the same way. As if she'd been killed by . . . a ghost."

# 2

Jed should have headed straight over to Christina's house, and in fact he had meant to.

But he didn't.

For some reason he found himself traveling down the road that led to one of the largest local cemeteries.

Beau Kidd had been laid to rest there. His parents and his sister, furious that Beau had been labeled a killer without a trial, grieving his death, had ordered a fine tombstone for him. A glorious angel in marble rested atop it, kneeling down in prayer.

It was dusk when he arrived, and the gates were closed, but the cemetery was one of the oldest in the area. Broken tombstones belonging to those who had served in the United States military as far back as the Seminole Wars could be found there. No one had ever spent the money for a high fence, so he was easily able to hop the low wall and enter. He knew this cemetery well. Too well, he thought.

Margaritte was buried here.

But he hadn't come to mourn at her grave or feel sorry for himself. Not tonight.

He was losing it, he thought. Visiting a cemetery, as if Beau Kidd could talk to him from the grave and offer him help.

No, he told himself. He had simply decided to check on the monument, that was all. In the years after the killings and Kidd's own death, the tombstone had been vandalized several times. Then Beau Kidd's mother had appeared on television and made such a tearful plea to be let alone that the vandalism had stopped. No requests by law enforcement or even arrests could have put an end to the graffiti and damage the way her softly sobbed plea had done.

He could see the angel as he headed down the path. What surprised him was that he wasn't the only one who had come to check on Beau Kidd's grave tonight.

There was a young woman standing there. He frowned, for a moment thinking it might be Christina Hardy. This woman, too, had long red hair, and she was tall, slim and shapely, with elegantly straight posture.

But when she turned as Jed approached, he saw that though she was attractive, her features were quite different from Christina's. For one thing, her eyes were a pale yellow-green color, not a brilliant blue.

He didn't recognize her, but she obviously recognized him.

"What are you doing here?" she snapped.

"Do I know you?" he asked bluntly.

"Katherine Kidd, Beau's sister," she said. "We've never met."

"No? Sorry, but I know who you are. You're an opportunist. You wrote a book about my brother. As if the events weren't painful enough."

"I wrote a work of fiction," he said. Why defend himself? He should just let her lambaste him. That might work out better for both of them.

"Why are you here? Do you want to hammer a stake into my brother's heart? Do you think he's alive and killing again?"

"I'm sorry. I'll leave."

He turned to go.

"If you're lost, your wife's grave is nowhere near here," she called after him.

He squared his shoulders and kept walking.

"Wait!"

He was startled when she ran after him. Her eyes were troubled when she awkwardly touched his arm to get him to turn around.

"Why are you here?" she demanded.

He hesitated. "I don't know, exactly. I guess . . . I wanted to think. Honestly, I don't know."

"Beau was never the killer," she said.

"How can you be so certain?" he asked.

"He was my brother."

He let out a soft sigh. "You do know that every homicidal maniac is some mother's son?"

"I know you investigated when you wrote your book. I know you were a cop. And I know you have a license now as a private investigator. You came here because you're feeling guilty for what you did to my brother's reputation. You want absolution? Fine. Prove that's not just a copycat out there. Prove Beau was innocent."

He stared at her, unable to think of anything to say.

"I'll pay you," she offered suddenly.

He shook his head. "No. No, you won't pay me."

"You don't really believe in Beau's innocence, do you? Not even now, with the evidence lying in the morgue," she said.

"I don't know what I believe right now," he told her honestly.

She shook her head. "I've read every word let out by the police, the newspapers, every

57

single source. No copycat could be so exact."

"I don't know yet just how exact he was," he said.

"I do. And I know that Beau wasn't a killer, no matter how guilty he looked. And you . . . you used him."

"I used a story, a real-life story," he said quietly. "And I'm going to investigate, but no one owes me anything. I guess that's why I was here tonight. This one is between the two of us, Beau and me," he told her.

He nodded and walked away again. When he looked back, she was standing where he had left her, looking bereft and alone.

"I'll keep you informed — when I can prove something," he told her.

He thought that she smiled as she lifted a hand to wave goodbye.

There was a low ground fog beginning to rise. Looking up, he saw that the moon was full. Odd night. Most of the time around here, the fog came in the early morning. Between the moon and the fog, the cemetery seemed to be bathed in some kind of eerie glow.

As he headed to his car, he thought about Sherri Mason, lying on the autopsy table. Sherri . . . tall, slim, with long red hair.

Before he knew it, he was heading back

into the cemetery. "Katherine!" he shouted, running.

She was standing by her brother's monument again. She looked up, startled.

"You need to get out of here," he told her. She stared at him blankly. "It's dark, and there's a killer loose. Where's your car?"

"Along the street, just past the gate."

"I'll see you to it."

"All right." She sounded unconvinced, but she didn't argue.

He walked her to the Honda parked by the curb. She must have arrived after the cemetery had officially closed, as well. She slid behind the driver's seat and lowered the window. He ducked down to talk to her, but before he could speak, she said, "I know, long red hair. I'll be careful, I promise."

"Thanks."

"I'm twenty-four, but I still live with my folks. I'll be okay."

He nodded as she turned her key in the ignition, and he watched the Honda's lights disappear into the fog.

He stood there for a long moment, feeling a strange sensation of dread grip his spine like an iron claw. Beautiful women with long red hair.

Christina Hardy fell into that category, as well.

■ ■ ■ ■

He had lost her tonight, thanks to the cop-turned-writer.

But he would prevail. He would behave normally. He was a special person, unique; amazing things went on in his mind. He could walk, talk, smile and act completely normal, and all the while he would be planning his next kill.

But there had been an almost frightening moment when he had felt as if he might combust, the opportunity had been so good.

She had been there, so appetizing.

He made himself breathe, told himself to function. There was his world, his inner world, and then there was the world beyond. Sometimes he could combine them, but it was over now.

Still, there had been those moments when he had almost been able to taste and feel the results of his brilliance. He had come here tonight by happenstance, unable to resist a visit to the grave of the man who had taken the blame for everything he himself had done all those years ago. And then . . . to see Kidd's sister . . .

It was too good.

She was such a pretty thing. All that lovely

hair . . .

Then he'd shown up.

Jed Braden was big and broad-shouldered, clearly capable of holding his own in a fight.

But that didn't matter. The point lay in his own brilliance, not in something as crass as a physical fight. He loved watching the dumb fucks chase their tails while he went gleefully about his business.

God, he loved the press. The newscasters were so grave when they talked about the latest killing. Then, with the switch of a camera angle, a smile instead of a somber look. Suddenly it was "Lots of fun on tap for Halloween this year."

But at home, watching their plasma TVs, the viewers would be reeling. No change in camera angle for them. A killer was on the loose. . . .

The experts were all baffled. It would never be like the crime shows. He was far too intelligent. There would be no solving his murders in a one-hour show.

How he loved the attention. His double life. Defying profilers and "behavioralists," knowing they were more confused than ever now.

And all thanks to his own brilliance.

Breathe. Be ready. Walk, talk, smile, and all while the other world lived on in his mind. The time would come again — and soon — when it would become real once again.

"Quit staring at me. You're giving me chills," Christina said to her cousins.

Mike shook his head, looking away. "I just want you to be careful."

"I am careful. I've always been careful. I never go anywhere with strangers. I'm street smart, honest. You guys know that," she said.

"Just keep your doors locked, okay?" Dan said.

"I told you, I'm always careful. I carry pepper spray, I don't talk to strangers and I don't open the door without checking through the peephole," Christina assured him.

The doorbell rang.

Christina jumped, then flushed in embarrassment.

Mike said, "I'll get it," and headed down the hall.

"Remember how much fun we had with this thing?" Ana said, returning to the original subject. Christina wasn't sure why, but she was sorry she'd kept the damn thing around. Ana seemed way too enamored of it.

"It's Tony from next door," Mike said

62

when he returned a minute later, two more people in his wake. "And his fiancée," he added, stressing the word.

Tony went over to Christina, took her shoulders and gave her a peck on the cheek. He'd been a gaunt, geeky boy, but he'd grown into a tall, well-built man. His eyes were gray, his hair sandy-colored, and his nose and ears were no longer too big for his face.

"Hey, Tony, thanks for coming," Christina said.

"Nasty fog out there," he said. "I couldn't even see your house from mine."

"Spooky," Ilona agreed.

"Christina, you remember Ilona, don't you?" Ana asked.

"We met at the funeral," Ilona said, stepping forward to take Christina's hand. She had a warm grip and sympathetic green eyes. She was slim, with long, straight blond hair and a pleasant way about her.

"Yes, of course we met," Christina said warmly. "Congratulations. I didn't know the two of you were engaged. When's the big day?"

"Oh, we haven't planned that far ahead yet," Ilona said.

"I say we ask the Ouija board," Ana suggested.

"I say we have a beer and some barbecue," Mike protested from the doorway.

"Oh, all right, but then we do the Ouija board," Ana insisted.

"What about Jed? Should we wait for him before we eat?" Christina asked.

"My dear cousin will get here in his own good time," Ana said. "He can eat when he gets here."

"Sounds like a plan," Christina agreed.

"Let's eat, then," Dan said.

"Worked up a real appetite being a fluffy, huh?" Ana teased.

Dan gave her a fake scowl as they all moved into the kitchen and started eating.

The conversation was general and pleasant as it moved from topic to topic. It turned out that Ilona had originally come from Ohio, which led to a discussion about the Rock and Roll Hall of Fame. Nice, easy stuff.

So why, Christina kept wondering, was she feeling so on edge?

Ilona asked Christina about her work, and she explained that writing advertising jingles was more difficult than most people thought, as well as a crucial element in selling the product. "If you can get people to remember a jingle, then they'll remember the product," she explained. As she spoke,

64

she could hear Dan, Mike and Tony talking about the murdered woman who had been found beside the highway.

When everyone seemed to have finished eating, Ana reached over for Christina's plate. "Done with this?"

"Cleanup time?" Dan said, noticing. "Let me help." He came over with a large garbage bag and they all tossed their paper plates into it. "Gran wasn't the type to let any of us get away without picking up after ourselves, right, Christie?"

"Right. But," she added, smiling to take any sting out of the words, "it's easier when all you have to do is grab a garbage bag."

"Gran made us scour her copper collection every Sunday," Mike put in, a nostalgic smile curving his lips.

"Yeah, and it was a pain in the butt," Dan said, and grinned at Christina. "You gonna keep all that copper glowing forever?" he asked. His eyes indicated the array of copper pans and molds lining the special racks their grandfather had constructed to hold the collection.

"Of course," she said.

"Better you than me," Dan told her, laughing.

"Christina was always the keeper of the keys," Tony said, lifting his beer to her.

"The keys?" Ilona said, puzzled.

"Christie was always the one who loved all the old family stuff," Tony explained. He sounded slightly impatient.

"Oh," Ilona said in a cool tone.

"I'm sorry," Tony murmured, pulling her close.

"Get a room," Dan teased.

Ilona laughed softly, blushing, and drew away from Tony.

"Why would they get a room when they have a perfectly good house?" Mike asked.

"Forget it, it's Ouija board time," Ana announced.

"The parlor is a mess," Christina said.

"We can just sit on the floor," Ana said, waving away her objection. "We'll start with Tony and Ilona. Maybe the Ouija board can give us a wedding date."

"Sure," Tony said with a shrug.

Ilona giggled. "Shouldn't we dim the lights or something?"

"Why not?" Mike asked with a shrug, moving to the switch that controlled the lights.

Dan made a sound as if a soft and wicked wind were moving through the room.

Christina, arms folded against her chest as she leaned against the arched doorway, groaned.

Ilona and Tony set their fingers on the planchette, which began to move, finally settling over the *J.*

"January," Ana breathed.

"It's gotta be at least July," Tony said. "We're just not ready yet."

"Look at that," Mike said as the planchette started moving around erratically. "She wants January, he won't be ready until July, and poor Mr. Ouija doesn't know what to do."

"You're pushing it," Tony accused Ilona.

"No — you're pushing it," Ilona protested.

"Don't take it so seriously. It's just a game," Mike said lightly, as if aware that a real argument was in the offing.

And that was all that it was: a game, Christina reminded herself.

"Fingers barely touching the planchette," Ana advised. "Christina, come over here and help me show them how to do it."

"Oh, all right. But we're not doing this all night," Christina protested. She flashed a smile at Ilona. "I want to learn more about how you and Tony got together. Who cares when the wedding is? We'll all have a good time whenever you choose to have it — if we're invited, of course."

"Of course you're invited," Ilona said.

"All right, all right," Ana said. "Just get

down here."

"Is it dark enough? Want it spookier?" Dan teased.

"That fog is spooky enough," Ilona said, and shivered.

"It's just fog," Christina said, barely managing not to shout. Damn. It wasn't like her to be so edgy, but it was unnerving to realize how closely she fit the description of the victim of a serial killer.

Either a copycat . . .

Or a maniac who had somehow escaped detection for twelve years.

"And don't forget the moon," Ilona added.

"Are you thinking werewolves?" Tony teased her.

"There are enough real monsters out there," Christina said. "There's no need to make up more."

There was a sudden uncomfortable silence in the room. She realized she had snapped out the words rather than simply speaking them.

"I'm sorry," she said quickly. What was wrong with her? It was just . . .

It was just that stupid Ouija board and the idea of talking to spirits. She suddenly found the past welling up in her mind, a vision that was far too real. She could see Gran, after her grandfather had died. Sitting in her chair, looking at her so somberly. She'd dreamed that she'd talked to her grandfather. A psychology professor had once told her that such dreams were defense mechanisms, a way to reconcile oneself to losing someone. But Gran had said, "It's dangerous. You have opened a door. . . ."

That was just Gran and the Irish speaking. She had never had such dreams again. Not even when she had lost her parents.

All of that was far behind her now. She was a perfectly rational, sane person, and it was just the Irish sense of fun that made them all pretend to believe in banshees and leprechauns and even dreams.

"Okay, Ana, let's show everybody how it's done," she said, then lowered her voice teasingly. "It was a dark and stormy night . . . no, it was a dark and foggy night, with a strange, full moon rising above the mist."

Her light banter didn't seem to be helping her mood any, she thought, and apparently it was obvious.

"You okay, Christie?" Mike asked.

"I'm fine," she snapped.

"My fault," Mike said. "I'm sorry, I shouldn't have —"

"Mike, I'm sorry. I didn't mean to snap at anyone. I guess I'm just tired."

"You're really okay?" Dan said softly.

"Yes, of course. Come on, Ana. Let's do this Ouija thing and be done with it, okay?"

"Hello, Ouija board," Ana said, as if she were greeting an old friend.

Christina forced a grin, then set her fingertips very lightly on the planchette, which took off, slowly spelling out "Hello, good evening."

"Is there a spirit in you tonight, Ouija board?" Ana asked.

"Is she for real?" Christina heard Tony whisper to Dan.

"Who knows?" Dan replied.

"Real? Real is what we make it," Mike put in.

Christina knew that she wasn't moving the planchette, so Ana had to be the one causing it to spell out the answer.

"Y-E-S," Ilona read softly.

"Who are you?" Ana asked.

They all stared as the planchette began to move again and Dan read aloud, "B-E-A-U-K-I-D-D . . . Bookid?"

"It must mean boo, kid," Mike said. "Boo, like Halloween. Kid, like a trick-or-treater."

"No," Dan murmured. "B-E-A-U. Beau, like a man's name."

"Like General Beauregard, the Confederate military leader," Tony offered. "Right?"

"Beau Kidd. The detective who was supposedly the Interstate Killer!" Dan gasped.

"You did that on purpose!" Mike accused Ana.

"The hell I did," she retorted adamantly.

"The thing moves by the power of suggestion," Mike said impatiently.

"Ask him what he wants," Dan said. "Watch — it will spell out, 'I was framed. I'm innocent.' "

"What do you want?" Ana asked the spirit softly, ignoring Dan.

Christina gritted her teeth, longing to lift her fingers from the planchette, but somehow she couldn't quite bring herself to do it.

The planchette continued to move.

It was Ana, damn her. She had to be forcing it.

But what was really unnerving Christina was that she didn't think Ana was forcing it.

Dan whispered behind them, "Puh-lease. You'd think we were still teenagers, telling scary stories out in the woods."

"Be quiet. It's spelling something," Ana said impatiently.

"H-E," Mike began.

"L-P," Dan finished.

"Help," Ilona breathed.

"Hang on, it's not finished," Christina said.

"They must be moving it," Tony whispered to Ilona. "But they're good. Spooky, huh?"

" 'Help,' again," Mike said. "It's getting kind of monotonous, don't you think?"

What other letters added to "help" would make another word? Christina wondered as the planchette kept moving.

" 'Help me please,' " Dan whispered.

The planchette was practically racing around the board.

Help me please help me please help me please. . . .

Then, suddenly, it came to a definite stop in the middle of the board.

The room fell dead silent, even the doubters momentarily spellbound.

A thunderous knocking broke the silence and brought a scream from Ilona's lips. As if in response, the planchette seemed to rise and soar straight into the air.

And then they heard the front door burst open.

# 3

"What the hell?" Dan demanded.

Jed stared back at his old family friend, wondering why he looked so spooked. Okay, maybe he'd opened the door a bit more forcefully than necessary, but it hadn't been locked.

Although even if it had been locked, he would have forced it open, anyway, he had to admit.

He was definitely on edge, he thought, but he'd also heard someone scream.

"You tell me," Jed said to Dan. "What the hell is going on in here? I heard a scream."

Dan rolled his eyes. "Sorry." He stepped back so Jed could come in and closed — and locked — the door after him. "Good to see you, Jed. The screamer was Ilona, Tony's fiancée. She got spooked after Ana insisted on playing with the Ouija board."

"That's why the dim lights, huh?"

"Uh-huh," Daniel agreed dryly.

By then they had reached the parlor and Ana leapt up and rushed over to meet him, giving him a quick hug. "You made it."

"I said I'd come," he told her, looking past her to Christina Hardy, who was slowly rising. She was one of those women with the ability to do normally awkward things with the sinuous grace of curling ivy. She walked over, a small smile on her face, and gave him a quick, friendly hug in greeting. "Welcome. There's still barbecue in the kitchen."

"Good. I'm famished."

"Hi, Jed," Mike said. "You know Tony, but have you met Ilona?"

Jed nodded toward the woman at Tony's side. They'd met briefly at the funeral. "Nice to see you again," he told her.

"You, too," Ilona said.

"Did you know Jed's a famous writer?" Mike asked.

"I'm not really famous," Jed said quickly, embarrassed.

"Speaking of which, guess what name those two —" Mike paused to indicate Ana and Christina "— just dredged up. Beau Kidd."

Jed frowned. Even if his nerves hadn't already been on edge, the name would have stung. Damn it, he thought. He hadn't caused what had happened to the cop. He had just built fiction around the facts of what had already happened.

Yeah. Fiction that clearly skewered the man.

"Beau Kidd?" he said, and he knew that his voice was harsh.

"Oh, Jed, don't sound so mad. We were just playing with the Ouija board," Ana said.

"After talking about the recent murder," Dan explained.

"Ouija board?" Jed said skeptically.

"Hey, blame Ana, not me," Christina said lightly.

"I'm telling you, it spelled out his name," Ana said stubbornly.

"Come in the kitchen, I'll warm up some food for you," Christina said.

"Don't bother," Ana teased. "He used to be a cop. He even eats cold pizza."

"Well you don't have to eat cold barbecue," Christina said firmly, then stared at him with those crystal-blue eyes of hers and smiled slowly. "Thanks for coming."

He shrugged a little awkwardly. "Sure."

She strode past him, smooth and sleek. He followed.

She was already reaching into the refrigerator by the time he stepped into the kitchen. She handed him a beer.

"So how's it going?" she asked after he thanked her, helping herself to one, as well, and leaning back against the counter. A subtle grin curved her lips. "When does your next book come out?"

He arched a brow. "Last month, actually."

"Oh. Sorry."

"That's cool."

"I should have kept up."

"Amazingly, the entire world doesn't rush out to the store the minute a book of mine comes out."

She flushed. "Yeah, well, I'm one of Ana's best friends. I should have known."

"Not even all of Ana's friends rush out the minute I have a book on the shelves," he assured her.

She smiled and dug into the refrigerator again. He realized with an inner smile that she had planned for his arrival as she pulled out a microwave-ready plate with chicken, ribs and corn on the cob.

He hadn't been lying when he'd said he was hungry. He'd showered, and the smell of the autopsy room no longer seemed to fill his nostrils.

But he couldn't forget the dead woman or what had happened at the cemetery.

Couldn't forget that Christina Hardy was a beautiful redhead.

He warned himself to get his thoughts under control. He couldn't let himself become obsessed with this, couldn't let it consume him and everyone around him.

"So how's it going in jingle land?" he asked. "What's your latest?"

Her smile deepened as she played with the dial on the microwave. " 'Come to the Grand, walk on the sand, hear the steel band, sunsets and glory, the minute you land,' " she sang lightly.

"That was you? I hear it all the time," he told her.

"It's a great resort," she told him. "I was given a comp weekend when I was hired, so I got to check it out for free. It's one of those all-inclusive places. Really nice. You step out from your private bungalow right onto the beach."

"Nice work if you can get it," he teased.

"As long as I am working."

"Well, this place is worth a mint," he told her.

"I'd panhandle before I sold this house," she assured him passionately, then seemed embarrassed by the emotion she had betrayed. She offered him a wry smile. "Hmm. And are you suggesting I won't get work?"

He laughed. "Never," he vowed solemnly.

The microwave beeped. She reached in

for his plate, and he walked over to take it from her. The scent of barbecue was strong, but her perfume was more alluring. He remembered how, years ago, he had thought she was a pain in the butt and wished she and Ana would go away.

Things certainly changed, he thought wryly.

She smiled and brushed by on her way to get him a fork, knife and napkin. His muscles tightened. Hell, yes, things changed.

Ana appeared in the kitchen. "Hurry up," she said to Christina. "You're the only one who can make that stupid Ouija board work."

"I wasn't doing anything," Christina protested.

Jed felt his muscles tighten again, and not in a good way.

"Beau Kidd?" he said to Christina.

She flushed. "I swear, I didn't make it do anything," she protested.

"Whatever you say," he said curtly.

He hadn't meant to be so brusque. She barely moved, but he could feel her stiffen from across the room.

"It's just that I worry, okay?"

She sighed. "I know. I'm a redhead."

"A beautiful redhead," he told her, trying

to atone.

"I'm a big kid, and I've lived on my own for a long time now. I don't do stupid things."

"Don't assume that all victims are stupid."

"I'm not. But I am careful," she told him. "Really." She was irritated. Why not? It was a good cover-up for being frightened.

She walked out of the kitchen, toward the parlor. He followed her, keeping his distance and stopping in the doorway.

"You made that name — Beau Kidd — appear," Mike said, staring accusingly at Christina.

"I sure as hell didn't," she replied, and her voice betrayed her annoyance. "Twelve years ago, I was thirteen and my mom turned the news off every time something came on TV that she thought I shouldn't know about. In fact, my parents used to argue about it. My dad thought I needed to be aware of what was going on in the world, but my mom just thought I was too young to know some things — no, a lot of things."

"You still must have heard the name," Dan said. He was sitting on the floor, back against the wall, arms folded over his knees.

"I'm sure I did, but a lot has happened since then, in my life and in the world," she informed him, her tone irritated. "I didn't move the planchette."

"Right. Beau Kidd did it himself, because there is no copycat killer and he wants us to know he's innocent," Mike murmured dryly.

"Maybe he didn't do it," Ana said. "And maybe his spirit did move the planchette."

"Now you're scaring me," Jed teased his cousin.

She frowned, staring at him with a stubborn set to her jaw. "Oh, right, Mr. He-man. There's no possibility that anything you haven't seen for yourself could possibly be real."

"What's the phrase? A ghost in the machine?" Tony said, his tone light, as if he were hoping to lift the tension that had suddenly filled the room.

"If there were a ghost here, it would be Gran, yelling at us," Dan said, grinning, and evoking smiles from the others at last.

"Was she mean?" Ilona asked.

"Heavens, no," Christina said. "But she had a very clear vision of right and wrong." She flashed a smile. "I don't think she'd be yelling. We haven't messed anything up."

"Well, she wasn't all that fond of the way I'm running my life," Dan said, shrugging. "I tried to explain to her that I intend to be more than Raccoon Ralph."

"And you will be," Christina said. "You're

going to be Zeus."

"Right. And Halloween is around the corner. I'll get to play some pretty scary stuff," Dan said.

"The three-year-olds are trembling in their boots," Ana teased, then suggested, "Why don't we ask the Ouija board when you'll get your big break?"

Mike groaned. "I'm getting another beer." He started down the hall, almost crashing into Jed, who was still standing in the doorway. "Beer?" he suggested.

"Yeah, sure, one more," Jed said, heading to the kitchen with him.

A few seconds later, they heard a loud and startled clamor from the parlor.

They frowned at each other and rushed back to the other room. Jed was in the lead, and when he reached the arched doorway, he was almost hit in the head with the planchette.

"Hey, who threw that?" he demanded. Ducking had saved him from a good shot right in the face.

"She did," Ana said, pointing to Christina.

"I did not!" Christina protested.

Ana met his eyes, looking more than a little scared. "It . . . it was like it got mad and flew cross the room," she said.

"Ana, get a life," Jed snapped.

"What's going on?" Mike demanded from just behind Jed.

"We asked it if Dan was going to get the part he wants," Christina said.

"And it spelled out 'help' again," Ilona said, eyes wide.

"They're pulling your leg, Ilona," Mike told her.

Ana let out a long, aggrieved sigh.

"Whatever. Let's put the stupid thing away," Christina said. Without waiting for anyone to agree, she reached for the box.

"Throw the stupid thing away," Dan suggested.

"Christina, throw an old treasure away?" Tony teased. "Never."

"It's a good thing I don't throw anything away. You might recall a box I packed up when a few people forgot about it after one Christmas dinner," Christina said, looking from Mike to Dan and smiling complacently.

"Yes, and we appreciate it," Dan said, then explained to the others. "We got bonds for Christmas one year when we were kids. We forgot all about them, but Christina stuck them in a box and held on to it. Our bonds matured and ended up being worth a bundle."

"And we thank her for it," Mike said, then turned to Christina. "Want me to help you pack anything up?" he asked as he turned up the dimmer switch.

"No, but thank you for the appreciation." She rose from the floor as gracefully as ever.

Dan yawned, then apologized. "Sorry, but I've got to go. I'm on first shift tomorrow. Costuming at seven in the morning for the eight o'clock breakfast. This was fun. Thanks, Ana. Christina."

"I should take off, too," Jed said, anxious to get away. He still couldn't get the autopsy off his mind, and the last thing he needed was to spend the evening at a party where the conversation kept turning to Beau Kidd.

"Christina, Ana, thanks for dinner, and, Christie, welcome to the neighborhood."

"Thanks for coming," she said, and walked over to him for a brief hug. There was still something reserved between them.

His fault, she decided as he waved to the others and started toward the door.

"This is your home, too, just like always," he heard Christina tell her cousins as they followed a few steps behind.

"Thanks, kid," Dan told her. "But one day you might have a sex life, and you wouldn't want us walking in on you."

"Let's go," Mike said. "I don't want to

hear about my little cousin's sex life, okay?"

"Would you rather walk in on it?" Dan asked.

"Outta here," Mike said firmly.

Jed was almost at the door, but he still overheard the last remarks from the group in the parlor.

"What the hell was with Jed tonight?" Tony asked.

"The Beau Kidd thing," Ana said. "When he wrote his book, he was sure Kidd was guilty, but now he doesn't know."

Jed headed out the door to his Jeep and gunned the engine.

Ana was right.

Ana left a few minutes later with Tony and Ilona. Dan and Mike had offered to drive her home, but Tony had assured them that he and Ilona would see her safely inside. Ana had bought her parents' house when they had retired down to their place in the Keys, so she'd never moved once in her life. And at the price of real estate, she was lucky — as Christina was herself.

Christina locked the front door as the stragglers left. One thing she didn't have was an alarm system. Something she should probably consider in the future, she decided.

There wasn't much to do as far as cleaning up; paper plates for food that had arrived in cardboard cartons didn't create much of a mess. She was done in five minutes.

When the water stopped running, the house seemed almost painfully silent.

She walked back into the parlor and immediately noticed the Ouija board. "You suck," she muttered. Her eyes moved over the many boxes littering the room.

For some reason, all those boxes made her feel uneasy. The fact that the house didn't have an alarm — which had never bothered her before — now made her even more uneasy. The silence weighed on her.

And she wished to God they had never played with the stupid Ouija board.

She found herself walking around, turning on every light in the house. She even turned on the plasma television in the living room, thinking the noise would be good.

The news came on instantly.

"As is common in such cases," an attractive young anchorwoman was saying, "there was evidence that the police didn't share with the public when the Interstate Killer was at work twelve years ago. The police have not yet commented on whether or not the murder of Sherri Mason shares any of those confidential similarities or not. As you may be aware, the Interstate Killer's spree ended with the death of the man who had become the prime suspect, Detective Beau Kidd. Kidd was familiar with two of the victims, who —"

Christina was tempted to throw the remote control across the room; she hit the power-off switch instead.

Groaning, she rechecked the front door, turned off the lights and started up the stairs.

She hadn't taken over her grandmother's room, and she wouldn't. It was going to be her guest room, she had decided.

"Beau Kidd, indeed," she murmured aloud in annoyance when she reached her own room. "If this house is haunted, it's haunted by Granda and Gran. Good people who loved me."

She had never felt afraid in this house, and she was angry that the night's events had left her feeling so unnerved.

So she was a redhead. There were lots of redheads out there, natural and otherwise. It was a popular color.

She locked her doors. She didn't go off with strangers. She was careful.

She looked around her room, the same room she'd always stayed in as a child. It had changed a great deal over the years. She had a new bed, for one thing — a Christmas present from a few years ago. It was a queen, with a handsome cherry-wood sleigh-style frame. Her dresser and wardrobe matched, as did the artfully concealed entertainment center.

She headed straight to it, turning on the television and finding a channel with nothing but sitcom repeats.

"So there. I will have no news tonight," she said.

Her voice rang strangely loud in the empty house. She was glad when the sound of the television filled the space.

She was even more pleased when a commercial with a jingle she had written popped up on the screen. "Ever soft, ever silky, ever gentle to the touch, oh, dear Biel's Tissue, we thank you very much."

Not poetry or even her most brilliant lyric, but it was a good, catchy tune.

She smiled, walked into the bathroom and slipped into the cotton sleep shirt that hung on the back of the door, then washed her face and brushed her teeth. A few minutes later she drew back her covers and settled beneath the clean, cool comfort of her sheets.

And she stared at the television, not seeing a thing.

She rose again and turned on the lights she had turned off earlier. She was certain that from the street, her house was lit up like a Christmas tree. She turned the television down, plumped her pillow and closed her eyes, hoping that the soft drone of the sitcom would help her sleep. It wasn't as if she had anything imperative going on early in the morning; she was just going to finish setting up the house and emptying boxes.

But she was tired. She wanted to sleep.

She tossed around for a while, forcing herself to lie still with her eyes closed, half listening to the television.

Then, head on the pillow, eyes closed, she felt a strange prickling sensation. She couldn't pinpoint anything different about the air around her or the sounds she was hearing. It was an old house, and it creaked. But she knew every creak, and she wasn't hearing anything she shouldn't have been.

But the sensation stayed with her.

She felt as if she were a child again, frightened as she watched a spooky movie, closing her eyes . . .

If this had been a movie, though, she would have felt compelled to open her eyes, but this was real life, and she fought the desire. If she kept her eyes closed, she would be all right. It would be like hiding beneath the bed or taking refuge in a closet.

I won't. I won't open my eyes, she thought. And it will go away.

But the feeling didn't go away, and finally she had to open her eyes and look into the shadows, just to prove that there was nothing there.

She opened one eye slowly.

It felt as if her blood congealed and her heart froze.

She closed her eye again. She must have imagined what she thought she'd seen. A shadow. A shadow in the shape of a man. Standing at the end of the bed.

Her frozen heart began to thunder.

A normal response, she told herself, given that there was a killer on the loose.

This was all nonsense, she thought. No one could possibly be there.

She opened both eyes, bolting up to a sitting position at the same time.

Someone was there.

A tall, solid, yet somehow shadowy figure standing at the foot of her bed.

Christina screamed and leapt out of bed, then practically flew out of the room.

She raced to the door, out to the hall and down the stairs. She burst out the front door, onto the porch and leapt over the two steps that led to the ground. She ran until she reached the end of the driveway, and then she finally turned back, gasping, checking to see if he was in pursuit.

It was difficult to see, though, because it was such a strange night. The fog was still lying low to the ground, while above, shimmering through with an illumination like silver, was the great orb of the full moon.

Instinct was kicking in. Fog or not, she would see him coming from the front of the house, and he clearly wasn't in pursuit. But she didn't have her keys. That was okay; she could just go next door to Tony's house, and she would be safe.

In her mind's eye, she pictured the figure coming after her, catching her, tackling her right before she could reach Tony's door.

Then there was a tap on her shoulder.

She froze.

Spun around.

Screamed.

He was there.

It was impossible, but he was there. He'd somehow gotten out of the house without her seeing and ended up behind her.

And he wasn't a shadow, either. Not only that, she had seen his face before.

It took her a moment to remember where she had seen it, and when.

Then she knew.

She had seen it, plastered all over the newspapers after Beau Kidd had been shot kneeling over the body of his latest victim.

"Christie . . ."

Did he say her name, or was it the breeze? Or was she only deep in some horrible nightmare where the dew-damp grass beneath her bare toes was ridiculously real and the face of the man before her was bizarrely vivid?

"Christie . . ."

The world seemed to be fading, getting lost in the fog.

"Please . . . help me."

She had never passed out before in her life, but she did then, dropping flat onto soft, wet earth, seeing nothing but stygian darkness.

# 4

"Hey."

Christina became aware of the deep, rich voice at the same time as she felt the chilling discomfort of the ground beneath her.

The sun was rising, she realized, feeling completely disoriented.

"Christie?"

She blinked. The sun created a haze as it burned off the last of the fog, so she blinked again, turning her head slightly to make out someone standing above her. For a moment she felt a resurgence of fear. But the sunlight was bright, and when she blinked a third time, her vision cleared and she finally saw who was standing there.

Jed Braden.

He hunkered down by her side.

"Are you all right?" His tone was anxious, harsh.

She realized that she was lying on her lawn and frowned.

"Are you hurt?" he demanded anxiously, his hands on her shoulders, his face close, his features tense.

"No, I'm not hurt. I'm fine."

She saw relief fill his face.

"Fine? Really?"

"Absolutely. I swear it."

"Thank God you're alive," he murmured.

She struggled to rise up on her elbows. "I guess I . . . fell asleep."

"You're joking, right?" he said. His voice hardened to a sharper edge. "You told me you were smart, remember? You said you didn't do stupid things."

She stared at him. She must have had a nightmare. She couldn't possibly have seen the ghost of Beau Kidd. There in the light of day, the idea was just too ridiculous. But she really was lying on the grass, so she really had run out of the house. And she had run because someone had been there. Hadn't he?

She blurted the words without thinking. "There was someone in my house."

Jed stared at her, slowly arching a brow. "Someone was in your house?" He sounded both concerned and doubtful.

"Yes."

Anxiety tightened his features. "So some-one broke in and chased you out, then . . .

93

forced you to sleep on the ground?"

She stared at him. "I'm telling you, there was a man at the foot of my bed."

"But you're also telling me you weren't attacked, right?"

"No. He was just . . . there."

"What was he doing?"

"Staring at me. I . . . felt him there, opened my eyes and saw him, then jumped up and ran out," she explained.

"You locked up, right? You made sure you locked up after everyone left?"

He stood then, and reached down to help her to her feet. He was in jeans, a knit polo shirt and a casual suede jacket, towering and at ease. "Christina, usually people run somewhere when they're running away from danger. They don't just curl up and go to sleep on the front lawn."

"I didn't just curl up and go to sleep!" she flashed angrily.

"Oh?"

"Look, I'm not kidding."

"Christie, bad things are happening," he said softly, dark eyes on her like onyx. "This is no time to crywolf."

"I would never do that," she said, her temper growing, her tone an aggrieved growl.

"All right, so exactly what happened?"

"I came running out here and . . ."

"And?"

"And I'm not sure."

His voice went very soft then. "You're sure you weren't molested in any way?"

Was she? She'd passed out cold. But she hadn't been assaulted or anything. She was certain of it.

"No. I wasn't hurt. I wasn't even touched," she murmured.

"Okay, so this man broke into your house to stare at you and then did . . . what when you ran out? Ransacked the place?"

No . . . somehow he moved faster than I did. He tapped me on the shoulder and scared me so badly I fainted. But she could hardly say that.

She lowered her head, lashes falling, flushing. "I'm not sure."

"Well, let's take a look around, huh?" He strode toward the house. For a moment she stood watching him; then she hurried after him.

"Jed, what are you doing here, anyway?" she asked.

"I came over to have coffee with Ana, and then I saw you lying out here." He motioned for her to stay on the porch, his face wearing a stern mask of warning.

"He could still be here," he said, and it

made sense — except that she knew he didn't believe her that anyone had been there in the first place.

But she knew he didn't dare ignore her. He might think that she was crazy, that she'd had too much to drink while playing with the occult, but there was a killer in the area, and he couldn't take chances.

"I think I'd be safer with you," she called as he disappeared into the house. "In all those slasher movies, when the guy goes off and leaves the girl she ends up dead!"

There was no answer.

She stood nervously on the porch, feeling like a fool. Despite the fact that this was Florida, autumn was well on the way, and she was chilled, standing there in her damp cotton nightgown and bare feet.

"Jed?"

There was still no answer. She looked around, since there was nothing else to do. The day was coming on nicely. By mid-afternoon, it would be hot. The sky was crystal-blue now, but no doubt this afternoon the thunderclouds would come rolling through.

Jed returned at last, startling her out of her reverie as he stepped outside and shook his head. "Nothing. There's no one in there now."

She let out a long breath. "Jed, it was real. He was real. I opened my eyes, and I saw a man standing at the foot of my bed."

"We'll walk through the house together," he told her, the expression in his dark eyes an enigma. "You can see if anything is out of place."

She followed him into the house. "Upstairs first?" he suggested.

Upstairs, the rooms that her family had claimed in earlier days were empty and undisturbed. Even in her bedroom, everything looked normal. The sheets were tossed back, as they had been when she bolted, but everything else looked just as she had left it.

"Anything?" Jed asked.

She shook her head.

He stared at her. "You and Ana shouldn't have been playing with that stupid Ouija board."

"Oh, so now you believe in Ouija boards?" she said.

"No. But I do believe in the power of suggestion."

They traipsed downstairs. The kitchen was tidy, thanks to her efforts the night before. There was a last garbage bag waiting to go out, but that was it.

In the parlor, the boxes remained where

they had been.

Too bad I don't have a ghost who wants to unpack for me, she thought.

No. She didn't have a ghost at all. Besides, if anyone was haunting this place, it would be Gran, just as they'd said last night. And she would be a stern but kindly ghost.

But of course there were no such things as ghosts, she told herself.

"So has anything been stolen?" Jed asked. "Or even moved?"

"No, I don't think so."

She couldn't help but wish that her hair wasn't sporting blades of grass, and that her cotton sleep shirt wasn't damp and hugging her uncomfortably.

"The silver isn't missing?" There was a dry note in his voice, she noticed.

"No," she said, increasingly upset.

Looking more disturbed than amused, he said, "Christie, if someone really had been in the house, either something would be missing or you would have been followed out and attacked on the lawn."

She glanced around the parlor, and then she frowned.

The Ouija board.

It had been moved; she was certain of it.

She had set it on top of some other boxes when they had finished with it the night before, but now . . .

Now it was back in the center of the floor.

"That moved," she said suddenly.

"What?" Jed asked.

"The Ouija board."

He groaned.

"I'm serious!"

He was so silent that she could have sworn she could hear every breath either one of them took and even their heartbeats.

"Sit down, Christina," he suggested.

She looked at him, puzzled. Then she realized that he was trying to be patient and had reverted to being a cop trying to calm a distraught citizen.

"Christina, I admit I wasn't a cop for all that long, but I never heard of anyone breaking into a house just to move a Ouija board."

She flashed him an irritated glance and stiffened, refusing to give him the satisfaction of sitting down as ordered.

"I'm telling you, when I went to bed last night, that box wasn't there."

"Sit down," he said again. "I can get you a glass of water or put some coffee on if that will help." He wasn't making fun of her, she knew. He was just treating her the same way he had when they'd all been kids and he had five years' advantage over them.

"Jed, I'm telling you —"

"No. Let me talk," he said.

He pushed her down into one of the big wing chairs and hunkered down in front of her, taking her hands. "It's hard. Trust me, I understand how hard it is."

"What are you saying?"

"Christie, you have Dan and Mike, but other than that, you've lost your entire family." His face hardened for a moment, and she knew why. He occasionally talked about his late wife, and sometimes he would smile or even laugh when he talked about something fun they had done.

But he never, ever spoke about the months of her illness or her actual death.

"I'm really not sure you should keep this house," he told her.

"I love this house."

"But you're dangerously close to being haunted by it. By the house itself, by the memories, good and bad, of all the years here. When I lost Margaritte, I stayed in the house for a while. I couldn't part with any of her belongings. They even sent me to a police shrink. Eventually I gave her clothing to charities that could use it and only kept a few special mementos. And I sold the house and moved, because it was the only way I was ever going to stay sane."

She stared at him and squeezed his hand in comfort. There were so many stages of grief: shock, disbelief, anger . . . no, fury. Then, sometimes, a dullness. Acceptance. Enough time to learn that you would never forget. A time to forgive. And then . . . not peace, as some suggested, but at least gratitude for those who tried to help you, and an ability to function and move forward, because that was somehow ingrained alongside the survival instinct.

But she had already accepted her grandmother's death. Gran had lived a long life, and every memory she had that revolved around her grandparents was good.

The house, if it had a personality at all, was good.

"I'm okay. Really. And I love this house. Gran left it to me because she knew that. I'll never sell it," she told him. "But thank you for your concern." She cleared her throat. At another time in her life, she mused, she might have been thrilled to have Jed Braden practically on his knees in front of her, but this moment was far too raw for that. "I'm all right," she said, indicating that she wanted to get up. He stood first, and since his hand was still on hers, he helped her up, too. "Do you want coffee? Or something to eat?" she offered.

He shook his head. "No, thanks. I need to get going. I have a few self-imposed deadlines today, but I'm only a phone call away if you need me."

He did think she was crazy, she thought. Or at least emotionally fragile right now because of Gran's death.

"We checked every room," she said. "There's no one here. And like you said, no one breaks into a house just to move a Ouija board."

He smiled a little ruefully and reached for her, pulling a blade of grass from her hair. "Call me if you need me."

"Sure. Thank you," she said, and smiled at him. Like hell, she fumed in silence. That damned Ouija board had moved.

She managed to keep her smile in place as she walked him to the door.

"Christina," he said gravely, then hesitated.

"I know. There's a killer on the loose with a thing for redheads. I'll be very careful, I swear."

"Sleeping on the lawn isn't being careful."

"I wasn't — Oh, never mind. It won't happen again."

"I really am here if you need me."

"Right," she said, thinking, I had such a crush on you once, buddy.

He was still crush-worthy, she had to admit. The character worn into his features by life made him a striking man.

The fact that he was obviously patronizing her was a sharp wake-up slap, however.

"Thank, Jed. Thanks. I will call if I need you — if there's a real problem," she assured him, and there was only a slight note of coldness in her tone.

If he heard it, he gave no sign, and left.

She closed and locked the door, then looked around. The house was silent. Then the old grandfather clock chimed out the hour of 8:00 a.m. and she jumped.

With an irritated sigh, she headed for the kitchen and the coffeemaker. While coffee brewed, she raced upstairs. She'd been wearing those damp blades of grass just a little too long, and she had too much to do that day to be hanging around in her nightshirt.

Maybe she was crazy, she thought as she showered. Or at least more fragile than she had thought, too open to suggestion.

Because he was right. No one broke into a house just to move a Ouija board.

Unless . . .

Unless they wanted you to think you were crazy.

Police Detective Shot and Killed Disposing of Victim.

Police Detective Beau Kidd Identified as Interstate Killer.

The newspaper headlines gave no indication that Beau had only been the alleged killer. A little voice inside Jed nagged at him guiltily, even though he knew, rationally speaking, that if the department, the news and everyone else had condemned Beau Kidd, there was no reason why he shouldn't have done so, too.

He had seen the story as terrifying, horrible, sad — and a lesson about how impossible it was to know even those closest to you, those who should be trustworthy. He had been completely convinced of Beau Kidd's guilt.

Now he was equally convinced he'd been wrong.

Why?

Sitting at his computer in his townhouse overlooking one of the area's natural lakes, Jed called up his files on the case. He stared at the names and ages of the previous victims as if some new truth would suddenly be revealed. Kelly Dunhill, twenty-four; Janet Major, twenty-eight; Denise Grant, thirty-one; Theodosia Wallace, twenty-two; and Grace Garcia, twenty-five. Only one of them, Grace, had come from the area, and she had been born in Tampa. The others had migrated south from four different states, Kelly from Tennessee, Janet from New York, Denise from Iowa and Theodosia from California. All had long red hair, ranging from strawberry-blonde to a deep, dark auburn. Their eye colors had been different, and their heights had ranged from five six to five nine. Each one had been found in the grass off one of the state's highways, naked, arms crossed over her chest. None had shown signs of torture, such as cigarette burns, but there had been bruises on the bodies, as if they had been pushed around when they were alive.

As if they had tried to fight their abductor.

They'd all been sexually molested, but no semen had been recovered; their killer had used condoms. Nor had there been any flesh beneath their fingernails, so there was no way to test for DNA. The killer had been very careful.

The "no's" were endless.

No fingerprints, no DNA, no footprints, no cigarette butts found by the dump scenes. Simple physiology said that something was left behind when two bodies came together. But not in this case. Nothing of any use whatsoever had ever been discovered. It was baffling, and had been seen as indicating that someone in law enforcement or forensics had been involved.

He read through everything he had acquired from the newspapers and police files, hoping to see something, anything new, a spark of information or even misinformation that might help him. There was nothing.

He decided to take a trip down to his old precinct.

Christina looked around the house while she waited for a new singer, a local girl named Allison Chesney, to show up to work with her on a new nonfat potato chip commercial. The promotions department at the giant food manufacturer had chosen her because of one of her previous jingles, which had been filled with "pep," or so her contact had told her.

She'd managed to get rid of the boxes, storing most of them up in the attic — a perk most of the houses in the area didn't have. She even had a basement, another rarity in the state. Going up to the attic and down to the basement had been a bit over-whelming. Why, she wondered, hadn't she realized just how much stuff she would find there? Despite that, there had been plenty of room for her boxes. In time, she promised herself, she would check out everything that was already there.

She sat down at the piano in the parlor, feeling happy as she ran through the jingle herself one more time. She was ready to try out Allison Chesney's sound, she decided, just as the doorbell rang.

Being smart, as she had promised every-one she would be, she looked through the peephole before opening the door. The young woman on the other side was a pretty brunette with flashing hazel eyes. As soon as Christina opened the door, she offered her hand with a shy smile. "Christina? I'm Allison."

"Hi, great to meet you. Come on in."

"This is your house?" Allison said in awe as she stepped inside.

"Yes."

"It's fabulous."

"Thank you. It's been in the family a long time," Christina replied. "Can I get you something before we get started? Tea? Cof-fee? A bottle of water?"

"Water would be great, thanks."

"Make yourself comfortable in the parlor," Christina told her, pointing the way.

She got a bottle of water from the kitchen and returned to find Allison standing by the piano, looking out the bay window.

"This is really spectacular," Allison told her. "I grew up in a place just like this."

"Really? Where are you from?"

"The Gainesville area."

"It's pretty around there."

Allison laughed. "Pretty quiet."

"It can't be too quiet. It's a university town," Christina reminded her.

"Yeah, and that's about it. But at least it's close to the action here. Well, action Florida-style. I thought I was so good when I was a kid that I was sure I'd be a big deal in New York by now," she said ruefully. "But that's not the way it happened."

"Don't put yourself down. I listened to your demo," Christina told her. "You're good." She sat down at the piano bench and smiled in return. "Or are you trying to tell me that doing jingle work is slumming it?"

"Oh, good God, no!" Allison said. "Not at all. It's just that . . . well, I guess it's this house and, quite honestly, you. What are you? About twenty-five?"

"On the nose."

"And you're so successful," Allison murmured.

"I'm paying the bills," Christina said, smiling.

"Did you ever want to compose great operas or something?" Allison asked, openly curious.

"Nope. I always liked writing little ditties. Must be my Irish heritage," she said dryly. "Quite frankly, I just got lucky with my first jingle and found a good agent. My cousin Dan is an actor, though, and he's still trying to get a break into the big time. Well, the bigger time, anyway."

"Really?"

"He's a few years older than I am, and he's done some great shows, but you know how it is. Every time something ends, you're looking for something new. At the moment he's playing Raccoon Ralph at the new park, but he's been promised a lead in their next main stage show, so he's feeling pretty hopeful."

"Cool," Allison said, looking more relaxed.

"So . . . ready to get started?"

"Can I hear you do it first? Just so I can get a sense of how you hear it?"

"Sure," Christina said, and sang, "Keep it off your hips, try our great new chips, Sanina's is a trip if you're looking for a chip."

Allison smiled broadly as she finished. "Cool," she said again, then apologized. "I'm sorry. There are other words in my vocabulary. Really."

"Not to worry. There's no reason to be nervous around me."

"Sure there is. You can fire me."

"I told you, I liked your demo. I really liked it. Okay?"

Allison started singing then, without waiting for the piano accompaniment. She had just the voice Christina wanted. Women would hear her and think they could be just like her; men would think there was suddenly something sexy about potato chips. Most important, people had to find it catchy enough to make them think about Sanina's Chips frequently.

"Great," Christina told her, and Allison blushed proudly.

They ran through it a few times with the piano, until Christina was more than satisfied that Allison could do the job.

"Okay, we've got an appointment with the Sanina's people at the recording studio next Tuesday morning, nine o'clock."

Allison nodded vigorously. "I wrote it all down the first time we talked. This is great. Thank you. Thank you so much!"

"Thank you," Christina told her as she

walked with her to the door.

"I'm going to be the voice for Sanina's Chips," Allison said happily.

"Let's both hope they're good, huh?" Christina said with a laugh.

Allison smiled and thanked her again, and Christina waved, then closed the door. As it clicked shut, she jumped.

Someone had played a note on the piano.

A single note.

A cold chill swept over her body. She swallowed hard. Something had fallen on the keyboard. That had to be it. Because there was no one else in the house.

She forced herself to turn and retrace her steps. She stood in the doorway and stared into the parlor. There was no one there. Of course not, she told herself. She'd known there was no one else in the house.

She walked into the room and looked at the piano. There was nothing on the keyboard. It was just as she had left it.

Feeling as if cold fingers were raking down her spine, she sat down and forced herself to hum the Sanina's Chips tune as she hesitantly picked out the notes on the piano.

Suddenly she stood abruptly and walked into the kitchen, then back around to the other side of the house to check the library and the dining room.

It was only midafternoon. The sun was out. The day was sparkling.

She walked up the stairs and into every room. She paused on the landing before going downstairs again.

"This is my house," she said aloud. "A good house, where good people, kind people, lived. And still live."

I'm talking out loud to invisible spirits, she moaned inwardly.

"And I'm heading to the coffee shop," she added aloud, then gave herself a shake. No more talking to the air.

Downstairs, she collected her purse and headed out, making certain that she locked the door behind her.


"Hey, it's the local big shot," Alex Mars, who had graduated with Jed from the police academy, called out.

"Hey there," Hal Rather, Alex's partner said, grinning and rising to shake Jed's hand.

"Hey yourself," Jed said, and looked across the room. Jerry Dwyer, looking haggard, was just coming out of the lieutenant's office.

"Jed," he said, grinning, as everyone in the room rose at once and came over.

"Hello, golden boy," Sally Griegs, the

communications officer, teased as she gave him a hug and a kiss on the cheek.

Lieutenant Tiggs came out of the office when he heard all the noise. He was tall and slim but tough as nails, as Jed well knew. He'd seen the lieutenant in action, before his promotion to his current status. Tiggs been attacked in a bar and turned into Jackie Chan. His attacker had wound up on the floor, begging to be cuffed and taken away.

"To what do we owe the honor?" Tiggs asked him.

Jed shrugged. "Frustration?" he suggested.

"You got that right," Jerry muttered.

"You're a civilian now, Jedidiah," Tiggs said, using his full name, just as, for some unknown reason, he always had.

"Licensed private investigator," Jed reminded him lightly.

"Hired by whom?" Tiggs asked skeptically.

Jed shrugged again. "A writer who might have gotten it wrong."

Tiggs stared at him and shook his head. "Has to be a copycat," he said quietly.

"A damned good one, then," Jed said.

Jerry shuffled his feet. "You know we can't give you anything that hasn't already been released — even if we had it," he said.

"Can it, Jerry," Tiggs said. "I know you

had him at the autopsy." He leveled a finger at Jed. "And I know you have copies of the old files. So if you find out anything . . ."

"You know damned well I'd never conceal pertinent information, Lieutenant," Jed said.

"Sometimes I think I know damned well," Tiggs said, "and sometimes I'm not so damned sure I know anything."

"Kidd's old partner —" Jed began.

"Retired. But of course I interviewed him," Jerry said, then added, "But no one can stop you from talking to the man yourself, unless he refuses to talk to you."

Jed looked at Tiggs.

"Be my fuckin' guest. I'd take help from hell itself right now, if it was offered."

Jed frowned. Sure, the new case had hit the papers like a bomb, but it wasn't as if months had gone by with a high-profile case unsolved.

"Troopers just called in a second body off I-4," Jerry said. "I . . . uh . . . I'm on my way to the scene now."

Tiggs threw up his hands. "Screw it." He stared at Jed. "If you don't ask, I can't say no."

He turned around and headed back to his office.

Jed followed Jerry Dwyer out to the street.

■ ■ ■ ■

Coffee cup in hand, Christina headed to a table outside the coffee shop. It was a pleasantly cool day. The sun was out, the sky was blue, and there was a gentle breeze just moving the air. Perfect.

She unfolded the newspaper she'd bought and idly read the local section, noting all the advertisements for the Halloween-themed events taking place at the parks. She wondered idly if Dan was going to play Raccoon Ralph with fangs or dress up as Franken-coon.

As she sat there, still looking at her paper, she suddenly realized that she wasn't alone, that someone had joined her at the little table with the umbrella overhead.

Then it started.

A sense of chills like icy water sweeping down her spine.

She didn't want to look up.

And yet . . .

She felt as if she had to.

The breeze stirred, and it was almost as if she felt a touch. A gentle, silken touch, nostalgic, poignant . . .

It was the breeze, she told herself, and finally looked up.

She exhaled, feeling like a fool. There was no one there.

Smiling in embarrassment at her own lunacy, she picked up her coffee and headed for her car. Ten minutes later, she turned down her street and pulled into her driveway.

The moment she was inside, she felt it again. That terrible, chilling sensation. As if she was not alone. As if someone was with her, watching her.

There's no one here, she told herself. No one. This was the same silly thing that had happened at the coffee shop.

Still, she immediately stepped back outside. She wasn't going in alone. She sat on the porch and tried Mike's number first, but hung up when she got his answering machine. She tried Dan next, and he answered.

"What's up, cuz?" he asked.

"What are you doing?"

"Watching TV, killing time till my evening shift," he told her. Then, carefully, he asked, "Why?"

She hesitated. "Is there any chance you can come over?" she asked him.

"I guess. Why?" he asked again.

"I . . . it's silly. I keep thinking someone is in the house," she admitted.

He was quiet for a minute. She heard him sigh. "Christie . . . are you afraid that Gran is haunting the house or something?"

"No!"

"All right. I'll be there in a few minutes."

She waited, wincing at the thought that she'd had to call her cousin to come over. But better to call him than do something stupid. Like go into a house where a murderer might be waiting.

Dan made it to the house in record time. She rose from the porch steps as soon as he pulled up and got out of the car. "Let's see what's up, kid," he said, stepping past her and entering the house. She followed him, but Dan was moving quickly. He cut a circular path through the ground floor, and she only caught up with him as he hurried up the stairs.

There was no one downstairs, and not a sound — other than the old floorboards creaking beneath their feet — could be heard as they went to check the bedrooms.

On the upstairs landing, Dan paused, hands on hips, staring at her. "Maybe you should sell this place," he said softly.

"No way," she said firmly. "Gran left me this place, and I'm not leaving."

With a groan, he checked the bedrooms one by one, then pulled down the stairs to the attic. It wasn't a spooky attic; it was well used and even well lit. There was a rocker by the little window that now looked over the neighbor's yard but had once offered a view of a sloping green hill. There were trunks and boxes, an old love seat and an overstuffed chair, and even a braided rug set between those so people could sit and play games.

It had always been a family home.

But there wasn't a hint of a stranger, a presence, or anyone who shouldn't have been there.

"Basement," she said.

Dan rolled his eyes impatiently. "Sure," he agreed, and they traipsed back down the stairs.

The door to the basement was in the kitchen. Christina hit the light switch, and they headed down into another bright, comfortable space. There was a Ping-Pong table in the center of the main area, surrounded by lounge chairs. There was a wet bar in the corner, and the laundry room was off to one side.

And nothing else.

"Okay?" Dan asked.

"Yeah, thanks," she said awkwardly. "I'm . . . uh . . . sorry I bothered you."

He set an arm around her shoulders,

pulled her close and lightly patted the top of her head. "Don't worry about it."

"Thanks," she said lightly.

"And . . . well, you are living here alone. You're right to be careful. Call anytime, Christie. I'll be here."

Back upstairs, she asked him if he wanted something to eat or drink.

"No, thanks. In fact, I'd better get going. I'm going to be doing some extra work at the park, so I need to go in for a costume fitting. I'm the Grim Reader," he told her. "Like the Grim Reaper, get it? You going to come see me read scary stories to the kiddies?"

"Of course," she told him.

"I'll call you later with my schedule," he said.

"Super. And thanks again."

She walked him to the door. He left with a wave, and she locked the door immediately, telling herself that maybe it was natural to feel uneasy in a house she'd never really lived in before, and never alone.

She walked into the parlor and sat idly on the piano bench, planning just to fool around.

There was music on the stand, she realized.

She frowned. She hadn't left any music

out. Had she?

No, damn it, she knew she hadn't.

Great. Who broke into a house to put music up on a stand?

She looked around the room. She was far from obsessive-compulsive, but . . .

Things had moved.

The changes were subtle. A chair facing in a slightly different direction. The drapes drawn back just a bit farther than they had been.

Her heart started to beat hard. She was tempted to leap to her feet and flee the house again.

She gritted her teeth, suddenly fighting tears.

No.

It had to be her imagination. Emotions seeping from her subconscious and coloring the world. There was no denying the fact that there had been far too much loss in her life.

"I am not running away again," she said softly.

Dusk fell as she sat there, unmoving.

Then she nearly jumped straight over the piano as a shrill noise suddenly reverberated through the house.

# 5

The first patrolman on the scene had done his job; a huge perimeter had been marked off around the body, keeping voyeurism from the highway to a minimum. Doc Martin was already on the scene, speaking to Jerry's partner, Mal O'Donnell, when they arrived.

O'Donnell swept a long gaze over Jed but made no protest at his appearance. Doc Martin gave both the newcomers a nod.

"You know I can't say anything definitive until I've completed the autopsy. But . . ." Martin let out a weary sigh. "This does echo Sherri Mason's murder to a T. She was definitely dumped here. I'd estimate time of death to have been very late last night or very early this morning. I'd say she was laid out before dawn."

"Jesus," Jerry muttered. "And it took this long for someone to spot her?"

"Over there," Jed said, pointing. "The

bushes. They hid her from the road. And let's face it, people going by at sixty miles an hour don't have time to notice much."

Since he hadn't been thrown out, he hunkered down by the body while the others digested the fact that the bushes had evidently hidden the victim from the road.

"He must have not have realized his mistake," Jerry said.

"I agree," O'Donnell said. "He likes — needs — the attention that comes from the bodies being discovered naked and posed."

"And vulnerable," Jed agreed. He realized that the cops and the M.E. were staring at him, and he knew why. Everyone knew he had copies of the old files. That he had interviewed scores of people for his book. That he'd become friends with the FBI agent who had profiled the killer for them.

Jed looked down at the dead woman. Her face was lovely; her brown hair long and highlighted with wide streaks of red. The strangulation marks on her neck were the only apparent giveaway to her violent end. She was stretched out naked, arms crossed over her chest, mummy-style.

Or in a way she might have been laid out in a funeral parlor.

"Patti Jo Buhler," Mal O'Donnell said quietly. "Twenty-nine. There's an employee

ID in her purse, which was found to the left there." He paused to point out the location where an officer had discovered her bag. "She's an entertainer at one of the parks."

"Usual victim," Jerry said dryly.

Jed stared at the girl. His heart seemed to lurch. Without the marks, she might have been sleeping. She almost looked as if she could open her eyes, smile and get to her feet. She might be at peace in death, but her dreams were over.

"Any other bruising?" he asked Doc Martin.

"I'm seeing a few spots where it looks like postmortem bruising will appear," Doc said. With a gloved forefinger he pointed to her arms. "See there? She was shoved around, but she wasn't beaten."

Jed looked down at what was left of Patti Jo Buhler. He'd seen all the crime photos when he'd written the book, and this could have been one of them. Like the others, she'd been a beautiful young woman with everything to live for.

But now . . .

He thanked God he was no longer a cop. That he wasn't the one who would have to inform her family. That he wouldn't have to feel their pain, so much greater than anything a cop learned to live with.

A redhead lying there. . . .

She could too easily have been Beau Kidd's sister.

Worse.

A flash of vision taunted his mind's eye, and for just a moment he saw Christina Hardy lying there.

He stiffened, then shrugged to ease the tension in his shoulders. He was getting too involved. Too wrapped up in this. Letting it eat him up inside.

O'Donnell's phone rang. He answered it, stating his name in a monotone, then listened expressionlessly for a moment. "Thanks," he said then, and hung up. He looked at the others. "Patti Jo was officially reported missing by her roommate two days ago, after they made her wait the mandatory twenty-four hours, so we can assume she was nabbed somewhere between work and home three days ago. A dozen people saw her leave the park. No one's found anyone who's seen her since."

"If we can get Tiggs's okay, I'd like to use the media," Jerry told his partner.

"Why the hell not?" O'Donnell muttered. "Nothing else is working."

Jed stood. "Time for me to go, but thanks for letting me in," he said to the two cops and the M.E.

"Sure. Just don't make us out to be the bad guys in your next blockbuster, huh?" There was a note of venom in O'Donnell's voice that surprised Jed. He'd thought the department had accepted that the Interstate Killer had been one of their own gone bad.

"Where are you off to?" Jerry asked Jed suspiciously.

"Gainesville," Jed told him.

"To see Larry Atkins?" O'Donnell asked sharply.

"Yes."

O'Donnell shook his head. "Atkins will swear on his life that he knew he was doing the right thing. What do you expect? That he wants to be known as a trigger-happy cop who killed his own partner?"

"Maybe these are copycat killings," Jerry said. "Hell, none of us were around back when it all went down."

O'Donnell looked away. He obviously wasn't pleased to have Jed around now. Too bad, Jed thought. Because if he felt like it, he could say he had been hired to look into the case.

Beau Kidd's sister was looking for the truth.

Jed felt a sense of uneasiness. It was imperative for them to solve this case quickly. This guy was piling up victims fast.

But there was something more frightening, more personal, about the current situation.

The killer was focusing on redheads. Like Beau Kidd's sister.

And like Christina Hardy.

Jed looked at his watch. Plenty of time. He had an hour- , hour-and-a-half ride ahead of him. Larry Atkins had retired to a farm outside Gainesville, where he kept retired racehorses that hadn't been successful enough to become breeding stallions or broodmares, horses that might have wound up in the glue factory. He was a homebody. His wife had died a decade ago, and his kids had gone to college out west and stayed there.

Most nights Larry could be found on his porch from about seven to nine, smoking his pipe in peace and quiet, and staring out over the acreage his pension had bought him.

Two killings. God in heaven, Larry had to have something to give him. It was as if this guy was carrying out a series of perfect murders, as if he were in law enforcement, forensics . . .

As if he were a detective assigned to this very case.

There was no such thing as the perfect

murder, Jed reminded himself.

"Tell Larry hi for me," O'Donnell said.

"Will do," Jed assured him, and he headed for his car.

"Hey!" O'Donnell yelled.

"Yeah?" Jed turned back.

"No secrets, no being a big man and thinking you're going to solve the case. You —"

"Yes, I know," Jed said patiently. "If I come up with anything at all, I'll be calling."

Christ!

What the hell did it matter who figured it out?

As long as the killing stopped. Now. Before . . .

He gritted his teeth and kept going to his car.

It was the phone. Nothing more than the phone.

Christina laughed aloud, then sobered, glad she hadn't hurt herself when she'd jumped off the piano bench with such force that it had tipped over. She'd forgotten that the phone rang as loud as a banshee's howl because Gran had been afraid she was losing her hearing.

"Hey, you," Ana said when Christina

caught her breath and picked up.

"Hey, yourself."

"What are you doing?" Ana asked cheerfully.

Sitting here afraid that I'm imagining really weird things. Or that I'm not imagining them and they're real, which is even worse.

"Working," she said instead.

"I'm coming over, and we're going out," Ana said.

"Oh?"

"You need to get out of that house," Ana said.

"Ana, I just moved in."

"You have to get away from your own company for a while," Ana said.

"Now, that's just mean. I actually like myself just fine," Christina told her.

"Great, well, then, do you still like me?"

"Of course I do."

"Good. Because I want to go shopping. I don't have anything to wear for Halloween. And I don't want to go out alone."

Did she really want to stay there? Christina asked herself. No.

"Give me ten minutes," she said into the phone.

As soon as Ana arrived, Christina ran out to her car and slid into the passenger seat, then stared at her friend and asked accusingly, "Okay, who have you been talking to?"

"About what?"

"Me."

Ana shrugged. "Well, I did get a call from Jed."

Christina groaned. "He thinks I'm crazy."

"Not true. He . . . cares about you."

"Don't be ridiculous. I've barely seen him in years."

Ignoring that, Ana said, "And then I happened to run into Dan at the gas station."

"My cousin thinks I'm crazy," Christina said glumly, then brightened. "Did he tell you he's going to be playing the Grim Reader?"

"No. Is he supposed to be scary?"

"Yeah, I think so. We need to go see him do his thing. Should be fun."

Ana shuddered. "And crowded."

"Not if we avoid the weekends and Halloween itself."

"We should make plans, then. There are only two weeks left until Halloween."

"My nights are fairly open," Christina told her. She thought about it for a minute. "In fact, they're completely open right now."

Ana giggled. "Mine, too. Hey, can he get us free passes?"

"I'm sure he can. So where are we going

tonight, anyway?"

"A place called Once More, With Feeling. They sell vintage stuff, and then for Halloween they bring in more costumes than anyone else in the area. You'll like it."

The shop was as eclectic as promised. Half of it was dedicated to the old, from fedoras to flower-child bell-bottoms. Then there were the costumes, as well as a selection of accessories that could be added to the off-the-rack offerings to individualize them.

"We should do a theme thing," Ana murmured. "You know, like Dorothy, Toto, the Tin Man and all that."

"Are we going trick-or-treating?" Christina asked.

"I want to go out, anyway. I'd love to win the costume contest at O'Reilly's this year."

"If you want Dan to come, you'll have to make sure he's not working."

"We'll just buy him a costume and hope for the best. Are you in?"

"Whatever."

"Okay, I'll be Toto," Ana said.

"I'm not carrying you around in a basket all night," Christina said.

"I know, but think about how great it will be. Every time you see people doing the Wizard of Oz thing, Toto is a stuffed toy. You never see a live Toto. And you'll be fabulous as Dorothy."

Christina shrugged. Ana was going through a rack of costumes, looking for what, Christina wasn't certain. She found herself watching the other customers, curious to see what they were picking up.

A group of college boys were gravitating toward the slasher costumes. One of them put on a Freddy Krueger mask, and started laughing and menacing his friends. It was quite an effectively creepy costume, Christina thought.

And when he had it on, he could have been anyone.

It was a sobering thought.

"Are you listening?" Ana said, breaking into her thoughts.

"What?"

"Pay attention, would you? Mike can be the Tin Man, and Dan can be the Scarecrow."

"We'll be missing the Cowardly Lion," Christina pointed out.

"I'll have to talk Jed into that one."

"You think you can get Jed to dress up like the Cowardly Lion?"

"Maybe not." Ana looked thoughtful for a moment. "We'll work on who dresses up as what later. He might go for it, though. He actually does have a sense of humor. Somewhere," Ana assured her dryly. "I'm going to pay for this stuff. Then we'll go."

"We'll split it," Christina told her.

After the costume shop, they headed down International Drive, Ana complaining about the tourists the whole way. "The traffic gets worse every day."

"It's October in theme-park land. What do you want?"

Ana was quiet for a minute. "Haven't they heard we have a serial killer on the loose?" she asked.

Christina was surprised by her friend's intensity. "Ana, most people never think they could be victims themselves. And most women can assure themselves they're not young or a redhead."

Ana looked at her worriedly. "You are."

"But I'm not a tourist," Christina said with a sigh.

"Here we are," Ana said. "And I'm starving."

They had reached O'Reilly's, a pub that predated the invasion of theme parks into central Florida. Family-owned and operated, it was currently in the hands of the third generation. The food was good and solid, and the atmosphere was friendly.

"Check out the pictures on the wall when we go in," Ana said. "You can see who's won in previous years."

"Yes, ma'am," Christina said meekly, smiling.

A friendly hostess showed them to a booth. They both opted for iced tea and shepherd's pie, the house specialty. When their drinks were delivered, Christina dutifully looked at the pictures on the wall, recently hung as a ploy to entice customers to make O'Reilly's their destination of choice on Halloween. First prize was a thousand dollars — and a place on the October Wall of Infamy.

"Oh, my God," Ana breathed suddenly.

"What?"

Ana pointed to the television behind the bar. Customers usually sat there to watch sports. But there was no game on tonight. Instead the screen showed a reporter, looking grim as he spoke live from the shoulder of a highway, where he was interviewing a police spokesman.

"Turn it up, please," someone at the bar said.

The entire restaurant seemed to go still as the police spokesman, a lean, older, authoritative man, spoke quietly.

". . . yet another victim. We are withholding her identity until her next of kin have been notified. We're asking everyone —

especially young women — to be careful. Don't go anywhere with strangers. Don't walk through dark parking lots alone. Many of the businesses in the area will be taking special precautions to ensure the safety of our residents and tourists. We're also asking for help. Be vigilant and report anything, anything at all, that looks suspicious. Be smart, be careful."

"Some people are saying that the Interstate Killer has come back to town," the interviewer said. "Are we looking at a copycat, or was a serious mistake made twelve years ago?"

"Beau Kidd was never convicted of any crime," the spokesman said. "But we don't know what we're looking at just yet. Be assured that we have every law enforcement agency in the state on guard, and if circumstances warrant, the FBI will be called in, as well."

Christina started when her dinner was set before her and looked up. Their waitress was a pretty girl with golden eyes, freckles and carrot-red hair. Her slight accent said she was Irish but had been in the States for a while.

"They aren't saying it on TV," the girl murmured with a shiver, "but some cops come in here all the time, and they talk.

Freddy MacGregor was just in, and he said that girl was a brunette, but she had red streaks in her hair."

Christina felt a sensation of dread come creeping over her.

"I'm dying my hair black," the waitress announced, staring at the television. Then she cleared her throat. "More iced tea?" she asked cheerfully.

Christina hoped to find out more about the murder, but the station was no longer broadcasting live from the highway. They'd moved on to interviewing little children in homemade Halloween costumes.

"Just great, isn't it?" Ana muttered in a tone that said it was anything but great.

"What?"

"All those kids in monster costumes. What happened to being a cowboy or a princess? All those monsters . . . when there's a real monster out there."

"There's always a real monster out there somewhere," Christina said. And that was the sad truth, she thought. Somewhere, at any given time, there was a monster on the streets. "And the scariest monsters look just like the boy next door," she murmured.

"I figured you'd be back," Larry Atkins said.

As Jed had expected, Larry had been sitting on his porch, a cool beer by his side while he puffed on his pipe. The pipe smoke had a pleasant aroma.

"That thing will kill you one day," Jed told him.

Larry smiled and ignored his words, using his pipe to point in the direction of his pasture. "You ever think about getting a horse, Jed? I just got a mare in — they were going to put her down. She didn't live up to her promise. Sweetest thing you ever want to see. She follows me around just like a puppy dog, as if she knows I saved her life. A horse would do you good, you know. Grab a beer from the cooler over there, make yourself at home."

Jed perched on the wooden porch fence and shook his head. "Thanks, but it's a long drive back."

"Yup. An hour and a half — just like the drive up here — and you decided to come on a whim, huh?"

"You haven't heard yet? They found another victim."

Larry stared at him and shook his head. "What the fuck is wrong with people? I drew my weapon twice when I was on the force. The first time I winged a guy so high on heroin that when he took aim at me, the bullet went about a hundred feet wide. And then . . . then I shot my own partner when I saw him with that girl. I gave him a warning, and that's when he drew his gun on me. But I tell you, even seeing Beau there with the girl, even knowing he was a sick psychopath, even then . . . knowing that I'd killed a man was a bitch. How the hell do people get so warped that they can rip up another human being and take pleasure in the pain?"

"If we had that one solved, we could start working on world peace," Jed told him.

"You came out here because you're thinking I must have made a mistake," Larry said, and scratched his chin thoughtfully.

"I saw the last victim not two hours ago," Jed said quietly. "I'm telling you, it looks like the same guy. Larry, did I miss something in the files? Can you think of anything, anything at all, that was particular to the Interstate Killer? Something to prove this maniac is a copycat?"

"Boy, wouldn't we both like that?" Larry breathed.

"Want to talk through it again?"

"Sure. I got nothing to hide. Beau had dated Janet Major, the fourth victim. I saw his face when we found her. He was green. At first I thought he was all torn up about it. But then, little by little, it comes out that the two of them had a real set-to over some other guy. She was seen leaving Beau's apartment complex the day before she died. None of us believed it could be him, but our lieutenant did talk to him. Beau admitted to me that the lieutenant was worried — he hadn't accused him, but he was about to take him off the case. So I did some background checks on the other victims and some sleuthing on my own . . . turned out he had at least met the other girls, as well. A few of the other detectives on the case were starting to look at him, too, especially after the point was made that we were looking for someone who knew what the cops would be looking for and knew how not to leave a trace. And we just couldn't find anything. You would have thought one of those girls would have managed to scratch the killer, but . . . nothing.

"He was dating the girl from Tampa, the last victim, Grace Garcia. We all knew it. When I came up, he had her in his arms, he was laying her out. I shouted at him, and he drew on me! What the hell else could have been going on?"

Larry's voice sounded tortured. Well, why the hell not? Jed thought. He was going through his own angst, and all he'd done was write a book.

Larry Atkins had shot and killed the man.

"Larry, other than Beau knowing the girls and being a cop, what was the other evidence against him?" Jed asked. "Run through it for me again."

Larry stared out at the field, puffing on his pipe. "No alibi," he said, and took a deep breath. "The way we saw it, and the FBI guy agreed with us, the profile was for a man in his twenties, a functioning psychotic, someone who smiled by day and went about his business. Hell, look how long Bundy got away with it." He shook his head. "Lots of times, you get the guy who's down and out, a car thief, a junkie. He looks weird, and people are afraid of him. Then you get the really scary guys, who look as normal as your dad or your brother, and everybody around goes, hell, no, he's a nice guy, he pats my dog on the head, he keeps his yard neat. Beau was that guy."

"So far, everything about these killings is the same as twelve years ago, the women disappearing, being missing for almost three days before they're found."

"Sounds right," Larry agreed, rocking in his chair, not looking at Jed.

"So here's the question. Where the hell is he keeping them?" Jed asked.

"We never found any evidence, but Beau

must have been hiding them in his apartment, tying them up, gagging them . . . until their time was up and he killed them."

"In his apartment," Jed murmured.

"We've been over this before," Larry said. "I wish I could think of something, something I've been missing."

There has to be something, Jed thought.

"I've been thinking about nothing else, ever since I heard about the murder of Sherri Mason," Larry told him. "I just can't think of a damn thing."

"Thanks for trying, Larry."

"You come anytime."

"I will. Thanks again."

"Think about getting a horse, Jed."

"I live in an apartment."

"Get yourself some land, get into horses."

"I'll give it some thought," Jed promised.

"I think I'm going to stay with you tonight," Ana told Christina when they reached her house.

Christina realized that she was staring at the house with foreboding, and immediately felt irritated with herself.

It was her house now; she was the keeper of the family seat. And she loved it.

"I'm fine. Really," she lied to Ana, hoping her tone was as convincing as her words.

"Maybe you're fine, but I'm not," Ana told her.

Christina turned to her friend in surprise. Ana did look upset.

They exited the car and looked around, then looked at each other, both silently acknowledging they really were somewhat nervous. But the night was clear and beautiful; there wasn't a trace of the fog that had rolled in the night before.

Christina unlocked the door, and they entered the house. "Want tea or something?" she asked.

"We just ate," Ana reminded her, then yawned. "I'm ready for bed."

"Sounds good."

Ana didn't seem to be afraid once they were inside, Christina noticed, but she herself felt just as uneasy as she had before. She assured herself that the door to the basement was bolted, then wedged a chair under the doorknob to brace it, just for good measure.

"I'm going upstairs," Ana called.

"Cool. Pick a room."

"Pick a room? You just move over, sweetie. I'm bunking with you."

"Thank God you're small," Christina teased.

She went to set the coffeepot timer for the

next morning, and it was then that she froze.

Someone had already done it.

The timer was set for seven-thirty, and the light was on.

Had she lost her mind? Was she doing these things herself and not realizing it?

She reached into one of the cabinets for Gran's old rolling pin and got the pepper spray out of her purse. Methodically, and alone, she searched the downstairs.

Nothing.

No one.

Nothing else out of place.

Still armed, she walked up the steps and went through every room upstairs except her own, determinedly looking in every closet and underneath all the beds. Though she realized that she was shaking, she decided to check out the attic.

Ana — comfortably clad in a pair of Christina's pajamas — came out into the hallway just as she pulled down the ladder.

"What are you doing?" her friend demanded.

"The coffeepot was already set," Christina said. "Someone's been in here."

Ana watched her, frowning. "Christina, no one breaks in just to set a coffee timer. You must have done it and forgotten."

"No, I didn't."

She started up the ladder and realized Ana was behind her.

"What are you doing?" Christina demanded.

"You're not leaving me alone down here," Ana said.

"Nothing's going to happen to you," Christina promised. "I searched the ground floor and secured the basement, and I've been all through the rooms up here. All that's left is the attic."

"You're still not leaving me down here," Ana assured her.

They went up the ladder, Ana on Christina's heels. Christina found the light switch and looked around. The attic was just as it had always been.

"There's no one here, Christina," Ana said. "Maybe it wouldn't hurt for you to see a therapist. I mean, maybe you're having short-term memory loss."

"I'm not," Christina insisted stubbornly. But what else could it be?

"Christie, thieves don't break in just to move things around and put the coffee on for you," Ana said gently.

"Let's get some sleep," Christina suggested firmly, ignoring Ana's unassailable logic.

Ana giggled. "If you've got a ghost who

brews the coffee for you, I want him to move in with me."

Christina groaned. "I don't need this from you, okay? Don't you dare mention a word of this. Promise me right now that you won't."

"Right. My lips are sealed." Ana hesitated. "Can we sleep with the television on?"

In a few minutes they were in bed, the hallway and bathroom lights still on, the TV tuned to a channel that ran nothing but sitcoms twenty-four hours a day. Pillows plumped, they settled down.

Ana was quickly and soundly asleep. Christina watched the television until she finally started to drift off.

Then it started again.

The feeling.

The feeling that someone was there. Standing at the foot of the bed.

Watching her.

Open your eyes.

No! she thought, ignoring what had to be an imaginary voice.

Christie . . . Help me, please. . . .

She opened her eyes.

The room was in shadow, strange contrasts of light and dark created by the glow emanating from the bathroom and the hallway, which still left so much in darkness.

But there was something.

A figure.

At the foot of her bed.

"Ana!" she cried, gripping her friend's arm.

Ana awoke, screaming. "What?"

The shadow . . . the figure . . . was gone.

Christina jumped up and ran to the foot of the bed, where she waved her hands through the air as if trying to feel something that clearly wasn't there. Ana stared at her as if she had gone mad.

Suddenly they heard a noise from outside, the slamming of a car door.

They stared at each other. Ana's jaw dropped.

Christina flew to the window, Ana right behind her.

There was a strange car in her driveway, parked on the far side of hers, so she couldn't see the make or model.

"There!" Ana gasped.

Christina looked, and then she gasped, too.

A tall, dark, menacing figure was standing on the lawn. And as she watched, it started moving toward the house.

# 6

"And ever since the coming of the creature to the cavern, eerie screams can be heard at night. No one dares enter, because the creature remains there still, deep in the earth beside the crystal waters . . . waiting."

Dan McDuff whispered the last word, then shut the book with a thump. To his deep gratification, several of the young women and two of the men in the audience jumped. He rose from the overstuffed armchair where the Grim Reader held court and swept a hand over the crowd, long black nails catching in the dim light. "Come back tomorrow night, if you dare, and the Grim Reader will offer you more tales of mystery, mayhem and the bizarre. Until then, good night, my children. Morbid dreams to you all."

To the accompaniment of a nice smattering of applause, he walked down from the dais and headed for the doorway hidden in a hollow tree in the Mystic Forest, leading to a stairway into the tunnel system that was reserved for employees only. As the Grim Reader, it wouldn't do for him to be seen mingling with the crowd before or after his appearances, though he did sit atop one of the floats in the parade, his oversize book on his lap, using his silver-tipped cane to point in sham threat at people in the crowd.

When he reached the men's locker room, he scrubbed off the white-and-gray face paint that gave him the look of an aging corpse, then showered and dressed. He was off for the night.

He let out an irritated sigh as he shut his locker. There was still no word on final casting for the new show, and he was starting to get frustrated. He really didn't want to be Raccoon Ralph forever. It didn't pay enough, for one thing. It wasn't that he'd gone through life wasting money, and he had the trust fund his grandmother had left him, but he was getting old. He needed something more substantial on his résumé. Either that, or he needed enough money to invest along with some of his fellow actors at the park who wanted to open their own theater.

He reflected for a moment that it was too bad Gran hadn't decided to sell the old house — he didn't even want to speculate what it was worth. Even a third of the profit from the house would have set him up. Hell, he probably could have opened a theater all on his own.

He smiled suddenly, wondering just how Christie was doing on her own in the old house.

As he left the locker room he bumped into Marcie McDonnagh, who was up for the part of Hera in the new Greek gods show and was also currently a fluffy by day and scary creature by night.

Marcie was pretty, with shoulder-length auburn hair and huge dark eyes. She was a talented dancer, as well, an area where he was lacking. His strength was that he could glance at a page of new music and know the melody before it ever left his lips.

"I wish they'd cast that new show already," she said, obviously as frustrated by the situation as he was.

"Yeah, me, too." He didn't tell her that he was relieved that she didn't know any more than he did.

She yawned. "Well, good night. See you tomorrow?"

"Yeah, I'm on."

She gave him a big smile. She really was pretty, he thought. Not to mention talented, and sweet.

She turned to walk away. "Hey, Marcie," he said.

"Yeah?"

"Be careful."

She shivered. "I know. Who can miss the news?"

"I'm on my way out. Let me walk you to your car."

She nodded. "Sure. Thanks."

As they walked, Dan slipped an arm around her shoulder. Maybe he wasn't the best dancer, he thought. But he had all the strength he needed.

"Oh, my God! He's coming!" Ana yelped.

The doorbell rang, and Ana turned to stare at Christina, who stared right back.

Then reason asserted itself.

"Burglars don't usually ring the doorbell," Christina assured Ana.

"But . . . it's so late."

"We were tired, so we went to bed. It's really not that late. Only around ten-thirty."

"You get a lot of visitors this late?"

"I've only lived here two days."

"Get the rolling pin and your pepper spray," Ana advised.

Though she felt foolish, Christina did as Ana had suggested. Then they crept down the stairs and toward the front door. When the bell rang again, they both jumped, and Christina almost stepped on Ana.

Christina stepped up to the front door and looked through the peephole, then let out a sigh of relief.

"Who is it?" Ana demanded, pushing closer and trying to get a look.

"Jed," Christina said in surprise, balancing the pepper spray and rolling pin in one hand so she could open the door.

Jed stared at them with arched brows as the door opened. "You two look like you've seen a ghost. Did something happen?"

"Someone made coffee!" Ana blurted.

"What?" Jed demanded.

Christina stared at Ana. So much for not saying anything.

"Nothing. Come on in," she said.

He looked warily at the rolling pin.

"Just a precaution," she said, blushing.

"And don't worry," Ana added quickly. "We searched the house."

Jed looked at Christina, and she couldn't tell if she was reading doubt or concern in the dark depths of his eyes. "Why were you searching the house this time?"

"Christina was convinced someone was here," Ana explained. "Someone who set the coffeepot to go on at seven-thirty."

This time Christina was certain the look he gave her was one of doubt.

"You think someone broke into your house to make coffee for you?" he inquired, trying to keep the skepticism from his voice.

She waved a hand dismissively and glared at Ana. "Don't worry about it," she muttered quickly. "What are you doing here so late?" she asked, forcing cheer into her voice. "Anybody want tea?"

"I'd love some," Ana said.

Jed shrugged, staring at Christina, who headed for the kitchen, tossing a question over her shoulder. "So what are you doing here, Jed?"

"I guess I just came by to check on you."

The others had followed her to the kitchen, where they perched on bar stools at the pass-through counter.

"We heard the news while we were out," Christina said. "That they found another girl."

She was certain she saw concern in his eyes. She let out a breath.

"A redhead," she murmured.

"Like I said, I just came by to say hi, make sure things were all right," Jed said, still staring at Christina with concern — and wariness.

"Well, it's nice to see you," Christina said,

privately thinking that she and Ana must be quite a sight, with tangled hair and scrubbed faces, and wearing pajamas.

Admittedly, he was just a friend, but still, she wished she looked a bit more dignified. Or even . . . sexy.

Not like the kid he had known forever.

"Did I wake you guys up?" he asked.

"No," Ana said. "We weren't asleep, we were staring out the window. We should have Jed look around the place, too," Ana said.

"There's no one here," Christina assured her.

"Because whoever was here just put the coffee on and left?" Ana asked flatly.

Christina stared hard at Ana again. Didn't her friend realize that she was adding to Jed's perception that she was crazy, or at least overemotional?

Christina knew that she'd had a crush on the guy all her life, which was making her current embarrassment worse, but she couldn't help it. She didn't want him thinking she needed serious therapy.

"No harm in looking," Jed told her. "I'll just take a walk through the house."

"I'll go with you," Christina said.

"Hey, you're not leaving me here alone," Ana warned them. "Haven't you ever seen a slasher film?"

"Not many," Christina said, and almost added, Real life is worse.

They followed Jed from room to room, floor to floor. Occasionally he asked Christina if anything looked odd or out of place, and once he asked if she could think of any reason why someone would come in to make coffee for her.

"The thing is," he said when they were once again in the front hall, "no one has broken in. Your lock hasn't been picked."

He was right, she realized.

If someone had been in the house, that someone had used a key. There was absolutely no sign of forced entry.

"Does Dan or Mike have a key?" Jed asked.

"I . . . I don't know. But I just can't see either one of them coming in to set up the coffeemaker."

"Then there's just one answer," Ana said softly.

Christina glared at her. "But I didn't do it." They were both staring at her. Irritated, she said sharply, "Whatever!"

Jed looked away and cleared his throat. She remained stubbornly silent. He looked back at her and asked, "What else could it be?"

"Dan's the type to play a practical joke," Ana suggested.

"Mike isn't," Christina replied.

They were all startled by a knock at the door, and Jed arched a brow questioningly. As if she should know who would be stopping by in the middle of the night, Christina thought, her irritation growing.

Jed opened the door to reveal Tony standing on the front steps.

"I saw all the lights on and came over to check up on Christina," he said, looking questioningly at Jed. "Is everything all right?"

"Everything's fine, Tony. Thanks for looking out for me," Christina said. "Do you want to come in? Would you like some tea or something?"

"Tony, you haven't seen anyone hanging around the house, have you?" Jed asked before Tony could answer.

"No, why?" Tony frowned in thought.

"No reason," Christina said firmly. "We're just a bunch of nervous Nellies, as Gran would say. So . . . would you like something?"

"No, no, I've got to get back. Ilona will be worried."

Christina smiled. "Thanks for checking on me," she said with genuine gratitude.

"Good night, then," Tony told them.

"Night," Ana echoed.

After Tony left and the door was shut, the three of them stood awkwardly in the hall once again.

"All right, I'm out of here, too," Jed said. He kissed his cousin on the cheek; then a beat passed before he took Christina by the shoulders and kissed her cheek, too. It was casual, one friend to another.

The warmth of his lips on her cheek seemed to rush through Christina like lava. Sensual. Sexual. She tried not to react visibly. Had her crush on the man always been this strong? It had always been there, that quality in him that made her want to be near him. Only now that she was older, she could see — no, feel — that she wanted so much more than just to be there in his shadow. The man who stood before her now was far more than just a handsome high school jock or a brooding Heathcliff on the moors. Shaped by the good and the bad he'd faced in life, as were they all, he was the complete package now, a man worth loving.

"Good night, Jed," Ana said cheerfully.

"Good night," Christina managed politely, then stood there with a pleasant smile plastered to her face. If only Ana were leaving and Jed were staying.

But that wasn't the way of things, and in a moment he was gone.

"Lock the door. Carefully," Ana said gravely.

Christina wasn't sure if a door could be locked carefully, but she slid both bolts home as firmly as she could.

"Let's get some sleep," Ana said.

"Let me just make sure the burners are off," Christina said. "You run on up."

"Not on your life," Ana said, and trailed behind her to check out the kitchen before they went upstairs, where they left the hallway and bathroom lights on again.

Christina was half asleep when Ana said, "It's strange, really. You've always been afraid of the dark."

"I'm not afraid of the dark," Christina heard herself reply, the response instant — and defensive. "I just hate it," she said, "when it's pitch dark . . . you can trip on things. You can't see."

"That's the point. For sleeping, anyway."

"Do you want more lights out?"

"Good God, no."

Ana fell asleep quickly moments later, while Christina found herself lying awake and wondering.

What was it about the darkness?

It could be the idea of the unknown, always lying hidden in the dark.

Or was it that, somewhere deep inside, to everyone, darkness meant death? Death without reprieve. Just a coffin in the earth, and nothingness . . .

She rolled over, and at last she slept.

Ana was a freelance makeup artist, a good one. She'd been offered a permanent position by all the local theme parks, but she preferred to work her own schedule. This being October, though, business was booming. There were haunted houses everywhere, and haunted houses meant hundreds of performers dressing up as zombies, mummies, vampires, movie killers and creatures from lagoons of every color on a daily basis. She complained as she dressed, "It's so busy! And I'm an idiot. A greedy idiot. I said yes to way too many people. I start off at one park this morning, then go to another in the afternoon, and then the park where Dan is working tonight."

"I don't get it. How can you do makeup for that many people every day?" Christina asked her.

"I don't do them all. I only do the major players. With most people, I help them at the beginning, teach them how to do what they need to. Plus all the parks have people in-house to fix up anyone who can't do it themselves. How about you? What are you up to today?"

"I'm going to have the locks changed, and I'm going to buy a dog," Christina told her.

"The locks being changed sounds good, but . . . a dog? That's a big responsibility. Who'll take care of it when you travel?"

"You'll come over and feed it."

"What if I'm traveling?"

"I'll find a good vet."

Ana stared at her, then shrugged. "A guard dog?" she asked.

"Yes," Christina told her. "And the bigger the better."

"The food will cost you an arm and a leg. A cat would be better, you know."

"I should go out and buy a guard cat?" Christina asked.

"Hey, Fuzzball can be ferocious," Ana said, defending her own beloved pet. Fuzzball had come from a shelter when Ana had been about twelve, and he was still going strong.

Fuzzball could be ferocious, Christina had to admit. He liked to lie in wait on top of a bookcase and whack people when they walked by. But he wouldn't — couldn't — bark if someone broke in.

"A dog. A brute. A massive German shepherd, maybe," Christina said. "I could look around for a trained one, I guess, but I'd rather go to a shelter. The people there can help me, I'm certain. So many pets need homes, and, anyway, what I mostly want is the companionship."

"A cat is a great companion," Ana advised.

"I want a companion that will warn me if someone is around."

"Suit yourself," Ana said with a smile. "I've got to get going. Oh, and whoever set the coffeepot? They did a nice job. The coffee was just the right strength."

In seconds she was out the door, totally unaware of how chilling her last statement had been.

Christina had planned to call a locksmith as soon as Ana left. Instead, she grabbed her purse and headed out to her car.

When she reached it, she hesitated and looked back. She loved this house. And she refused to let herself become terrified of it. And she wasn't, she realized. She didn't think there was anything evil about the house itself, and yet . . . she was still afraid.

Afraid for her own sanity?

Maybe.

She could move out, she supposed. If this were a movie and bad things were happening in a house, she would be irritated with the people who lived there, thinking that if they had any sense at all, they would move out.

But this was real life, not a movie, and to move out . . .

To move out would be to betray everything that had meant anything in her life, everything that had formed her. It would mean abandoning her past and all her wonderful dreams of the future.

A dog, she decided, would solve everything. A huge one that would strike fear into the heart of any would-be invader, human or otherwise.

Her mind made up, she drove away.

It was frightening to see just how much alike the victims looked when they were lying on the autopsy table, Jed thought.

She was lying there as if she were sleeping, but this was the forever kind of sleep.

Doc Martin was droning on about tearing and bleeding, and the absence of fluids, fibers or any other trace evidence that might help. Like the other victims, she had been manually strangled, a clear indication that the killer had strength. There were signs of force once again, but no signs of torture.

Jed stood silently by Jerry's side, listening.

160

Doc Martin had spent a long time telling them what they didn't have, but the fact that they didn't have anything still gave them something.

The killer wore gloves, but not cloth gloves, that would have left fibers behind.

Were they looking for a doctor or a nurse, both of whom would have had easy access to plastic gloves? Or, for that matter, a dishwasher?

The women had been forcibly taken and raped, but not tortured before death. The high, the climax, was in the killing.

"She was beautiful, huh?" Jerry said softly.

She certainly had been, Jed reflected. Young and beautiful, with long hair highlighted with brilliant red.

Doc Martin continued to talk into his recorder as he prepared to open the corpse, and Jed turned away, striding from the autopsy room. He didn't need to see the invasion of her body; he didn't need to be there at all. If they learned anything new, anything pertinent, he would hear about it soon enough.

He wasn't optimistic, though. Their killer was clever, and so far they had found almost nothing scientific with which to work if and when there was a suspect. It was a case now for the most basic kind of detective work, and that meant hitting the street and asking questions.

He was surprised when Jerry followed him out. Jerry looked a little green, which was strange, since he'd seen dozens of autopsies. As soon as they got outside the building, Jerry lit a cigarette.

"Thought you quit," Jed said.

"I only smoke after I've been in there," Jerry said as he drew heavily on his cigarette, then coughed. He took another drag. No cough that time. "Think this guy knows his victims?" he asked after a minute.

"I don't know. He either knows them or he has the kind of charm that puts them at ease. Think about Ted Bundy. Young women knew there was a dangerous predator out there, so he made himself look completely nonthreatening by wearing a fake cast, then lured his victims into helping him."

"So you think this guy is pretending to have some kind of a handicap?"

"I think it's a possibility," Jed said. "Unless he knows them or snatches them before they can fight free, it's either a fake handicap or he has some other way to appear to be nonthreatening."

Mal O'Donnell joined them then, and Jed arched a brow at him. Doc Martin couldn't have finished with poor Patti Jo so quickly.

But even Mal had apparently decided that staying to the bitter end would be pointless. He scowled at the other two men. "He said he'll call us later about the tox report and her last meal," he said.

"They won't find alcohol or drugs," Jed predicted.

O'Donnell looked irritated. "Hey, you gave up the cop thing, remember? Unless you got the killer, keep your opinions to yourself."

He shoved past them both, and Jerry looked at Jed. "He's just pissed because the FBI are on their way," he said. "The heat we're getting is unbelievable."

"I can believe that."

"You get anything, call me," Jerry said.

"Will do."

Jerry handed him a sheet of paper before heading after his partner. "Don't be pissed at Mal," he called over his shoulder. "We're going to be dragged through the official ringer this afternoon, and you get to walk away."

When Jerry was gone, Jed looked at the paper he was holding. It held a list of names and addresses. Patti Jo's friends and co-workers, and the last place she'd been seen alive.

The newest theme park, Jed noted.

And Dan McDuff was listed as one of her coworkers.

There was a new animal shelter in the area where Christina was certain she would find the ideal companion. The place ran on donations, and she was happy to give a large one. And because they had so much land, they were able to take in large dogs. Perfect.

From her car, she could hear the barking. Most of it was coming from the many wired-in runs that surrounded the main building. Some of it was coming from inside.

Christina headed in, where she saw a harried-looking young blonde behind a counter, and a middle-aged couple on their way out, beaming and leading what looked like a large Belgian shepherd. There. Just the kind of dog I want, Christina thought.

"Hello," the woman behind the desk said.

"Hi. I'm Christina Hardy, and I'm looking for a dog."

"What kind of dog are you looking for?" the girl asked her.

"Honestly? A guard dog," Christina told her.

The young woman sniffed. "You and every woman in the county," she said, shaking her head. "The thing is, we don't want fright-

164

ened people taking our pets, leading them on, making them think they're loved — then dumping them back here when the killer is caught." She shivered. "If the killer is caught."

"I promise you, I have a big house and a big yard. I won't be bringing back my dog," Christina vowed.

"You'll have to fill out an application, then wait to be approved, no matter what," the blonde told her.

"Okay," Christina said.

"We do a thorough background check," the woman warned. "Take a seat, Miss Hardy. And fill this out," she added, handing over a clipboard holding the application.

Christina did as ordered. When she went to hand the application back, she noticed that there was a stack of papers on the counter, applications bearing a large stamp that said they'd been approved.

The door to the runs in the back of the building suddenly burst open, and Christina heard a ferocious bark.

The girl behind the counter cried out in alarm. "Oh, no! It's Killer!"

Jed returned to his town house first, where he forced himself to be methodical and read over the twelve-year-old files from the original case first, focusing on the victims' lifestyles.

Janet Major had not been an entertainer, though she had worked in the business office of one of the local dinner shows. Grace Garcia had worked in a nearby restaurant as a singing, tap-dancing waitress. The others had worked at the theme parks, full- or part-time.

Surrounding every venue was an enormous parking lot.

Had they been taken from the parking lots? How? By force? Or had the killer appeared so trustworthy or nonthreatening that they never even suspected him?

Jed looked at the résumés of the two recent victims, both of whom were also connected to the entertainment business in some way.

Even so, he didn't think it was the show-business aspect that drew the attention of the killer. He thought it was the killer's ability to get to the women that made them the victims he wanted. He jotted down notes about the last time each woman — then and now — had been seen alive. As he stared at his notes he realized that, in his own mind, he was convinced.

Beau Kidd had never been the Interstate Killer.

So why had he drawn his weapon when Larry Atkins approached him?

Jed left his house and headed for the new park. Things were going to get a lot trickier now, since he didn't have a badge. However, he had learned long ago that the impression of authority was often worth more than authority itself.

When he reached the park, he was quickly given access to one of the entertainment managers, and he accompanied the man as he made his rounds to check on the performers. He learned that Patti Jo had been playing a vampire princess before she had scrubbed herself clean of makeup and headed out. She had been seen in the locker room by one of her best friends, Marcie McDonnagh, who had herself left soon after, and no one had seen her since. Not even in the parking lot. The trail ended right in the park.

"This is so awful," Ben Smith, the entertainment manager, told Jed. "October is such a big time of the year for us, and these killings are going to scare off the tourists." They passed a tall man adjusting a bloody pirate mask. "Hank, tuck your hair in," he snapped.

"Yessir, Mr. Smith," the pirate called back.

"One of your employees has been brutally murdered, Mr. Smith," Jed reminded him.

At least the man had the decency to look ashamed at that point. "I know, and it's terrible, but I assure you, the park is totally innocent of any wrongdoing. We allow nothing sexually explicit on the grounds, we stop serving alcohol an hour before closing . . . we're working hard —"

"To be a contender?" Jed cut in.

"I'm being serious. Patti Jo didn't get into a car with some stranger in a monster mask," Ben Smith said.

Jed tended to agree.

They had reached the employee cafeteria, and Ben Smith pointed to a woman at a nearby table. "That's Marcie McDonnagh. The guy with her is Dan — Daniel — McDuff. I'll introduce you and you can speak to Marcie. If she wants to speak to you, anyway. She was pretty shaken up by the whole thing. And she talked to the cops just a little while ago."

Jerry and Mal had probably made this their first stop, Jed realized. "It's all right. I know Dan. I'll introduce myself," Jed told Ben.

Smith nodded distractedly and looked at his watch. "Great. If you need anything else . . ."

I won't be bothering you, Jed thought. "Thanks," he said aloud as Smith turned and left.

Dan McDuff looked up and frowned when he saw Jed approaching. "Hi," he said when Jed reached the table. The pretty redhead at his side looked up curiously, and Dan made the introductions. "Marcie, this is my old friend Jed Braden. Jed, Marcie McDonnagh, one of my co-workers. Jed, what the hell are you doing here?" Dan frowned. "Are you . . . are you working on the last . . . ?" He didn't say the word *murder,* but he might as well have, because the word seemed to hang in the air, anyway. "But . . . you're not a cop anymore." He seemed truly puzzled.

"I'm working it from the private sector," Jed explained, and looked down at Marcie, who grew pale.

"Sit down," Marcie said. "I'll tell you what I told the cops. I ran into Patti Jo after her shift. We talked about going to a Halloween party on the thirty-first, after we got off. She was in a good mood. Then she headed to the employee parking lot, and that was the last time I saw her." Tears suddenly welled in her eyes.

"Thank you, Marcie," Jed told her.

"She wasn't stupid!" Marcie blurted out. "She wouldn't have gone off with a stranger."

"Marcie, it's all right," Dan murmured, looking helplessly at Jed. There was a slight spark of irritation in his eyes, as if he were saying, She's already been through this with the cops. Just how bad do you want to make her feel?

"Honest to God, she just wouldn't have gone off with a stranger or with anyone she didn't trust," Marcie said. "Oh, my God! I have a shift tonight," she said, as if she'd just realized it.

"Me, too," Dan told her. "So I'll walk you to your car, and I'll follow you home."

"Point me to the employee parking lot?" Jed said.

Dan nodded. "I'll do better. I'll take you to the exit Patti Jo used and point the way to the lot where they found her car."

Marcie gave him a hug before they left. Were the two of them just friends? Jed wondered. Or more?

As at all the parks, the hall was part of an entire network that ran underground, so the comings and goings of the employees never had to intrude on the excitement above. The walls were painted with creatures, some friendly-looking, others grotesque, to indicate which section of the park they were beneath, and the corridors seemed to go on forever, with doors to dressing, locker, meeting and dining rooms along the way, as well as storage rooms and offices. Sometimes the halls were empty. Sometimes they were passed by a horde of people.

Finally they reached the door Patti Jo had used, which opened onto a huge parking lot enclosed by a fence. In the distance, Jed could see a guardhouse at the gate. Surrounding the lot were trees, nothing but trees. The new park had been built far enough away from the other parks that it was practically in the woods.

"Did you know her well?" Jed asked Dan.

"Pretty well," Dan said softly.

"And?"

"She was nice. She got along with everyone." His voice hardened. "But like Marcie said, she wasn't a fool."

"So . . . she walked out to the parking lot and she wasn't seen again until she was found off the highway?" Jed murmured to himself as they headed back to the cafeteria.

"It's scary, huh?" Dan said, studying Jed. "What do you think it is, then? The ghost of Beau Kidd, come back to kill again?"

"I don't think ghosts commit murder," Jed told him. "But then again, what the hell do I know?"

"If I can help in any way . . ." Dan offered.

"Sure."

"This is personal for me now, you know?" Dan said.

"Yeah," Jed agreed.

The two men said goodbye outside the cafeteria. Jed looked inside before he left. Marcie McDonnagh was still sitting where they had left her. A redhead. Jed could almost picture her lying on the autopsy table, just as Patti Jo had been today, as Sherri Mason had been earlier . . .

Redheads. Beautiful redheads.

Were they all interchangeable in the killer's mind?

He swore softly, afraid. As soon as he could get a signal, he flipped open his cell phone and called Christina's house.

No one picked up.

He ran for his car and started driving as quickly as he could in her direction.

Irrational? Hell, yes. But a sense of dread was growing within him, and he was powerless against it.

## 7

"Ha," Christina said, opening her front door.

Killer, woofing loudly, ran in ahead of her.

"I have a dog now!" she called out. "A ferocious dog. He will bark and rip out the throat of anyone who dares to sneak in to play a prank on me."

There was no answer from inside, not that she'd really expected there to be. In fact, as she entered, she couldn't help but feel slightly foolish, especially because there was nothing out of order.

She let out a soft sigh, following the dog through the house. He was curious and wanted to explore everything.

After they finished the circuit, she set down a bowl of water for him in the kitchen. Killer lapped up a bit, then stared at her, his tail wagging a thousand beats a minute. "So, you like it here?" she asked.

He wagged his tail some more.

The phone rang, and Killer gave one sharp bark, as if in warning.

"Hello?" she said, picking up the receiver. Killer barked again.

"It's me. Dan. What the hell was that?" her cousin demanded over the line.

"My dog."

"Dog?" he said with a groan.

"You're going to love him."

"Right. I'm going to love some big, slobbering beast that will eat my shoes if I step out of them," Dan said.

"You'll love him, trust me," Christina said. "So, what's up?"

"I'm just calling to check up on you. You didn't answer your cell when I just tried you."

"Sorry, I left my bag in the front hall when I came in," she told him. "So what has you so worried?"

She heard him let out a long sigh. "Didn't you hear about the latest victim?" he finally asked. "Christie, she worked here. I knew her."

"Oh, Dan, I'm so sorry," Christina said.

"I'm worried sick about you and Ana now."

"Don't be. We're smart, and careful and now I have a dog."

"You gonna be around later? I worked the

174

early shift today, so I've got some time before I have to go back for my Grim Reader duties."

"I'll be here. Come on by if you want."

"Jed was here earlier."

"He was?"

"Seems he thinks he's a detective again."

"He is, a private detective. I guess he's wondering if the case was ever really solved."

"Yeah. Well, you take care, understand?"

"Of course."

She hung up, but she had barely replaced the receiver before the phone rang again. This time it was her cousin Mike.

"Christie?"

"Yes. What's up, Mike?"

"Nothing, just calling to see if you're okay."

"I'm great. Thank you."

"Glad to hear it. Um . . . you don't have any late nights planned, do you?"

"No, I don't. And yes, I know another woman was killed. But guess what? I bought a dog."

"A dog."

"You know. Woof, woof."

"Great. I guess. A big one?"

"His name is Killer. You'll have to come meet him."

"I'll do that. Seriously . . . you need to be careful."

"I will. I promise. Dan's going to come by later to meet Killer. Why don't you come, too?"

"Sure. If I can get out of here at a reasonable hour. Listen . . ." His voice trailed away. "Take care, okay?"

"You, too."

She rang off and stared at Killer, who was still madly wagging his tail. He cocked his head at her, and she let out a sigh. She had gotten her dog, but it was too late now to get a locksmith out until tomorrow. Not that it mattered. The only two people who had keys to the house were her cousins. Who loved her. Who were worried about her.

She was still going to have the locks changed, she decided.

But for tonight . . .

"I have Killer," she murmured.

He looked up at her as if he were hanging on her every word. Then his tail stopped wagging and he began to bark like a mad thing before he turned and raced toward the front door.

As he ran, she heard the doorbell chime.

She strode to the door and looked out. She felt as if her heart caught in her throat, then was annoyed with herself for the pleasure that swept through her.

Jed.

She told herself not to get carried away. He was Ana's cousin. It only made sense — especially after last night — that he felt obliged to check up on her.

"It's all right, Killer," she murmured as she opened the door. He stood by her side, wagging his tail but still barking maniacally.

"Shh, it's all right," she told the dog again. "Jed, what a surprise. Come on in."

Jed stared at the dog, then stared at her. "Killer?"

"Are you coming in?" she demanded with a sigh, then started for the parlor without waiting for an answer.

He followed, but not before closing and locking the door in his wake. He found Christina sitting on the piano bench, but she indicated that he should take one of the comfortable wing chairs.

As soon as he did so, Killer jumped onto his lap, tail wagging as he tried to shower Jed with kisses.

"Killer?" Jed asked again.

"When I adopted him, that was already his name."

"Christina, this is a Jack Russell terrier."

"I know."

"Sit," Jed firmly ordered the dog. Killer

177

did so, sitting calmly on his lap and staring at him as if he were the most marvelous human ever to occupy the earth.

"He's very well behaved," Christina said.

"I . . . uh, don't want to burst any bubbles here, but Jack Russells aren't what usually come to mind when someone is thinking guard dog," Jed told her, looking a little bemused. His hair was slightly ruffled, and the rueful smile tugging at his features was extremely attractive, she thought.

"He has a great bark," Christina said, defending her dog.

"Yes, he has a great bark." Jed cleared his throat. "Were they all out of German shepherds?"

"They were."

"I see."

"He wasn't second best or anything. They had lots of bigger dogs. It was just that he came flying out and . . . and . . ."

"And picked you," Jed said.

"Kind of," Christina agreed.

"And the idea is that he'll warn you if anyone comes around?"

She smiled. "Why are you so worried? You don't believe anyone has been here. You think I'm emotionally disturbed."

"Not emotionally disturbed," Jed protested. "Just . . . hurting," he said after a moment.

He patted the dog for a few moments, which somehow kept the silence from growing too awkward as it stretched between them.

"I hear you were out at the new park," she said at last. "Dan told me the second woman who was murdered was one of his friends."

"Yeah," Jed said, looking down at the dog.

"Are you . . . investigating?" she queried.

"Sort of."

"But you're not on the force anymore," she reminded him.

He lifted his eyes to stare at her then. "Actually," he said, "I have a client."

"A client?" she echoed with a frown.

"Beau Kidd had a younger sister."

Christina almost fell off the piano bench. "Beau Kidd had a younger sister . . . and she's hired you to investigate?"

"Go figure, huh?" he murmured.

"But . . . your book really did kind of . . ."

Her voice trailed away weakly.

"I know."

"So what's his sister like?" she inquired.

"I haven't really gotten to know her," he said.

"Did she . . . call you up? How did she find you?"

"We were both in the cemetery," he said as he picked up the dog and stood, then set Killer down on the floor. "Congratulations on the new addition to the family."

She ignored his last comment and said, "You met Beau Kidd's sister in the cemetery — and she hired you?"

"Kind of."

"But . . ." she began, and then the rest of the words froze in her throat. The cemetery was one of the oldest in the area, but it was still accepting the dead. Her grandparents were both there, as were her parents.

And so was his wife. He must have been at Margaritte's grave.

He stared at her, and a strange look came over his face. When he spoke, his words sounded harsh. "Actually, I don't know why, but I went to see Beau Kidd's grave."

"I see," she murmured, though she didn't see at all. He seemed so distant, all of a sudden, even though she'd known him for so long.

She admitted that she had spent most of her life being fascinated with Jed. When he had married Margaritte, she had told herself that he was just Ana's older cousin, someone she'd idolized but not someone she'd ever really hoped to end up with. She had a life, loved her music, had a few serious relationships along the way.

And yet . . .

He'd always been there for her. Strong, quiet, always saying the right things.

As she watched him sit there, she knew that she loved the contours of his face, the power of his build. But that wasn't why he stayed in her mind, like something etched into her heart.

There was something deeper in him. In those eyes, in the sound of his voice, in his soul, his mind.

Something that made her long to see him.

Something that made her draw back when she did.

He seemed to be deep in thought, but finally he spoke. "There's a chance Beau was innocent. If so, I need to do everything in my power to help clear his name. Naturally his sister wants the same thing."

"Damn it, Jed, none of it was your fault. It wasn't your case. You're a writer."

"I'm a private eye, when I choose to be," he said coolly. "I have the license to prove it."

"But . . ."

"But what?"

"I don't know," she said at last. "I think getting involved in this could be dangerous."

He walked over to her and, to her surprise, lifted her chin with his thumb. "I can't help feeling that not looking into it could prove to be even more dangerous," he told her. He stepped back then. "Well, I guess I should get going. The, uh . . . hmm, is it really a whole dog?" he said lightly, teasingly. "The little mutt is great."

"Killer," she said indignantly.

"Killer. Right."

He smiled.

She was in love, she thought.

"If he'll keep you from imagining that things in the house are moving around, he'll definitely be worth his Alpo," he told her.

Her spine stiffened. "Right. Thanks so much for coming by, Jed."

"You should probably get those locks changed, though, you know."

"I was already planning to. Maybe I should lock up my imagination, too," she suggested.

"Christie, I wasn't trying to —"

"It's all right."

"Yeah, well . . . those locks are older than the hills. Who knows who has a key? Your gran might have given them to anyone. It won't hurt to change them."

She nodded and rose. "For the moment, I'll just have to use the locks I have."

He took the hint. "Take care."

With Killer in her arms, she followed him to the door. The dog whined as she watched Jed head down the walk to his car, then looked at her.

"Yeah, I know, he looks great, sounds great, even smells great. But he can be a real asshole," she told the dog.

Killer just wagged his tail.

Michael McDuff's offices were on International Drive, and he was very glad to be far away from the insanity of the parks. He liked what he did; he made a decent income by putting together the pieces of a production: talent, direction and money, even costuming and effects, but he was grateful he didn't have to be physically on the spot when everything merged. On the side, he'd also been working on the creation of a children's show, driven by a desire to overcome the prejudice he so often saw in the business.

All the parks employed actors, and they weren't usually discriminated against because of color, nationality, religion or sexual persuasion. But there was a pecking order, and it wasn't controlled by talent but by what amounted to luck: who'd been on a TV show, who had been in a commercial, who had at least been in a park show before, all the way down to the hopefuls with no experience at all but lots of drive and often more talent than those at the top.

Far too often he had to deal with a nasty little ten-year-old who thought the world owed her everything because she'd lucked into the role of fairy princess, or a fifteen-year-old who bossed around his parents and made sure to tell everyone he was tops because some commercial director thought he looked cute drinking a big glass of Florida orange juice. He wanted to create a show that gave lots of children with real talent a chance to get experience, so they would have a chance, now and later, to showcase that talent not just locally but anywhere there were performing jobs.

For now, though, he was done for the day, and he was glad of it. He felt tired of everything and suddenly anxious to get out, head to a pub, watch a football game.

Closing his desk drawer, he hesitated. He knew, of course, why this day had been so bitter.

Angie.

Angie, who still went by McDuff, since she thought it looked better on paper — and in lights — than Vladilovskya.

He felt his hands knot into fists and made

a point of straightening his fingers. Angie. Tall, slim, silicone-breasted Angie.

He'd paid for that silicone.

Just as he'd paid for the tummy tuck — not really necessary, he'd been told by her surgeon — and the liposuction. He'd been madly in love. He'd met her when she'd auditioned for a show he was putting together, and she'd fallen in love with him, too. Until she'd gotten the role. And a few other roles. And the boobs, the lipo and the tummy tuck.

Then she'd started to gain a reputation, even gotten a small role in a movie.

And he'd been out on his heels like an old, used-up has-been.

Her name had come up in a meeting today. He'd done all he could to keep his mouth closed. He hadn't dissed her, even agreed that she might be right for a role in a Christmas special one of the networks had asked him to pull together at the biggest theme park in the area. A role that could lead to more and better — and bigger — things in the future.

About to rise, he paused when he heard a tentative knock on his door. "Yes?" he snapped.

To his amazement, she walked in. Angie McDuff. His ex. Tall, slim and now all but perfect. Her eyes were huge and light green, and her hair was tinted to the color of burnished copper, though she'd been a brunette when he'd met her.

"Mike," she said softly.

"Hello, Angie. I was just on my way out."

"Sure. I just came by to say thank you."

"For what?"

"I hear that my name came up today and you . . . agreed that I have the right look, and that I have talent."

"And?" he said flatly.

"Well . . ." She stumbled over her words. "Thank you."

He folded his hands on his desk. "This is business, Angie. Just business. I make big bucks for putting the pieces together. If you weren't right for the role, I would have said so. You don't owe me any thanks."

She smiled awkwardly. "You sound like a Mafioso. 'It's just business,' " she said in a mock-gruff tone.

He shrugged. It was hard to look at her, but he forced himself to meet her eyes. Something shot through him. A spasm of unease.

Yeah, right.

He couldn't see her without remembering what it was like to sleep with her.

But that wasn't it. . . .

"You're welcome. Is that what you want to hear? Fine, you're welcome, and I wish you the best of luck, but there's only so much I can do. Hell, my own brother is on pins and needles waiting to hear if he got the role he wants. I only have so much control."

"More than you think. Thank you again, Mike."

He nodded. "Sure. Like I said, good luck to you."

She smiled. "One day, maybe you'll forgive me."

"Forgive you?" he said, as if puzzled. "Most of the time, I don't even remember you," he lied.

He could see her stiffen. "Sure. Thanks. Bye."

She turned around and left, and he sat, listening to the sound of the closing door. Then he rose — and followed her.

The power of suggestion was a very strange thing indeed, Christina thought after Dan left for his late shift at the park.

She had never been one to go to a cemetery regularly. She didn't believe that visiting a grave meant visiting the soul of a loved one. Remembering was the greatest honor she could offer the departed; speaking about them, even laughing about their foibles, kept them alive. She visited the cemetery when it felt right, not on a schedule.

But Jed's visit had gotten under her skin.

She and Killer were going to do just fine, she decided. The little Jack Russell was a bit on the hyper side, but that was good. It meant he would notice — and bark at — the slightest disturbance. It was also good that he was already two years old. The woman at the adoption center had assured her that he no longer ate shoes and anything else he could find. But the best thing about Killer was that he was so affectionate, so eager to please. He didn't object when she clipped his leash onto his collar when she headed out with him. She had seen dogs in the cemetery before, so she figured as long as no one had a fit, it would be okay to take him with her.

"Hey!" someone yelled as she stepped out her door. Tony and Ilona were in front of Tony's sprawling ranch-style house, throwing a Frisbee back and forth. Ilona paused after her greeting and waved at her, sending the Frisbee sailing toward her front yard. Surprised, she lost her grip on the leash, and Killer took off running.

To her astonishment, the terrier went flying down the porch steps and across the lawn, then made an impossible leap into the air — and caught the Frisbee.

"Wow!" Ilona shouted, hurrying over.

"Did you see that?" Tony exclaimed, hot on her heels. He grinned at Christina when they came to a stop in front of her and put his arm around his fiancée's shoulders. "Good God, where did he come from? The dog circus? That was amazing. Is he yours?"

"He's mine, and I'm as amazed as you are," Christina assured him.

"You adopted him?" Ilona asked, looking down at Killer, who was wagging his tail, Frisbee in his mouth.

"Yes, I just got him today," Christina said. "His name is Killer."

Tony looked at her. "Killer?" he said politely, but his lips were twitching.

"Hey, he was already named when I got him," she said.

"Well, he is killer good with a Frisbee," Tony said. "You could enter him in a contest. I bet he'd win, and some of those contests pay good money."

"He's a pet. He doesn't have to make money," Christina said.

"He obviously loves to play, though. You should let him play with us sometime. Of course, you're welcome to play, too," Ilona told her, grinning.

189

"I'm not as good as he is," Christina admitted.

"We'll make allowances for old times' sake," Tony assured her.

She laughed. "Okay, we'll see. Meanwhile . . . Killer, give that Frisbee back. We're off."

To her amazement, the dog immediately obeyed.

He went over to Tony and whined until Tony hunkered down and took the Frisbee. "Thanks, buddy."

"Have fun," she said, leading the dog toward her car.

"You, too," Ilona called.

"And, uh . . . be careful out there, huh?" Tony added.

"Will do," she assured him, feeling heartily sick and tired of everyone's concern, no matter how well meaning it was.

She drove to the cemetery. Killer sat in the passenger seat, staring straight ahead, totally well behaved, just as he had been when she had first taken him home. He remained seated, giving only one little woof when she paused by one of the vendors near the entrance to buy two large bouquets of flowers.

She parked outside the gate, because some of the lanes were so narrow and winding that it was possible to get blocked in.

She looked around. Everything was quiet. Great oaks dripped with Spanish moss. The land actually rolled gently in every direction. Carved angels and cherubs rose above many of the tombs. The cemetery was really quite beautiful, she realized. Peaceful.

Sadly, she knew the way to her family plot far too well. Granda had built the mausoleum surrounded by a cast-iron fence when they had first come to America, and it was an impressive sight, with a large stone angel rising above the ornate building marked McDuff/Hardy.

At the moment the mausoleum held four sarcophagi. Anyone else who wanted to be buried inside would have to start piggybacking on the others. She could go in, she knew, but instead she set one bouquet outside, where her parents were buried. She was at peace regarding her grandparents' deaths, but she didn't think she would ever feel the same about her parents. They had been robbed of so many years of life and had deserved so much more.

Killer, who seemed to recognize the solemnity of their mission, sat quietly at her side while she mouthed a little prayer. She looked at the dates carved into the stone marking her parents' grave and touched them, whispering a little "I love you" to each.

She didn't believe they heard her any more clearly here than they would anywhere else. This was just . . . a courtesy. More for herself than for them.

She held the second bouquet in her arms, but she wasn't sure where she was going with it.

She turned around and froze, feeling as if a cool breeze were washing over her.

Of course she was sure. She knew exactly where she was going.

It wasn't far.

Suddenly, just as clearly as if it had been the day before, she remembered back to her grandfather's funeral. She remembered how many people had been there, compared to the single couple who had stood by the other grave, the woman weeping pitifully.

She remembered how, when they had gone, she had walked over to the grave and cast a single flower onto the casket.

She hardly noticed Killer trailing along as she wended her way between graves, past markers and cherubs, crosses and angels, to that other grave.

Beauregard Kidd.

Beloved son and brother.

And the date . . .

He had died the same day as her grandfather, and he had been buried on the same day her grandfather had been buried.

And no one had come to his funeral because he had been suspected of being a serial killer.

The breeze picked up.

At her feet, the dog whined.

She set down the last bouquet of flowers. "I hope that justice is served, Beau Kidd, and I pray for your family. For your sister." She had been raised in the Catholic Church, so she crossed herself and added, "And I pray for you, Beau, and your immortal soul."

Suddenly the breeze turned cold, and Killer whined again.

And darkness arrived in a rush.

She ducked low and scooped up Killer, then hurried out to her car. All the way home, she mocked herself for being a fool. But once inside with her little dog, she felt better. With all the lights on, the house felt brighter. Even normal.

She admitted that she actually felt at ease. All because of a little Jack Russell with an enormous personality.

She spent some time experimenting with a few ideas on the piano, Killer at her feet. Then, right when she was in the middle of something she thought had potential, he leapt to his feet and began to bark. She jumped, but a minute later, when she heard the doorbell, she smiled.

"Killer, you're the best," she said to the dog as she went to answer the door. "Hello?" she said when she got there, peering through the peephole.

"Christie?"

It was Dan, and she opened the door. He looked tired and depressed.

"I'm so sorry about your friend," she told him with a big hug.

He shook his head. "It's not that I knew her that well, it's just . . . things like that, they just don't happen to people you know, you know what I mean?"

"I do. Come on in."

"Why don't you come out? We'll get something to eat."

"I really don't want to leave Killer alone just yet."

"Killer. Right. Your monster guard dog." He almost smiled as he looked down at the terrier by her feet.

"He's a great guard dog. He barks when anyone comes near me."

"How about fast food, then?" Dan asked. "We can park and eat in the car."

"Sure."

They took his car, and by the time they'd gone to a hamburger drive-up window, then parked, Dan was smitten by the dog.

Killer was obviously interested in hamburger, but he waited very politely to be offered a bite.

"I thought you were getting a big dog," Dan said.

"I thought I was getting a big dog, too."

"He's great."

"Hey, did you hear anything about the new role yet?" she asked him.

"Zeus? Nope. I think the park's getting nervous. Who knows? Tourism may plummet. There may never be a part, because there may never be a play."

"Have you pushed Mike to help?" she asked him.

"Mike can't do anything now. He's finished with his part of it. He did recommend me, of course. And I did a damned good audition. So . . ." He winced suddenly.

"What?"

"I think Patti Jo was up for a part, too."

She let out a long breath and stopped herself from telling him that she was sorry. He knew it already. And it wasn't as if anything she said could make it better.

"Are you going to be all right going home tonight?" she asked him.

"Of course." Dan glanced at her. "Are you going to be all right in that old house by yourself?"

"I'm not by myself," she assured him with a laugh. "I have Killer."

When they got back to the house, he went inside with her, and together they walked through the rooms, making sure no one was there and nothing was out of place. She really only did it to make Dan happy. She was certain Killer would have pitched a barking fit if there had been anyone in the house.

But she thanked Dan and gave him a good-night peck on the cheek, then locked the door behind him and went to bed feeling confident, the little dog at her side.

"Yup, kiddo, you get to sleep on the bed," she told him when he sat on the floor looking wistfully at the mattress.

She lay down, amazed at how tired she was and just how ready she was to go to sleep. Then again, she hadn't had much sleep since she'd moved in.

She was just dozing off when she felt the dog move. Felt him rise and heard him sniff the air. Suddenly he hopped down from the bed.

"Killer?" she whispered, too nervous to call it out.

She slipped out of bed and started down the stairs, feeling the heavy silence of the house. She started to call out his name again, but the sound died in her throat. When she reached the front hall, she hesitated, listening.

She heard a little whining sound. Not a bark. Nothing that sounded like either pain or agitation. It actually sounded . . . affectionate.

"Killer?" she said, and followed the sound into the parlor.

A scream froze in her throat.

A man was there.

Solid. Real. Sitting on the piano bench and stroking her dog.

He looked up, and her pent-up scream tore from her throat.

A look of distress crossed his features, and he rose, reaching out to her. "Please, don't scream. Help me."

She shook her head, another scream tearing from her lips. Because she knew who he was. Beau Kidd.

Except Beau Kidd was dead.

"Please . . . I need help," he told her.

But she hardly heard him, because the world was spinning, fading. As she sank into oblivion, the last thing she heard was Killer's whine of distress.

# 8

Sitting at his dining room table, Jed spread out the files and notes he had accrued, the past on the left, the present on the right. And in the center, a list of the various commonalities he had come up with.

Most of the women were in the entertainment business in some way — but nothing sleazy like stripping or pole-dancing. But he still didn't think it was their employment that had drawn the killer — or killers — to them.

The hair?

Every single victim had red hair or noticeable red highlights, whether natural or artificial.

The latest victim had last been seen leaving work.

He paused and flipped through his notes. Grace Garcia had last been seen leaving a shopping mall. He kept flipping. All the women had disappeared in parking lots,

whether coming or going. None of them —
and the police had searched their apart-
ments thoroughly — had been abducted
from home. The killer was taking them
when they were in close proximity to the
safety of their own cars.

Therefore the killer either appeared trustworthy or was someone all the victims had
known.

The second option didn't seem likely. No
one had discovered any common acquain-
tances between the women killed twelve
years ago, much less between them and the
newest victims.

He found himself pulling out an old file
concerning the investigation following Beau
Kidd's death. The detective who had written up the majority of the notes, a man
named Bill Grimsby, had apparently taken
Larry Atkins's word regarding the final killing, but he had checked out Beau's alibi for
the death of the other woman he had dated.
At the time she had been taken, he had been
at his family's home. His parents had sworn
that he'd been there almost all day, a
Saturday, helping his father take down the
hurricane shutters, then had stayed for dinner.

Jed had wanted to interview Grimsby
when he was writing his book, but had never

gotten the chance, because Grimsby had retired and headed out on a sailboat somewhere in the Pacific Ocean.

Jed put the file down and picked up the phone to call Jerry.

"Got anything?" Jerry asked glumly when he picked up.

"Yeah, but mostly just the obvious. We know he likes redheads, but beyond that . . . These women are walking away with someone they trust. They know him, or he has the ability to make them believe in him, just like we said earlier."

"There has to be a connection," Jerry said disgustedly. "We're doing the legwork. Asking all the right people the right questions. But the last two victims . . . they were happy as little larks, heading home, then . . . they were reported missing, their cars found abandoned . . . and then . . . well, you've seen the way they ended up. So far, we haven't got squat."

"You've got enough to save a few lives," Jed told him. "You need to speak with your public affairs person. Warn women matching the description not to go anywhere alone and not to trust strangers, no matter how harmless they seem. Get it on the air. It might to do some good."

"Yeah," Jerry murmured.

"What?"

He could almost hear Jerry sigh at the other end. "People will ignore us, think they're safe, think they know better. This killer — he'll find another victim."

"Make it hard on him."

"The thing is . . ."

"What?"

"If he doesn't kill again, if he doesn't make a mistake somewhere along the line, we'll never catch him," Jerry said.

Jed was silent for a long moment, then asked, "Jerry, do you know anything about Bill Grimsby? I know he retired, but have you heard anything about him coming back to the States?"

"I don't know anything, but you might want to call Larry Atkins."

"Why would Larry know?"

"Hell, no one ever told you when you were writing that book?"

"Told me what?"

"Bill Grimsby and Larry Atkins were tight. In fact, I think they're distant cousins or something like that. Give Larry a call. Maybe he can tell you where Bill has gotten himself off to."

How the hell had he not known that, and how the hell had that fact been ignored? Jed asked himself in shock. The officer verifying the facts regarding another officer who had fired his weapon and killed his own partner had been a buddy — maybe even a relative — of that same officer?

Surprised, disturbed and angry with himself as well as everyone else, Jed somehow kept a civil tone as he told Jerry to have a good night, then rang off.

He drummed his fingers on the table, wishing he still smoked.

How the hell had that information been ignored?

Everyone had wanted the case to go away. People wanted to sleep nights. They had all wanted it to be true that the killer was dead.

He looked at his watch. It was late. But not late enough. And since he was never going to sleep, what the hell? Might as well drive.

She felt Killer's cold little nose against her cheek. Frowning, she struggled to open her eyes.

When she did, she gasped, ready to scream again as she struggled to get up, desperately trying to get away from the man who was hunkered down by her side, an anxious expression on his face.

He couldn't be real, she told herself. She had utterly lost her mind, and no dog was protection against that. Her poor little dog of one day was owned by a woman who was totally insane, living in a fantasy world where the dead came back to life.

She stared at him. "Go away. I do not see you," she begged.

"But you do see me. And you saw me before."

"Never."

"You didn't see me, all those years ago?"

"What are you talking about? No — don't answer me. I'm getting up, and I'm leaving. Hell, I'm going to have myself booked into a lunatic asylum."

He reached out, as if to help her rise.

"No," she cried softly.

Killer barked happily, as if this were some kind of a game, and looked from her to Beau Kidd.

Beau Kidd.

Impossible.

But it was Beau Kidd. She knew his face. Was it from the newspapers? It had to be. They had never met. And she had never seen him before.

Except . . .

Except at the foot of her bed the other night. Except at the table at the café. Except out in her yard, when she'd passed out. Passed out and been found in the morning.

By Jed.

Who was certain she was crazy, or at least emotionally disturbed.

She stared at him and told herself that she had to be dreaming, that in reality she was still passed out on the floor.

"Go away. You're dead. You can't be here. You don't know me, and I don't know you. Now, go away," she repeated.

"You do know me," he said stubbornly. "And," he added softly, "you know damned well that I can be here."

"What?" she murmured.

He smiled. He had dimples, and he was very good-looking. And she was insane.

"You put a flower on my grave," he told her. "Don't you remember? At the cemetery. You saw your grandfather. He came to you. And then you put a flower on my grave."

She shook her head. "I never saw my grandfather after he died."

Beau sighed. "But you did."

"Please, I'm begging you, go away," she pleaded.

He looked weary, defeated. "But I need your help," he all but whispered.

"I'm going to close my eyes, and you're going to go away. When I open my eyes, you'll be gone," Christina said, and she closed her eyes tightly.

She opened them.

And to her amazement, when she opened them, he was gone.

She swallowed and stood, leaning on the wall, afraid to move away from it. Afraid that if she tried to stand on her own, she would merely slip back down to the floor, into oblivion.

Killer was still there, looking up at her with his trusting brown eyes. He barked, then whined and drew even closer.

"Killer, huh?" she said to him. "You didn't even bark at him. You befriended the . . . the enemy," she said. "No, not the enemy. The guy who wasn't even here. You're supposed to be protecting me," she chided him.

But could anyone or anything protect her from herself?

She looked at her watch. Eleven-thirty. But she didn't want to be alone.

She was getting dressed and getting out of there.

"Come on, we're going upstairs," she told Killer. No need. He followed her, then waited on the bed while she washed her face, pulled on a navy knit dress and stepped into a pair of sandals. She grabbed her purse and made sure she had her cell phone. Suddenly she realized that the television was on.

Had she left it on?

She didn't know and didn't care. Not anymore. It was a proven fact. She was insane, which was leading her to believe she was seeing the ghost of Beau Kidd. There was no denying it now.

Her hand was on the remote, but she hesitated. A newswoman was talking about a police warning for woman — especially young redheads — to avoid being out alone and steer clear of strangers.

She flicked off the television. "I have a dog now," she said weakly to the dark screen, then headed back down the stairs. She had just reached the front door and was going for the handle when Killer began to bark.

Christina screamed.

Someone was there, right on the other side of her front door.

There were no good games on at eleven-thirty at night. Didn't matter. Michael McDuff was happy enough to sit on a stool at O'Reilly's, staring at ESPN while the good games were recapped. His family had always come here, and a man didn't have to drink at a place every night to lay claim to a bar stool. He was on his third Guinness, a big mistake, considering he had a meeting first thing in the morning.

"Hey, handsome, don't you think you should maybe get some food into your system?"

He spun around. Mary Donahoe, with her bright eyes, cheerful smile and unruly carrot-red hair, was standing at his side. He smiled. "Guess you're right, Mary. Perhaps I should have something to eat."

"Good call. What'll it be?"

"Shepherd's pie, I guess."

Mary cocked her head at an angle, staring at him. "A young lady in here the other night ordered the same thing, and I just realized there's a likeness between the two of you."

He laughed. "Must have been Christina. My cousin."

"Ah, I knew there was a lot of family. I've not been here so long myself, but I hear from O'Reilly."

"Not so much family now. Everyone's dead except me, my brother, Dan — the truly charming one — and my cousin, Christie. She just moved up here, and she's living in the old family house."

"Nice. It's good to have family," Mary said.

"What about you?"

"My family is all back across the great old

ocean," she said lightly. "I miss them."

"So you live alone?" he asked.

"Aye, me and me cat." She laughed and turned toward the kitchen.

He caught her arm before she could walk away. "Mary, don't leave here alone, you hear me? It's not safe."

She touched her curling mop of hair. "Well, it's true it's red," she said. "Still, I'm a careful girl."

Mike shook his head. "Please, don't go home alone."

She smiled. "Well, if you're still here when me shift ends, you can see to it that I get safe to me car, okay?"

"I'll wait until you're off," he told her grimly.

She smiled. "Shepherd's pie, sir. On its way."

"What the hell?" Christina heard an angry voice ask from outside.

She was almost paralyzed with relief. Quickly — before he took it into his mind to break it down — she opened the door. "Jed," she breathed.

"You were screaming!" he said accusingly, then stared at her, frowning as he noticed that she was carrying her purse and her keys. "You're going out?" he asked incredulously.

"Um . . . yeah."

"Where the hell do you think you're going at this time of night?"

She drew her brows together, trying to think of a reply. Her hesitation etched a deeper frown into his forehead.

"Christie, where were you going?"

She sighed, opening the door wider to let him in. Killer barked happily. He obviously loved Jed, who continued to stare at her questioningly from the stoop.

"Out," she finally said.

"Out where?"

"Out anywhere."

"Have you lost your mind?" he asked her.

"Maybe," she murmured.

"If you need something . . . need to go somewhere . . . I can take you," Jed offered.

"No . . . just, uh, come on in. Shut the door. I guess I don't really need to go out."

"Christina, you're scaring me," he told her.

"I'm sorry."

She had started walking down the hall, toward the parlor, when his hands fell on her shoulders and spun her around. He was close. She was overwhelmed by everything about him. Not just his scent, which was always clean and somehow richly masculine. There was also his height, the perfect complement to her own. The heat, the vitality, emanating from him.

She'd always had a crush on him, but it was getting worse. Deeper. Sexual.

She caught herself staring at his chest. At the cool striped cotton of his casually tailored shirt. She looked up slowly into his eyes. He had the greatest eyes. Dark. Bottomless. Hard sculpted features that added to the sexual allure of the man. He was clearly concerned as he stared back at her. He wasn't mocking her. Not at that moment.

She opened her mouth, feeling the need to say something to keep him from thinking she was stark raving mad. But he just kept staring back at her, as if . . .

He tilted her chin, and it wasn't just to look into her eyes.

She felt his mouth on hers, the merest touch, and it was as if intoxicating waves of heat rushed over her, filled her, fused into her body, blood and bone. She strained to reach higher, standing on her toes. She felt his lips brush hers again, not real, too real. . . .

She pressed against the steely heat of his chest, shifting until her lips were fully beneath his. His arms went around her then, crushing her against him. His lips were no longer a whisper of air; they were crushing, like fire, hungering for and consuming her mouth.

In a thousand years, she never could have dreamed of this. . . .

It wasn't real, she thought. This was the kind of thing that happened only in dreams, in fantasies.

But it was real, and it felt as if all the events in her life had led her toward that moment. She was touching him, stroking the incredible contours of his face, warming herself against the fluid heat of his body. She was all but melded against him, except, annoyingly, for their clothing, which neither of them seemed to be getting out of the way fast enough. The moment somehow felt both amazingly graceful and yet ridiculously awkward.

In dreams, in reality, her fingers trembled as she touched him. As she did all those things she had longed to do for so many years. She felt the texture of his skin, traced the structure of his bones. She pressed against him with the entire length of her body, feeling a new weakness wash over her, along with a new strength, a new life. Her fingers played over his shoulders and around to his nape, then down his back. And all the while she tasted his kiss, tasted his tongue, reveled in the power and sweep and naked sensuality of that touch.

His shirt lay discarded on the floor, and she traced her fingers over his bare chest. Her shoes were off, her dress tossed on top of his shirt.

They'd been standing in the hallway, and then suddenly they weren't. At first she was leading him up the stairs, and then it was as if he grew weary of their slow progress and paused long enough to sweep her straight off her feet. She met his eyes as he made his way up the steps. She was preternaturally aware of the intensity of his gaze and barely even noticed the softness of the bed as they fell down onto it. She had ached for this for so long, her feelings submerged beneath pride and dignity and self-preservation.

As his mouth traveled across her flesh, her undergarments seemed to melt away, and she realized she had no idea where they'd gone.

Lights blazed throughout the house, but she didn't care. The only thing that mattered was the amazing sweet fire of his kiss, the heat of his caress against her naked flesh, the pressure of his body, arms, hips, sex . . . hard against her. She was desperate, starving, to return his every touch. But he was the more experienced lover. There were moments when she lay still, almost like a deer in the headlights, all but paralyzed by the sensations the liquid trail of his tongue and the sweep of his hands aroused upon her flesh.

God, yes, he was good.

God, yes, he knew what he was doing. . . .

The tiniest sensation in itself might have been enough to make her insane, just the feel of his frame next to hers, the brush of his hair against her flesh, his slightest movement. But there was more, so much more: the way his body moved against hers, the friction, the strength, the ease. He was everywhere. Kissing her ankles. Sweeping his tongue on her collarbone. She shivered at the power of his hand stroking down the length of her, at his fingertips on her inner thighs. Then his lips again, caressing her breasts, her abdomen, her hip, followed by a series of liquid caresses low on her belly, high on her thighs, directly between them, a touch of sheer madness, not of this world. . . .

She pressed her own lips against his flesh, tasted and teased, shuddering against him. She felt caught in a whirlwind, riding her tremors to climax, exploding like shards of shattered crystal, then riding that exultant wave again. She slid her ragged touch downward, stroked and caressed as he had done, until he sat up and she felt herself lifted in the steel vise of his arms, then brought down until at last he was inside her.

He held her hands and lifted their arms over their heads, then wrapped her arms around him and held them there, and all the while the dark enigma of his eyes seemed to pin her in place. She thought that she couldn't know a man better, and yet, for just a moment, she had to wonder if, even now, she knew him at all.

But then she was writhing, aware of nothing but the rise of desire and the feel of him within her, the kiss of coolness in the air, the surge of heat that seemed to rise like a ground fog around them. As he thrust and she arched against him, the friction of flesh upon flesh teased and tormented, awakening a desperate and almost unappeasable hunger, until, as mercurial and thunderous as a burst of diamonds in the air, she felt her climax sweep over and through her again, leaving her trembling against him, shaking and . . .

Cold.

The air was cold.

Her flesh was warm where he touched her,

so cold where he did not.

And the light . . . The room was so bright. She loved the light, but it meant there was no sweet darkness in which to hide. She didn't know whether she should be blasé or embarrassed . . . whether she'd even done this right. . . .

He shifted and drew her down against him on the bed, fingers smoothing her hair, touching her face so gently.

Oh, God, what should she say now?

Somehow he kept the moment from being awkward. "You do like it bright," he said softly, with both bemusement and affection.

She tried to match his tone. "Too much?" she suggested, as if they were sharing tea and she had just poured the milk.

"Well, I guess I'd find it a bit difficult to sleep this way," he told her.

Not if you were going mad, she thought. Not if you believed you had a ghost in your house. The ghost of a vicious murderer. Even then, a little voice inside asked, But had he ever been the murderer people said?

Suddenly she bolted up to a sitting position.

He was leaning back, one elbow crooked behind his head. He stared at her, puzzled.

"I forgot about Killer," she said. "Where did he go?"

"I closed the bedroom door. He's cute and all, but not . . . well, you know."

She smiled for a moment, then swallowed uneasily. "I . . . uh . . ."

"Yes?"

She decided to spit it out. "Jed, I was on my way out before because I was . . . because I didn't want to be here."

Because I thought I saw a ghost and I was terrified, she added silently.

He smiled, reaching out, touching her hair. "I understand that feeling," he told her softly.

No. He didn't. He understood how it had hurt to go on living where he had made his home with Margaritte. But she wasn't hurting. She was scared.

His smile turned rueful, and he arched a brow. "That wasn't all just because I, um, happened to be here and make a convenient distraction, was it?"

"Good Lord, no!" she said in horror.

He had dimples in both cheeks, she noticed. They looked really nice when he smiled, and suddenly she was scared again — in a whole different way.

"Jed, could you . . . would you stay tonight?"

"If you need me," he said, his eyes on hers again. There was no smile in them.

216

She felt her own lips curve slightly. "What if I just wanted you to?" she asked.

"That would be fine, too," he said. "But I get the feeling that you really do need me tonight. And that's okay."

She curled against him, not daring to speak. She didn't trust anyone enough to tell them how deeply afraid she felt. Certainly not Jed, not tonight.

But fear didn't matter right now. Not when his hand was strong and gentle when he touched her. Not when his arm around her offered security, a bastion behind which she could hide from the world.

She lay there in silence and shivered slightly, feeling the air around them grow colder. He pulled her more tightly against him and reached for the covers.

How strange . . . She knew that if he stayed, the feel of him against her would arouse her again. But for the moment she heard his words like a whisper, as if from far away.

"Poor thing. You're just exhausted, aren't you?" he murmured.

She nodded. It was true. Sleep had been so lacking in her life. Well, sex had been lacking, as well, but now she felt as if she had feasted and exhaustion was taking its toll. She settled herself in his arms and closed her eyes.

A moment later she felt his breath as he whispered, "Christie . . . the lights. Will you be all right if I turn just a few of them out?"

She smiled and managed a nod, though she didn't open her eyes. She wasn't afraid of the dark. She wasn't afraid of ghosts. She simply wasn't afraid.

Not with him there.

# 9

When Christina woke up, Jed was gone.

There was a flower — a hibiscus she was sure had been plucked from a bush in the front yard — next to her pillow, along with a note. *You were sound asleep, so I set the coffee for eight. Nothing strange — it was me.*

She bit her lower lip, hugging the covers close. No *Had a wonderful time* or *See you later* or even a *Thanks for the memories.*

But there was a flower on her pillow. And he had stayed until morning.

A short woof drew her attention. Apparently when Jed had left, he'd opted to leave the bedroom door open. Killer was at the foot of the bed, sitting and watching her, his head cocked at an angle she was beginning to recognize and that always seemed to suggest that the terrier knew something she didn't.

"Did he feed you, buddy?" she wondered aloud. "Anyway, I'll just hop in the shower, then get some coffee, and . . . well, if I'm ever going to get paid, I'd better start working on some ideas."

She hurried into the shower, where she hugged her arms around herself, dismayed at the occasional bouts of trembling that came on as she stood beneath the water. Sex happened all the time, she was certain. Well, for some people, anyway. She couldn't let herself read too much into it.

Despite that electric attraction she'd felt to him forever . . .

Was he still in love with his wife?

Some people, even some men, believed there was only one perfectly matched person out there. Only one love to last a lifetime. One that was like a knife embedded in the heart, one soul to match another soul for all time. Interesting theory. What if Jed was that one for her but Margaritte had been that one for him?

She emerged from the shower and dressed quickly, noticing that Killer was no longer waiting for her. As she pulled on a pair of jeans, she heard him barking downstairs. Not a harsh, defensive barking, just one of his excited "woof-woof" things, as if a friend were there.

She felt a strange chill and a sudden desperate need to hurry downstairs.

As she reached the landing, she heard her piano being played. Okay, she thought, apparently Jed hadn't left after all. He was downstairs, playing her piano.

Did Jed even play the piano?

She rushed into the parlor and came to a dead stop.

Killer was actually sitting on the piano bench, next to the man who was playing.

Beau Kidd.

He turned to face her, and she felt the familiar rush of fear — no, terror — sweep over her, like a dark blanket blacking out the world.

*No!* something inside her pleaded.

She leaned against the wall to keep from falling. "Who are you really?" she demanded harshly.

Killer wagged his tail. Great. She might have fallen in love with the little terrier, but he was proving to be no guard dog.

"You know who I am," the man at the piano said. "Please . . ."

He started to rise, and she lifted a hand to stop him. "No, stay right where you are."

He did, and though she couldn't stop leaning against the wall for support, she managed not to pass out.

"What are you doing here?" she asked.

"You let me in," he said softly.

She shook her head. "Oh, no. No, no."

"But you did."

"The Ouija board?"

He smiled. "More than the Ouija board, I think."

"I don't see dead people," she said.

He smiled, lowering his head. He'd been a nice-looking man, she thought, with an easy smile. "I've never forgotten the kindness of that flower on my grave," he told her.

"You're here because of that?"

"Who knows exactly why I'm here?" he murmured, and ran his fingers over the piano keys.

Killer gave a happy bark.

She shook her head again, hoping to clear her vision and find him gone. "You're not here. You can't be here," she said desperately.

He stood up. "I need your help."

She inhaled deeply, staring at him. "Because of the murders."

"I'm obviously not the killer."

"And what does that have to do with you being here, in my house?"

"You're . . . unique."

"Yeah? Well, I don't want to be unique."

"You have a gift," he said.

"I don't want any gifts," she assured him.

"Too bad. It's yours whether you want it or not," he told her.

"What do you want me to do?" she asked him.

He lifted his hands. "I'm innocent."

She felt a chill overtake her. "So who is the Interstate Killer?" she asked.

He stared at her in frustration. "I don't know. But I swear to you, that's no copycat out there now. The killer who struck twelve years ago is at it again."

She swallowed. "I am going crazy. That's the only explanation."

He was impatient now. "No, it's not."

"Do normal people see ghosts?" she demanded.

"Define *normal*," he said.

She let out a sound of irritation. He wasn't there. She was creating him in her mind, just as she had undoubtedly created that vision of her grandfather in her mind, all those years ago.

She turned her back on him and walked down the hallway to the kitchen, where she poured herself some coffee. When she turned around again, she started.

He was in the kitchen with her, leaning against the counter.

"You say you're here because you're innocent and you want me to help you somehow," she said. "Well, you're in the wrong place. I can't help you. I write advertising jingles for a living. I'm not a cop, and I don't speak to the dead. We're not all that far from Cassadaga. It's a charming little town founded by spiritualists. If you pop on over there, I'm sure there are plenty of people who would just love to talk to you."

He shook his head. "I can't."

"Why?"

He shook his head again. "I don't know. Maybe it has something to do with the flower. You did see and talk with your grandfather, you know. He was a great guy."

"You knew my grandfather?" she asked, skeptical.

He grinned. "We'd have coffee now and then at a doughnut shop down on International Drive."

"Why didn't I know that?" she asked.

He shook his head. "Why should you have known it? We weren't best friends or anything. We just used to chat some mornings over doughnuts and coffee."

She studied him closely. He looked real. Flesh-and-blood real.

He couldn't be. But then again, the alternative was just as ridiculous. Why would someone pretending to be Beau Kidd break into her house? Not just pretending to be him, a dead ringer for him.

Admittedly, this was Orlando in October. Costumes and makeup were plentiful. But how could anyone make his face resemble a newspaper photo to a T?

She smiled. "I'm going out now. When I come back, you're going to be gone."

"But I won't be."

"If my cousins put you up to this — if this is some kind of a joke, or worse — you'd better be gone when I get back."

Brave words. If he was a killer, she had certainly provoked him.

"Don't you understand?" he asked her sadly. "I can't go. And I need your help."

"Don't you understand? I can't help you."

"But you can."

"I'm going to burn that Ouija board."

He smiled. Sadly. "Won't do you any good," he told her. Then his grin suddenly turned deep and real. "Which is it? I'm a very strange kind of home invader — made up to look like Beau Kidd and put up to these wicked deeds by one of your cousins. Or I'm a ghost, tied to this house because you live here, and I can't just go away."

"Neither. I just have an overactive imagination," she insisted.

"You know that's not true."

"I can't help you. I'm not a cop."

He was quiet, staring at her. Then he said, "But you were sleeping with one. An ex-cop, anyway. Actually, the ex-cop who maligned me so badly."

"I'm going now," she said.

"You can try to run away," he said. "But you can't really go anywhere. We all learn that at some point."

"Enjoy your philosophizing," she told him. "Now . . . goodbye."

"Goodbye," he echoed, then gave her a thumbs-up sign. "You've stopped blacking out on me, at least. We're moving in the right direction. I knew this would work out, because whether you want to or not, you already know that ghosts are real. When you were a child, you weren't afraid. Remember? You need to reopen the door on those memories."

"Goodbye," Christina said firmly, then turned to her new pet, who was sitting just inside the kitchen doorway. "Killer, come on. We're going."

Instead of obeying, the dog walked over and stood next to Beau Kidd, whining mournfully.

"Now!" she snapped to the dog.

When he didn't budge, she picked him up and, without looking back, headed down the hallway, Killer in her arms. She slammed the front door behind her and made a point of locking it.

She got in the car and headed straight for a café, where her first order of business was to pull out her cell and call a locksmith, who agreed to meet her at the house in an hour. Her cousins were in the clear, she decided, but it still made sense to get new locks for the place.

The dignified gray-haired man stood stiff and unyielding in the doorway.

Jed wasn't sure just what he had expected. Of course Beau Kidd's father was going to be anything but glad to see him.

"I know who you are. I know exactly who you are," Forest Kidd said bitterly.

"I'm sorry if I offended you, sir —"

"Offended me? That trash you wrote did more than offend me."

"It was a work of fiction," Jed said.

"As if that's any excuse."

"The thing is —"

"The thing is," Forest Kidd said angrily, "my son has now been proved to be innocent!"

Jed let out a soft sigh. "Sir, many people think this is a copycat killer."

The older man swore, then turned and strode down the hallway of his single-story ranch house, but he left the door open, so Jed shrugged and followed him.

He went on back to a pleasant family room. Glass doors led out to a pool area, and an open counter separated them from the kitchen.

"Sir," Jed said, taking a seat across from Forest Kidd, "you said you were with your son when at least one of the killings took place. Whoever did kill those women — and whoever is killing now — isn't being quick about it. He rapes his victims repeatedly before finally murdering them."

"You think I don't know every aspect of this case?" Kidd demanded.

"On the contrary, I'm sure you know as much as I do," Jed said.

The older man shrugged, blue eyes sweeping across his backyard. "I come from one of the real old-time families around here. My great-grandparents were up in Jacksonville during the Civil War." His gaze fell sharply on Jed. "That's why I've never left," he said. "Thankfully, it's a transient area now. People coming and going, working at the parks for a while, then moving on. Otherwise, we'd have had to leave. Even though no one ever proved that Beau was guilty of a damn thing. My son was shot and killed, and as far as everyone was concerned, that was it. His partner — Atkins — he was pretty broken up. He came to see us, and at least there was an inquiry, but none of it mattered. Beau was dead — and branded. The killing stopped, and no matter what I said or did . . ."

"You said your son was with you when one of the women was killed," Jed said, hoping Forest might be willing to discuss the subject now.

Forest Kidd leaned forward and folded his hands before him and stared hard at Jed. "I said it because it was the truth. My wife said it, and my daughter said it. No one called us liars right to our faces. They just gave us those pitying looks that said they thought we were liars. And that was it." He leaned back again. "So what are you going to do? Write another book?"

"I'm trying to find out the truth," Jed said.

"Is that supposed to make me care?" Forest asked bitterly.

Jed stood up. "I think you already care, Mr. Kidd. You have a daughter. A beautiful daughter with red hair. I think you have to care, and that's why you let me in."

Forest Kidd stood, a tall man, almost eye level with Jed, who rose along with him.

"I care. But I've just told you everything I can, everything I told the police before. My

229

son didn't do it. The police were desperate. They were grasping at straws. The community was terrified, and there was Beau, a perfect suspect. He'd been seeing two of the girls, and he was leaning over the corpse of the last victim. I don't believe he ever drew his weapon on his partner. I don't care how sincere and wounded and agonized that bastard likes to look. There was never any reason for him to pull a gun." Forest Kidd stared at Jed belligerently.

Jed frowned. "So you're saying that even if he had been the killer, discovered there with the body, he could have just pretended he had discovered the corpse?"

"Bingo. You're a lot brighter than those louts down at the precinct."

"You suggested that to the cops?" Jed asked. He'd never seen it in any of the notes. He hadn't interviewed Forest Kidd or the family when he'd written his book. He had been writing fiction, for one thing, and he'd been convinced that the family of a serial killer would hardly want to talk to him about their beloved son. Not when they were still denying what everyone else was taking to be the God's honest truth.

"Is there anything else you can tell me?" Jed asked quietly.

Forest Kidd stared at him for a long moment. "Ask my daughter, Kitty, about the truth," he said softly. "Katherine. I hear you met her in the cemetery. She said you were there at Beau's grave."

"I saw your daughter there, yes."

"She seemed to think that you . . . well, hell. She seems to believe you're a decent guy."

"I'm trying to discover the truth, Mr. Kidd."

"Here's the truth. You ask any member of my family. Beau couldn't have been guilty. He lived in a small apartment. And trust me, they searched it. They looked and looked and looked for a hotel or motel where he might have stayed, where he might have held a woman and abused her until he killed her. They didn't find anything. And you know why? Because there was nothing to find. Beau wasn't guilty."

"Thank you," Jed said.

"You prove it," Forest Kidd told him as Jed started down the hallway. "You know, if you can prove it, maybe you can live with yourself again," Kidd called after him.

Jed didn't respond.

"I know your wife died of cancer," Kidd said. "No man out there can change that. And that includes you, Mr. Braden. But maybe you can change things for the better if you prove that Beau was innocent. Go for it. Please."

When Jed reached the front door and looked back, Forest Kidd had disappeared.

Jed let himself out.


Dan was at the door of the old family house, about to ring the bell, when he saw Ilona come outside. She saw him, too, and waved. "Hey, there!" he called to her.

"Hey!" she called back, but she didn't come over. Was she looking at him suspiciously? he wondered.

"Have you seen Christie?" he asked.

"She went out a while ago," Ilona told him.

"Did she say where she was going?"

Ilona shook her head. "I didn't ask her. I just happened to see her car drive by. Can I help you? Hey, don't you guys all have keys to that place?"

"I'm sure I had a key at some point," Dan told her. "Oh, well. It's not that important. I had some spare time before work, and I just thought I'd stop by."

"I see," Ilona said.

Dan felt a cold sweat break out at his nape. She was looking at him suspiciously. "Well, I guess I'll get going," he said.

"Good to see you, Dan."

He nodded. "Tell Tony hello for me, okay?"

"Absolutely."

He got into his car. Just as he did, he saw Christina coming around the corner. She waved to him cheerfully as she pulled into the driveway.

Ilona was still watching them, Dan thought as he got back out of his car and waited while Christina stepped from hers, a cup of take-out coffee in her hand.

Her new dog jumped from the car. He barked happily at Dan, his tail wagging.

"Hiya." Christina walked over, and gave him a hug and a kiss on the cheek. "What's up?"

"I had about an hour, so I thought I'd stop by."

"Cool. I'm waiting for the locksmith."

"Oh, yeah?" He looked at her questioningly. "You really think Mike or I would break in just to play a joke on you?"

"Of course not," she told him, shaking her head. "I just don't know how many keys might have wandered out over the years. That's all."

"Good point," Dan said.

When they went into the house, it seemed to Dan that she was behaving strangely. She kept walking around, looking into every room, almost as if she expected to catch someone there.

"Are you all right?" he asked her.

"Of course."

"Do you think the dog — and the new locks — will be enough?"

"Enough?" she asked him.

He shrugged. "I don't know. I'm feeling edgy, I guess. The newspaper headlines, the warnings on the news . . . I knew her, Christie. I knew Patti Jo."

Christina walked over to him, setting an arm around his shoulders. "I'm okay, Dan. I'm really okay. I'm always careful, and I've got Tony and Ilona right next door."

Just then the dog began to bark. He really did sound quite ferocious, Dan thought.

The locksmith was at the door.

While the man worked, Christina played some of her newest tunes for Dan. He'd worked for her a few times, and he liked doing jingles. She had a nice voice herself. They had both loved singing with their grandfather when they were kids.

"Shit!" he swore suddenly.

"What?"

"Work. I've got to go. The Grim Reader has a gig tonight."

When she walked him to the door, the locksmith was just finishing.

"All right. You got good old Killer and your new locks, so I'm out of here. Don't forget, you said you'd come see me."

"I'll talk to Ana. Tomorrow night?"

"Sounds good to me. I'm off Saturday."

"Maybe we can have a get-together here again."

They hugged briefly, and he left. He was halfway down the path when she caught up with him, holding out something toward him.

It was a key.

"Should I have this?" he asked her.

"Of course. Someone else has to have the key to the house. What if I lock myself out? And I've told you and Mike, this will always be your house, too."

He hefted the key in his hand.

He shouldn't take it, he thought. He wasn't sure why, but he just had a feeling he shouldn't have the key.

"Christie . . ." he murmured.

"Take it and get going. You have to go to work."

He nodded. "All right. Love ya."

He hurried on to his car.


Jed called Jerry and arranged to meet him for coffee.

When Jerry arrived, he looked at Jed hopefully. "Anything?"

"Nothing — other than the fact that I'm convinced Beau Kidd never murdered anyone. I can't even find anything that resembles real evidence against him. When Larry Atkins shot him and Beau died, that seems to have created the case."

Jerry looked at him and shook his head. "Okay, say you're right. So whoever is out there kills five women. Then he lets twelve years go by and starts again. Now what?"

"That's where you come in."

Jerry groaned.

"Come on, you guys have to be on this already. Whoever the killer is, no, I don't think he stopped, not unless he was in prison or otherwise out of commission. Maybe he slowed down. Maybe he left town. Maybe he even changed some of his methods. I don't know. But the facts on Beau Kidd are clear. The man was railroaded."

"Hey," Jerry protested. "You're the one who wrote the book."

"Yeah, a novel. And I was suckered in by the fact that the man was dead and the killings had stopped."

Jerry leaned back in his chair. "What's up with this? You get bought off by the family or something? I hear the sister is really

236

good-looking."

"She is. I've met her," Jed said. "She's a beautiful redhead."

Jerry threw up his hands. "There you go. Maybe it was Beau and it was some Freudian thing."

"Jerry, she was twelve when this whole thing started," he said.

Jerry picked up his coffee cup, giving Jed a morose look. "I have a twelve-year-old daughter, Jed. You should see the way she dresses, the way she acts. It's scary."

Jed shook his head impatiently. "That's not it. And you don't believe it, either. That's why you called me. That's why you let me back in on this."

Jerry shrugged.

"I need everything you get, Jerry. You can talk to the FBI, looking for links to deaths in other states, and I need to know what you find out."

Jerry nodded, looking down at his hands. "Do you know that the FBI believes there may be hundreds of serial killers at work in the United States at any given time?" he asked wearily.

"I do."

"Do you know how many are never caught?"

"Jerry, we're going to get this one," Jed

told him.

"Actually, I have a meeting tomorrow with a behaviorist, if you want in on it. Tiggs, he doesn't care if you make an appearance."

"Great. I'll be there."

Dan and the locksmith were both gone. But once she had locked the door behind them and headed down the hall, she hesitated, her footsteps slowing with dread. Then she squared her shoulders and forced herself to keep going to the parlor.

And when she looked into the room, he was there.

Once again Beau Kidd was at her piano, petting Killer, who was clearly fond of him.

She groaned.

Beau turned and grimaced ruefully. "I'm sorry," he told her softly.

"Can't you go haunt someone else?" she asked him. "Someone who could actually help you?"

He shook his head. "I can't. I . . . I have a connection to you."

"Just because I tossed a flower on your grave when I was a kid?" she asked.

"Well . . . that, and the Ouija board," he said. But he looked puzzled. "That and the Ouija board . . . and something else. But I don't know what. Only that there is something else, another link."

"If we discovered that link, would you go away?" she asked hopefully.

He lifted his hands. "If you would just help me . . ."

"I can't help you. I would help you if I could. But I'm not a cop."

"Jed Braden could help you help me."

She ignored that and sat at the far end of the piano bench, setting Killer on her lap. "It's so strange," she murmured. "Killer seems to know you're here."

"Dogs have special senses," he said. "Cute pooch, too."

"Yeah. My Rottweiler," she joked.

He grinned. "You knew no one was breaking in, right? I was trying to be a good guest, trying to be helpful and make the coffee and stuff."

"You nearly gave me a heart attack."

"But I didn't," he said softly. "Because you knew."

She shook her head. "I knew not to play with that stupid Ouija board," she said.

"Maybe you should play with it again," he told her.

Scowling fiercely, she stared at him.

"Or, maybe a séance," he suggested.

"What?"

"A séance might be good."

"You . . ." She pointed at him in exasperation. "You really have to go away. People already think I'm some kind of emotionally fragile flower. I don't need a damn ghost hanging around, driving me crazy for real."

She stood and headed for the kitchen, but he followed her and leaned against the wall, wistfully watching her.

"You can't ignore me, you know."

"I can't? Watch me." She started singing.

But then she felt him. He had set his hands on her shoulders.

She spun around and stared at him. "What?"

"You can't ignore me because I'm not just talking about clearing my name," he said very softly.

"No?" she whispered.

"No. I'm talking about saving the lives of all the other women some monster out there is planning to murder."

# 10

Files and notes were spread out before Jed when the phone rang. He picked it up and said, "Hello?"

"Jed? Jed Braden?"

He didn't recognize the female voice on the other end of the line.

"Yes, this is he."

For a moment there was silence. He kept his number listed and sometimes got calls from nuts. Was this one? "Who is this?"

"Katherine."

"Katherine . . . ?"

"Katherine Kidd."

"Of course," he said, wondering why he hadn't realized who it was as soon as she said her first name. "Hello. How are you?"

"Fine. I wanted to know . . . how are you coming along?"

He hesitated. "How am I coming along? Fine. I guess you know I went to visit your father. I no longer believe your brother was guilty. But I'm not a cop. And though I believe I know who the killer wasn't, I'll be damned if I have any idea who it is."

"Thank you for that. It means a lot." She hesitated. "Would you have coffee with me?" she asked softly.

"I'm not sure —"

"Right. You don't think it would be such a great idea to get personally involved with a client. I'm not looking to go on a date," she told him. "But if we talked . . . I think I might be able to help."

"Where should I meet you?"

He couldn't see much that was going on inside the house. The old lace Victorian curtains hid pretty much everything, other than the shadow of her figure as she moved from room to room.

He should have gone inside when he had the chance. Too late. Now all he could do was watch. But he loved to watch. He always watched first. Half the pleasure was always in the anticipation. And talking and sharing, of course.

But tonight there was no chance to talk, so he settled for watching her as she moved through the old house.

She was so pretty. Just his type. Tall, with that rich, red long hair. And those eyes . . .

But since he couldn't see any of those details tonight, a lot had to be left to his imagination. What he could see, even with the curtains in the way, was the elegance of her movements.

He felt a deep hunger, a pain that was almost agony, seize him. If only . . .

No, not tonight. Not tonight.

But the jaggedly slicing pain shot through him again. He had to have something, someone, to ease this agony.

He should go home, he told himself, and from there he could take care of everything.

He calmed himself by reminding himself that the time would come. And thinking that he could make history repeat itself . . .

That was even better.

Christina sat on the floor in the middle of the parlor, a box in front of her, and looked around warily. Beau Kidd was nowhere in sight. She hadn't seen him since he'd followed her into the kitchen. Of course, even when he was gone, she couldn't stop doubting her own sanity.

She dug into the box in front of her, glad that Gran had never thrown anything away. The box was full of newspaper clippings, including the entire local paper from the day of her grandfather's funeral. She took a moment to read the memorial to him that had run right on the front page. Unfortunately, her grandfather's article had been shortened to make way for a long recap about the just-identified Interstate Killer. She read through it carefully, searching for clues.

Each girl had been on her way to or from her car when she disappeared. All the cars had been found abandoned in the same parking lot where the victim had left it. Other than that and the fact that all the women had been young, attractive and red-haired, there were no clues at all.

She set the paper down and sighed. No wonder everyone had been so willing to believe that Beau Kidd had been the murderer. The evidence pointing to him had been slight, but it was more than they had to incriminate anyone else.

Depressed over reaching a dead end, she decided to go through some of her own boxes and see what she could organize. Almost immediately, she came across a huge article from the Miami paper about a treasure ship. One of the divers who'd found it was a friend of hers, Genevieve Wallace. She remembered going down to the Keys for her friend's wedding and meeting several people who worked for something called

Harrison Investigations, a firm specializing in paranormal research. Now, why hadn't she remembered that sooner?

She jumped up and headed to the dining-room table, where she'd set up her computer. As soon as she got online, she began to search for Harrison Investigations. Their Web site certainly made for interesting reading. They sounded like nothing less than real live ghostbusters.

She clicked on the Contact Us link, then hesitated and instead picked up her cell phone, went through her contacts and called Genevieve.

"Christina!" Genevieve said happily when she answered. "How are things going up there? Are you finding enough work?"

"Work is fine. With all the theme parks, it's an advertising Mecca."

"You're safe, though, aren't you?" Gen asked, suddenly serious. "The news media down here keep talking about those highway killings."

Christina paused for a minute. "Actually, that's sort of what I'm calling you about."

"The highway killings?" Gen asked, puzzled.

"I met some friends of yours at your wedding. The ones from Harrison Investigations."

There was a brief silence; then Gen said warily, "Yes?"

"Gen, I need help."

"In what way?"

"I have a ghost living in my house." She rushed to get the words out, then waited for Genevieve to laugh at her.

"Are you joking?" Genevieve asked sharply.

"No."

There was another silence. Then Gen asked, "Do you know who this ghost is?"

"Beau Kidd," Christina said.

Again silence. Then, "You're really not joking?"

"I wish I was." She hesitated, then asked, "Do you think you could call them for me, since you know them and all?"

"I'll make the arrangements as soon as I can," Genevieve told her. "In the meantime . . ."

"Yes?"

"In the meantime, be careful. Don't trust anyone, even people you think are your closest friends, your nearest relatives. Okay?"

Christina felt a chill and bit her lower lip. The locks were brand-new. She was safe.

"I'll be very careful. I promise."

They met in a café right on International

Drive. Katherine Kidd was already there, a large iced tea in front of her, when Jed arrived. He greeted her, went in for a cup of black coffee, then joined her at the table. This town was certainly tourist central, he thought, dodging the crowds on his way. Across a dozen lanes of traffic, he could see the dramatic facade advertising a dinner show. More signs touted an Arabian horse show and various theme parks. Two feet from where they were sitting, a wire rack held brochures and coupons for dozens of area attractions.

Once upon a time, and not so very long ago, the only thing here had been orange groves.

"Amazing, isn't it?" Katherine said to him. "They all know there's a killer out there, but they just keep going, no matter what. In a small town, a college town, something happens and everything comes to a stop. But here . . ."

He reached across the table and took her hand, squeezing it. "Have you thought about the fact that you fit the profile of the victims?" he asked.

She nodded. "Of course. That's one of the things driving me crazy. Some people think my brother was some kind of sicko who was trying to kill me with every victim. It's ridiculous. I was just a gawky kid when everything happened." She shook her head as if to clear it of unhappy thoughts. "You said you believe my brother was innocent," she told him.

"Yes."

"Well, here's something you should know. He didn't start dating either one of those women until after the killings began. I doubt if you'll find that in all your files. I think the case was a personal thing for Beau — because of me. Because I said something about how the killer kept going after girls with red hair. So he started warning women who fit the description, and that's how he ended up dating two of the victims." She looked around and focused on a poster advertising the seasonal goings-on at one of the parks. "You'd think that they'd stop some of this gruesome Halloween stuff, what with a killer being out there and all," she said.

"It's hard to stop a money machine," Jed told her.

As they talked, he saw a woman entering the café who looked vaguely familiar.

Tall. Long reddish-brown hair. He knew her from somewhere, though he was sure it had been a very long time since he had seen her.

"All right, so the news you have is that Beau didn't know any of the victims until he tried to protect them," Jed said.

Katherine nodded. "And because of that, I think someone out there thought Beau would make a good scapegoat."

"Do you think the killer might have been Larry Atkins?"

She let out a long sigh. "Maybe."

Jed mulled that over for a moment. Larry Atkins certainly had a remote place where he could be hiding women now. . . . But where had he lived twelve years ago? Jed thought back to his previous interviews with the man. Larry had lived in a town house. That didn't clear him, but . . .

The woman left the counter carrying a to-go cup with steam emanating from it. She paused by the table. "Hi, Jed, how are you doing?"

Who the hell was she, and how did he know her?

Katherine smiled, rising slightly, extending a hand. "You're Angie McDuff. I saw you on TV a few days ago."

Angie McDuff. Mike McDuff's ex. How the hell could he have forgotten her? Though, admittedly, it had been a few years, and she had a lot more red in her hair than when he had seen her last.

"Thanks so much," Angie said to Katherine, sounding genuinely pleased to have been recognized.

"Hi, Angie, how are you doing?" Jed said.

"Good, thanks. Though not as well as you are, it seems."

"I beg your pardon?"

She smiled. "Your face has been all over the news."

"Great," he murmured.

"They can't keep that book of yours on the shelves. I mean, I know it was fiction, but you know how people are. They're interested in anything with a hint of scandal attached to it. I bet you'll be getting a lot of calls soon, people wanting to interview you about Beau Kidd and what you think is going on now. Was Beau railroaded while the real killer got away, or is the current murderer a copycat?"

"Angie, this is Katherine Kidd," he said politely. "Beau Kidd's sister."

Angie gasped, turning a mottled shade of red. "Oh. I'm so sorry. I didn't mean to bring up bad memories."

Katherine shrugged. "It's all right."

"Well, nice to meet you. Jed, good to see you again. I think I saw your cousin Ana a few months back. And I heard that Mike's cousin, Christina, has moved to town." She flashed him a broad smile. "I bet she'll find a lot of work here, and she's going to need vocalists, of course."

He tried to keep his smile in place. Angie McDuff never stopped.

"Put in a good word for me, will you, if you run into her?" she asked.

Was she kidding? But he kept his smile in place. Christina Hardy was one of the most loyal women in the world. No way would she hire her cousin's ex, not that he was going to tell Angie that. "Sure," he said, and left it there.

Angie waved goodbye to them both with another smile and walked away.

As soon as the other woman was gone, Katherine started speaking as if they'd never been interrupted. "My brother was good friends with Larry Atkins, but still . . . All I know is that Beau wasn't guilty, and Larry's the one who shot him."

"He was kneeling over one of the victims. And he drew his own weapon," Jed said.

"You could at least talk to Larry again."

"All right, why not?" Jed told her. So what if he'd just been out there? he asked himself, thinking again about the amount of land Larry Atkins had now. It was hill country out there, too. Maybe there were a few secret places out on the property.

Katherine set her hand on his, breaking into his thoughts. "Want to see me home?" she asked softly. Suggestively.

He glanced at her hand. If this invitation had come a week ago . . . ? But it hadn't, and things were different now. "I'll follow you home, see that you get inside okay," he told her.

She drew her hand back. "There's someone else?"

In the past years, there had been a number of someone elses, he thought. This could have been the same. But it wasn't.

"Yes, there's someone else," he said huskily. "But I'll be happy to see you home."

She rose, then hesitated, shaking her head. "Actually, I don't think I'm heading home after all. I think I'll go down the street and see a movie. But thanks. And thank you so much for agreeing to see me. Please, after you've been to see Larry Atkins, will you give me a call and tell me how it went?"

"Yes," he promised her.

"You'll call no matter what?" she asked, her tone afraid and hopeful all at once.

"No matter what," he promised.

With a wave, she was gone.

Beau Kidd was back. He sat on the floor with her, going through clippings, while

Killer dozed on the couch. "There just has to be an answer," he said.

She gazed up at him, gritting her teeth. He hadn't been there . . . then he was. "You were the lead detective on the case," she reminded him.

He shook his head. "Yeah, and as soon as I wanted to keep an eye on a girl . . . she died."

"Beau, did you draw your weapon on Larry Atkins?" she demanded.

He paused, staring blankly out across the parlor. "I drew my weapon. But not on Larry."

"What do you mean?"

"The killer was there."

"The killer was there? Who was it?"

"Obviously, I don't know."

She stared at him as if he had taken leave of his senses. "But you said —"

"It was night. Dark. Someone had called in a tip about shadows moving by the highway, so I called Larry and told him to meet me there, but I reached the location first. I thought . . ." He paused, and ghost or not, the look that flashed across his face was one of pure agony. "I saw her, and I thought she was still alive, so I ran over to her. But then I heard something, so I drew my weapon. I thought that the killer was still there. She was . . . she was still warm, you see," he said very softly.

Killer suddenly stood up and barked once, his tail wagging.

The doorbell rang.

Christina leapt up as Killer barked again, excited, anxious to go to the door with her. "It has to be someone I know," she explained, starting for the hallway. But when she turned back to see if Beau had heard her, he was gone.

Killer barked again. "And they make fun of you," she told him affectionately as they reached the front hall. "You are a good guard dog."

She hesitated at the door. Somehow, she knew it was Jed, maybe because Killer was already so pleased. Her heart thundered as she looked through the peephole.

It was Jed.

"Hey," she said as she opened the door, trying to sound casual.

"Hey, yourself," he replied as she stepped back to give him room to enter. He hunkered down immediately to pet Killer, who seemed positively ecstatic.

Then again, Killer seemed to like her ghost just fine, too. She turned, anxiously looking down the hallway. Was Beau Kidd still there somewhere, just keeping out of the way?

She suddenly felt very awkward, and just a little worried. She sure as hell couldn't tell a man like Jed Braden that she had a ghost in her house. No need to give him any more reason to think she was seeing things. And yet . . .

The ghost was real. He wasn't just in her mind. He wasn't.

But she didn't like the idea of the ghost listening in on their personal conversation. Or their personal . . . other communication.

"So what's up?" she asked, leading the way into the parlor. Might as well see if Beau had reappeared, she thought. "I was actually going to call you later. I promised Dan that I'd go see him doing his Grim Reader thing. I was going to get hold of Ana and ask her to go with me tomorrow, and I was hoping you would come along."

"You're going to the new park?" he asked, his voice fierce, and he was frowning.

"I told you, I promised Dan I'd go."

He followed her into the parlor and looked around at the multitude of boxes. "I guess they're still doing all the Halloween stuff — despite the danger," he said, and it wasn't a question.

"Everyone has to make a living," she said.

He took a seat on the piano bench, looking around some more. He froze when he spotted an old article on the Interstate Killer. "What have you been doing?"

"Just going through stuff," she said.

"Tell me you're not getting involved in this case," he demanded.

"I'm just sorting out some old clippings."

"What you need to do is stay as far away from this case as you can," he said harshly.

Surprised by his tone, she shook her head. "You seem to be getting involved," she pointed out.

"I used to be a cop."

"So you should know that cops are grateful for any help they can get. If someone could figure out —"

"They might be in a lot of danger," he said.

She hesitated, and in the silence she could have sworn she heard some of the clippings rustling around.

"Everyone is in danger until this killer is caught," she said.

He leaned forward. "Christie, you write advertising jingles for a living."

"And I'm a redhead," she said coolly. "I'd like to see this solved."

He stood, agitated. "Look —"

"Beau Kidd didn't do it," she heard herself say.

"And how the hell do you know that?"

"I just . . . I just . . . Well, look at what's happening now. I just know he's innocent," she said stubbornly. When he didn't deny her words, she whispered softly, "You agree, don't you?"

"Agree?" he demanded.

"That Beau Kidd was innocent," she said more loudly.

He stared at her as if puzzled by her vehemence. "In my opinion? Beau Kidd was not guilty."

She smiled. "And the cops have to know that, too, right? So they must be looking for someone who was here then and is still here now."

"That would be logical, yes," he said.

"Maybe you could figure out the relationship between the victims then and the victims now," she said.

He groaned. "Great. All the law enforcement officials on this case, and you think that hasn't occurred to anyone yet?"

She flushed.

"Christina . . . why is it you suddenly seem to feel as if you have to personally make sure someone solves this and exonerates Beau Kidd?"

Not knowing how to answer that without sounding as if she needed to be locked up in a padded room, she changed the subject and asked, "Hey, how about some dinner? We could call out for pizza, or I could throw some eggs on the frying pan. . . ." She paused. "You look kind of worn-out," she told him. "Like you need a good meal."

He shrugged, clearly not about to tell her what was really on his mind. Then he let out a sigh. "I just had coffee with Katherine Kidd," he told her.

"Katherine Kidd?" she said.

"Beau Kidd had a sister," he said.

"I remember. She was about my age. You know, he was buried the same day as my grandfather. I remember . . . I didn't know whose grave it was, but I saw his parents there. His mother was sobbing. I didn't see his sister there, though."

"Maybe they wouldn't let her go," he said. "There was so much hatred for Beau at the time, so many people who believed he was a killer."

"So has she hired you to work the case?" Christina asked.

"No one needed to hire me for this case," he told her, then straightened his shoulders. "So, did I hear something about dinner?"

"Want eggs and toast?" she suggested.

"Sure."

She turned and walked to the kitchen,

leaving him standing there.

A minute later, she felt hands on her shoulders and froze.

Beau or Jed?

She spun around. It was Jed, pitch-dark eyes meeting hers. "I don't want to talk about this all the time," he said. "I don't want it to become an obsession, do you understand?"

"Right," she murmured. "Um . . . do you want wine with your eggs?"

"Whatever you want."

"Do you mind running down to the basement?" she asked him.

"Sure." He turned away and headed for the stairs. She reached for a spatula, then jerked when she felt a touch on her arm.

This time it was Beau Kidd.

"What are you doing here?" she demanded, irritated.

He looked hurt, but all he said was, "Thanks."

She shook her head. "You didn't need to haunt me. He's on it already."

He was quiet, looking perplexed. "I can't help it. The flower on my grave, the Ouija board . . . there's a connection between us, though I have to admit, I don't get it, either."

"Well, I've got company, so there's no

time to figure it out. Would you just go somewhere else?"

They could both hear Jed's footsteps on the stairs.

"Got a thing for him, huh?" Beau teased.

"Go away. Please?"

He let out a sigh. "I sure would love to see Kitty . . . my folks."

"Try wafting over there, why don't you?"

He grinned.

"Who are you talking to?" Jed called.

"I was just talking to the dog," she returned, glaring at Beau.

Jed reentered, and when she looked back to where Beau had been, he was gone. Jed poured the wine while she finished the eggs. "I saw an old acquaintance of yours tonight," he told her.

"Oh?"

"Mike's ex-wife."

"Really?" Christina felt herself stiffen. She couldn't help it. Angie had hurt Mike. She'd cheated on him and hadn't particularly cared that he'd found out, or that she'd hurt him. He'd been head over heels in love with her, and she'd used that to her advantage. They hadn't had any kids, but Mike was still stuck paying alimony.

"What did she have to say for herself?"

"She wanted me to suck up to you," he

said flatly.

Christina stared at him, curious. "Suck up to me? Why?"

"Because you're going to be looking for singers."

Christina laughed suddenly. "Wow. I don't think of myself as being particularly vengeful, but . . . well, she could suck up to me from now to eternity, and I still wouldn't use her."

"So I figured."

"I do think Mike is finally over her," Christie said as she dished out the eggs, saving some in the pan to give Killer later. As she set their plates out on the dining-room table, she realized that she was nervous.

Just what had last night been? A moment's insanity? The natural result of so many years of pent-up attraction, at least on her part?

Or was he here now because this was the beginning of something new, something different, for both of them?

She saw that she still had the Harrison Investigations home page up on the screen. Embarrassed, she closed it and got ready to shut down the computer, but just then a breaking news alert suddenly flashed on, and she gasped.

"What?" Jed demanded, just as his cell phone began to ring. "Another body?" he asked, staring at the screen while he flipped his phone open.

She shook her head. "No, no . . . not a body. A missing woman."

A woman she knew.

"Yeah, Jerry, thanks. I just heard about it," she heard Jed saying, though she couldn't seem to pull her eyes away from the screen. Then Jed strode into the living room and turned on the television. Immediately, the missing woman's face popped into view.

She was pretty. She was young.

She had long red hair.

And a voice like a lark.

"I know her," she told Jed as he snapped his phone closed. "Her name is Allison Chesney. I was supposed to record with her on Monday."

"She won't be going anywhere on Monday," Jed told her.

"But the computer only said that she was missing."

"She's been found," he said grimly.

# 11

He watched. Waited. Analyzed their body language.

They were both young, attractive, the man obviously in a hurry, the woman just as obviously anxious. The man was talking, his expression firm. He was clearly the kind who tended to speak with authority. When she responded, he could see that she was the type to defy authority. But pretty, so very pretty . . .

And then they kissed. Not the kind of peck a husband gave his wife when he was in a hurry. Not the kind of halfhearted kiss a man gave a woman when he was already long gone mentally. It was a kiss like a promise, brief, but filled with the future. Then the man left, and from his vantage point, he heard the lock snap.

He drew a deep breath and smiled. She was alone.

But this wasn't the time. Not yet. It would

come soon enough.

He left his hiding place and walked down the street, waving to the occasional passerby as he headed for the house, for the woman who knew him.

He felt as if his patience was paying off and things were finally going his way. All these years . . . He felt gleeful, like laughing. If they only knew.

Oh, if they only knew. . . .

All the victims looked so much alike when they were laid out on an autopsy table. But it wasn't the resemblance in death that drove the killer. Jed was certain of that. The sex, the power he wielded and the humiliation of his victims before death . . . those were what mattered to their murderer. And then, after death, they were left naked. And posed. But this murder was different.

This one felt far too close.

"Come on, Doc, tell us something," Jerry pleaded.

Doc Martin shook his head. In sadness? Frustration? Jed couldn't tell. Then Doc spoke. "Bruising . . . there, on the arms. And ligature marks on the wrists and ankles — see? That's a change in MO. Maybe she refused to cooperate or almost escaped or something. She was gagged, too. You can see the marks, here. She lost a hunk of hair, too. Probably pulled out while she was being dragged around. Cause of death . . . just the same. Manual strangulation. Nothing found near her. She was killed elsewhere and dumped by the highway."

"She didn't reach home two nights ago," Mal O'Donnell read from his notes. "But her sister thought she was with her boyfriend. The missing persons report was filed yesterday afternoon, and —"

"She was found by a family who pulled over because they didn't think their four-year-old would make it to the next rest stop," Jerry finished. "God . . . the uniforms said the little boy couldn't stop screaming. There's a kid who's going to be in therapy."

"What is that?" Jed asked when he saw Doc Martin frown and pick up a pair of tweezers. Then he saw what Doc had seen: something in the girl's hair.

"Grass. A long blade of grass," Doc Martin said.

Mal O'Donnell produced an evidence bag. "We'll get it analyzed," he said glumly.

"Who knows? Maybe someone will figure something out," Doc Martin said.

"Yeah. That it's grass. Ever seen a grassier frigging state?" Jerry demanded morosely.

"She was lying in the grass when she was

found, but . . . was it that grass?" Mal O'Donnell wondered aloud, looking at Jed.

"This is the third young woman — this is getting very bad," Doc Martin said, then began to recite the details into a tape recorder.

It was like déjà vu, Jed thought. They had heard it all before, but each time, it seemed to cut more deeply into the soul.

Killer had to go out.

Christina had stayed inside after Jed left, reading everything she could find on Harrison Investigations, but eventually Killer's whining got to her.

At least he was housebroken, a fact she could appreciate.

"Okay, boy. I'll wait on the porch," she said as she opened the door, then stood outside, and let him race up and down the front lawn. October could be such a strange month, she thought. During the day it could actually feel hot, but at night the breeze swept through, cooling everything down to the point that it could actually feel cold. She felt that chill now as she stood there waiting for Killer to do his business.

Suddenly the chill grew even worse, almost unnatural.

"Killer!" she called. "Let's go!"

She saw that the dog had gone dead still, standing with his nose in the air, sniffing. He was as rigid as if he were a lawn statue.

"Killer?" she repeated, a little less firmly. She looked around, trying to see what had caught the dog's attention, but she saw nothing. Despite that, she felt deeply chilled and had an uncomfortable sense that she was being stalked. "Killer, now!" she snapped.

When he still didn't move, she ran up behind him and scooped him into her arms, then ran toward the house as if she were being chased. She slammed the door closed behind her, and her fingers trembled as she slid the bolt home.

She turned, looking around to see if Beau Kidd was there. Maybe his presence was what was making her so uneasy. But no sooner had she walked through the downstairs and assured herself that he wasn't in sight than the doorbell rang. Somehow she kept from screaming as she hurried to the door and looked through the peephole.

Michael.

She exhaled in relief and opened the door. "Are you all right?" he asked, a smile fading from his lips, a frown furrowing his brow as soon as he saw her.

"I'm fine."

"You're not fine. You look . . . white."

"Um . . . have you heard the news?" she asked him.

"No, why? What's up?"

"They found another victim of the Interstate Killer," she said.

"Oh, God. That's awful."

As she stepped back to let him in, Killer barked. "Killer, this is Michael."

"Killer?" Michael said, arching a brow.

"Oh, shut up and come in. That was the name he had when I adopted him. Can I get you something? Did you just leave work?"

"Just a few minutes ago, yeah. I was working late. I talked to Dan earlier, and he said you promised to go see him as the Grim Reader tomorrow. I figured I'd just stop by now and make sure you were all right, and ask if I can crash the festivities. Is it okay if I go with you guys?"

"Of course. If it's still open."

"Still open?" Mike said.

"Didn't you hear me? They found another dead woman."

"Did she work at Dan's park?" he asked.

"No, in fact . . . she was going to work for me," she told him.

"Oh, Christie!" He took a step closer and threw his arms around her, pulling her close. "I'm so sorry. I mean, someone you knew . . ."

She accepted his hug for a minute, then pulled away when Killer gave a nervous bark. "It's okay, boy," she chided him. "This is your cousin Mike."

"I am not a dog's cousin," Mike said indignantly.

"Be quiet. You'll hurt his feelings," she said lightly, then turned to lead the way down the hallway. Once again she felt that eerie sensation and paused.

She nearly jumped a mile when her cell phone rang.

It was in the dining room, she realized. "Hang on," she called over her shoulder to Mike as she hurried into the dining room. Mike followed, and she noticed absently that he was wearing a trench coat. He looked like such an executive, she thought as she flipped open her phone and said, "Hello."

"Hey, you all right?"

It was Dan.

"I'm fine."

Killer started to bark, and the doorbell rang again. She frowned. What was going on tonight?

Mike shrugged. "I'll get it."

She smiled her thanks and returned her

attention to the phone.

"I saw that they found another dead woman, Christie. Another redhead," Dan said. "I'm worried about you."

"I'm fine."

"Because you have Killer?" Dan said doubtfully over the line.

She looked up. Mike was returning, and Ilona Nelson was with him. Christina smiled at her while still listening to Dan. She mouthed the words, Where's Tony?

"Tony is still next door," Ilona said cheerfully.

"You have a houseful?" Dan asked over the line.

"Your big bro is here, and now Ilona."

"Tell them hi," Dan said.

"Dan says hi," Christina repeated. "Mike says he's going to come with us tomorrow night," she explained to Dan.

"Yeah? Cool."

"Where are you going?" Ilona asked.

"To see Dan as the Grim Reader," Mike explained.

"Tony and I will come, too. If that's all right?"

"Of course they can come," Dan said, apparently having heard the entire exchange.

"Dan says of course you guys can come." She frowned and turned to Ilona. "Neither

270

of you has to work?"

Tony owned a bar and restaurant on International Drive, where he worked most nights, and Ilona helped out.

Ilona shook her head. "Nope, we're off tomorrow."

"We're all coming, Dan," she said into the phone, feeling a sudden desire to scream.

The Interstate Killer had claimed another victim, someone Christina had known, and they were talking about the next evening's social events.

At least she wasn't alone, waiting for Jed to come back from seeing Jerry. Before he left, he'd told her to lock herself in and not to open the door for anyone. But Killer had needed to go out, and she could hardly have refused, could she? And Mike and Ilona weren't exactly strangers.

Mike took the phone from her. "Hey, Dan. Christie isn't having a great night. Have you seen the news? She knew that last girl who was killed."

She took the phone back. "I'm okay, Dan."

"Christie, I'm so sorry. I know how you feel. I was friends with Patti Jo. This is getting . . . scary."

"I'm okay, honest. We'll all see you tomorrow night, okay?"

"Okay. Love ya, cuz."

"You, too," she said, and hung up.

Ilona offered Christina a sympathetic smile. "I'm so sorry," she said softly.

"Thanks."

"Well, I guess I'd better get back. Tony will be waiting, and . . ."

"And?" Christina said.

Ilona glanced at Michael. "Well, your cousin is here now, and you have that little cutie," she said, indicating Killer. "Tony worries about you, that's all. I hope you know we're both next door anytime you need us."

"Thanks," Christina said. At the moment her head was pounding and she wanted everyone to leave. "Mike, will you walk Ilona home?" she asked. "I think I'd just like to be alone for a while."

"Sure," Mike said. "Meet you here tomorrow night?"

"Sounds good," she said.

As soon as they left, Christina locked the door behind them, then got the feeling that someone was behind her. She spun around and stared at Beau.

"Stop that," she snapped. "I mean it."

"Stop what?"

"Showing up out of the blue like that," she told him.

"But . . ."

"Knock. Rattle chains. Do something," she said.

Christina heard a car door slam and looked out the peephole.

Jed was back.

She watched him get out of his car. She could almost feel Beau wince behind her.

"He . . . he went to see the body," he whispered softly.

"How do you know?"

"I was a cop. I know how a guy looks when he's seen what a killer has done . . . and he can't stop him."

"You have to get out of here."

"I don't think he can see me."

"But I'll forget and talk to you, and he'll think I'm insane," she said, and turned slightly.

He was smiling, but his expression was pained. "You've accepted it, haven't you? You have a gift. You can see ghosts. You can talk to them."

"Go away, please."

"I'm gone."

She believed him and swung the door open as Jed approached the house. He walked in, but when she would have touched him, he lifted a hand. "Can I use your shower?" he asked.

"Of course."

He knew the way, so when he headed upstairs, she went into the kitchen, where she hesitated, then poured a large whiskey.

Irish medicine, she taunted herself.

And maybe it was, in a way. If so, this was certainly the right time for it.

She walked up the stairs to the bedroom. She could hear the water running as she walked into the bathroom. He was sitting on the shower floor, the water cascading over him.

"Jed?"

He didn't seem to hear her.

She opened the frosted door. Forgetting her clothes and her shoes, she stepped in and hunkered down by him. As the water poured over them both, she could smell the heavy scent of soap. Somehow she knew that he had scrubbed with it, then scrubbed again.

"Hey," she said softly.

He looked at her then. Looked at her as if he had just realized she was there, fully clothed and totally soaked.

"Christie," he murmured. "Christie, I'm so sorry. I shouldn't have come here."

"But you did. Now, come on out of there."

She stepped out herself, turning off the water, then handed him a towel. He seemed impatient with himself then, all masculine and silent again. Wrapped in a towel, he found another one, drying her off as he stripped her of her wet clothing. She had meant to offer solace; instead, she found herself swept up in his arms and carried into her room, where he set her on the large upholstered chair by the bed. Then he found some logs in the basket beside the fireplace and set them in the grate on the hearth. It took him only a moment to get a fire started. She thought how striking and grave he looked, his features hard and chiseled in the light of the fire, and she wondered about the thoughts that went through his head. He'd been a cop. He'd seen so much.

But that didn't mean that what you saw couldn't tear at your heart.

"Are you okay?" she asked. "I brought you a whiskey. There, on the night table."

He glanced at her with just a trace of amusement in his eyes. "A whiskey, huh?"

She shrugged.

"Thank you."

He swallowed the generous shot she had poured without a breath, then winced slightly. He poked the fire, then walked over to her. She didn't know what to say, so she didn't speak. She simply stood and opened her arms. He stepped into her embrace and just held her for a long moment, then sat down on the bed with her on his lap.

It seemed to her as if they sat there for a long time. She had the odd feeling that he was seeing today's dead woman. He was seeing the years gone by. Seeing his wife, so young to be so ravaged by disease. So much loss.

And he'd been as helpless to save her then as he had been to save the dead woman today.

She wished that she knew the right thing to say to him.

Life isn't fair.

It sounded so trite, but at the same time, it was so true.

She never did speak, because at last, he touched her face. Lifted her chin. Found her lips. It seemed as if a storm, a tidal wave of heat, washed over her, as if the hot spray of the shower was once again beating tumultuously against her.

His lips were crushing, almost violent. His hands were steel-strong, his passion volatile.

Suddenly the tempest ebbed, and his movements turned sweet, then wicked and wild. Before . . . there had been hunger and the thrill of exploration. Tonight it was as if the floodgates had opened. She couldn't taste enough of his flesh, his sex, couldn't ride hard enough against him. He was equally forceful. She had never felt so completely part of another human being, entwined as if they were one.

She soared to a sudden climax, drifted in the still-volatile aftermath of what they had shared. She had barely calmed before she felt him moving above her once more. His eyes were darker than any abyss, his features tense with concentration. But this time his mouth was gentle, questing, as his tongue teased her collarbone and breasts.

He slid into her once again, then withdrew. His mouth began to ravage the length of her, but slowly. Slow torture. Prolonged seduction. She wrapped her fingers around his sex. Played him. Her teeth and tongue danced over his shoulders, down his chest, tasting the salt on his skin

No words were exchanged in the darkness of the night. In the end, he simply wrapped his arms around her, and she curled against him tightly. If she spoke, she would break the spell, she thought, so she just closed her eyes and allowed sleep to come, knowing he was with her.

Knowing that as much as she wanted him, as sweet as it was to be with Jed, it was equally true that she did not want to be alone.

She slept like an angel.

■ ■ ■ ■

Awakening, Jed rose up on one elbow and watched Christina sleep. Her hair was a true auburn, and as it splayed across her pillow, the touch of the sun turned it into a cascading torch. Her lashes, however, were darker, and they swept over her cheeks to add a touch of mystery. He felt a catch in his throat. And in his loins. But he didn't intend to wake her, so he only continued to watch her, feeling a flush of warmth, thinking how lucky he was, and yet afraid to think of what that meant.

At last he rose, impatient with himself.

He'd known her forever, and he'd cared about her. How could he not? She was Ana's little friend. Ana's little friend who had grown up tall and stunning, elegantly built, with huge blue eyes. When he thought about it, he realized that he'd been involved with her forever.

But he'd been in love with Margaritte.

If he was in love again . . .

Did that make him disloyal?

He didn't want to think about that, so he strode into the shower. He had loved his wife; there was no question about that. And it had been torture to watch her die, little by little, day by day. He'd never been disloyal then. Never been anywhere but at her side. Fighting. Hoping.

But in the end, fighting and hoping hadn't changed a damn thing.

There had been other women since then, of course. He hadn't lived like a monk. But Christie was different. This could hurt him. She could hurt him. Hurt him badly.

He couldn't stay away. He wanted her far too much. Needed her, craved her . . .

Damn it, he didn't want to think about it.

He finished his shower and got dressed, and then the dog followed him downstairs, where he turned on the television, checked his watch. He called Jerry, who invited him to come sit in on a meeting with the FBI, then found the dog food and fed Killer. Damn, but he was a cute little mutt.

He left, carefully making sure that the lock caught once he was outside. It was better when the door was double-bolted, but it was broad daylight. And the dog did bark like blue blazes when anyone came near the house.

There was dead silence when Jed opened the door to the bare-bones conference room at the police station. He knew some of the officers, didn't know others. Undoubtedly a lot of the men didn't think he belonged, but Tiggs handled the situation for him.

"Anyone who doesn't know him, this here is our celebrity ex-cop, Jed Braden. He's a licensed P.I. now, and he's working for Beau Kidd's family," Tiggs announced.

A murmur went around the room.

"Damn it, you're kidding," someone whispered. "After that book?"

"Yeah, ironic, huh?" Jed said, moving in to take a seat at the back and looking around the room. Mal O'Donnell and Jerry were seated up front. Doc Martin was there, too, along with another twenty-plus cops, some local, but at least six of them from the state police.

One of the younger detectives leaned over to bring Jed up to speed. "That's Gil Barron talking. He's FBI, but he seems to have a handle on real life."

Exactly what that meant, Jed wasn't sure, but he nodded his thanks, then listened.

"It's pretty obvious that our perp is targeting a certain type of woman. Whether we're looking at the same guy as twelve years ago or a second killer, the victim is young, right around twenty-five. She's not a prostitute. She either is an entertainer or works with entertainers."

"That narrows it down. Doesn't he know

this is theme park heaven?" one of the cops muttered.

Gil Barron obviously overheard, but he didn't seem disturbed. He only smiled. "It's a bitch, huh? I wish I could tell you something new. I can only reiterate what we do know. We've profiled this guy, and we think the murderer is employed, and that he makes a decent income. He's not old. Personally, I see the same ID in the killings, which would suggest that Beau Kidd was innocent. The murderer is snatching women and hanging on to them, so either he has a place to stash them where their screams aren't heard or he's keeping them drugged, or perhaps it's a combination of both. It appears that, for the most part, they've been snatched from public places. This would suggest that they're going with the killer with smiles on their faces. I hate to say it, but we're looking for the boy next door."

"I hear that Beau Kidd was the typical boy next door," one of the younger officers interjected.

"Profiling isn't an exact science," Gil Barron said. He was tall, lean and had an unlined face. He didn't look like the kind of man who dealt with sick minds on a daily basis, Jed thought. "The killer may be married, may even have a family. And I'll repeat.

My personal opinion is we're looking at the same guy from twelve years ago."

Forgetting that he was no longer a cop, that he didn't really have a right to be there, Jed voiced his question. "What the hell has he been doing for the past twelve years, then?"

Gil Barron nodded in approval of the question. "I was just getting to that. We've pulled records from the national database. Three women disappeared and were found in similar circumstances in Georgia, near the Florida border, eight years ago. God knows why they were never associated with the earlier vics. I suppose most people thought the Interstate Killer was dead and just never thought about him. A recent international search pulled up a similar scenario just two years ago in Jamaica. The women — there were three of them — were black, but they all had their hair highlighted red. And though none of those killings were ever solved, the victims in each location did have a connection. In Georgia, the victims took piano lessons from the same teacher. In Jamaica, all three women worked in the same restaurant. We're looking diligently for something specific that connects our recent victims to the earlier women — if, indeed, we are looking for the same killer."

Gil talked for a while longer, then Doc Martin got up to talk about the autopsies and the change in MO with the last victim. The meeting broke up then, and Gil Barron found Jed. "Good book," he told him.

"I'm not so sure," Jed said.

Barron shrugged. "Don't beat yourself up. It was fiction."

"Yeah. Fiction."

Barron smiled. "You're hungry to end this. That's a good thing. Tiggs seems to think so, too. Well, good luck to all of us, huh?"

"Yeah, thanks."

In the morning, she woke alone.

Or almost alone.

When her eyes opened, she started violently, grabbing her covers, and stared at Beau Kidd, who was in the massive upholstered chair where she had sat the night before.

"This is very interesting," he said without preamble. "First a woman who worked where your cousin works is killed, then a woman who was working with you."

"What the hell are you doing in my bedroom?" Christina demanded angrily.

Beau waved a hand dismissively. "What are you worried about? He's gone."

She shook her head, closing her eyes. "Get

out of my room. I'd like to take a shower and get dressed."

"You're forgetting how important this is," he told her.

"Never," she said softly. "Like you said, I knew Allison Chesney. There's no way I can forget."

"You are going to the wake, right?"

She arched a brow. "You know when it is?"

"Not for a few days."

"And you know this how?"

"Braden had the television on before he left. Oh, and he fed the dog."

"Did he put the coffee on for me?"

Beau smiled. "Well, he did make coffee, but I chucked it and started over. I know just how you like it."

"Great. Now, get out of here. Please."

She could only suppose that he had done so, since he disappeared. She rolled out of bed, showered, dressed and headed downstairs. In the kitchen, she poured coffee, and it was just the way she liked it, damn it. A minute later, the phone rang.

"Hello?"

It was Jed. "Christie, your grandfather played guitar for fun sometimes. Played his guitar and sang at a local pub, right? I seem to remember hearing him a year or so before he died."

"He used to play at O'Reilly's. It was a real hangout for the Irish in the area. It's still there."

"Thanks for the info."

"Why? What's up?"

"I'm not sure. I'm just looking at all kinds of stuff. You just keep your door locked, okay?"

"I always do." As she spoke, Killer started to bark, followed by the doorbell. It was uncanny how he always knew ahead of time when someone was coming. "Someone is here."

"Don't open the door till you know who it is," he said, but she had already set the receiver down.

# 12

"I don't believe it," Dan breathed. He was standing in front of the bulletin board, staring at the piece of paper announcing the casting for the new show had been done. He touched the sheet reverently.

Zeus, main: Daniel McDuff. Stand-ins . . .

He didn't see who would be standing in for him. He didn't care. He couldn't believe it. His own name was there, and he was too excited to think past that.

"Congratulations!" someone said, and he turned. The face in front of him was blurred. Tears? he thought. No, it couldn't be.

"Thanks," he said, and his voice was hoarse.

Other people came by, and the congratulations continued to flow. It was incredible. His life was incredible. He was so happy. . . .

"Patti Jo was up for this show," someone said, and Dan swallowed, wincing. How could he have forgotten?

But . . . oh, hell. He had made it! He couldn't help the huge smile on his face, couldn't help feeling as if he had conquered the world.

"Christie?"

Jed knew she hadn't hung up on him, that she had just set the phone down, because he could hear the dog barking and some kind of commotion.

"Christina!"

She didn't pick up the phone again, and, swearing, he headed out, unable to explain the sense of sheer panic he was feeling.

"Gen? My God — I can't believe you're here!"

"Christie!"

It was so good to see her friend, it seemed almost impossible. Genevieve was standing on the front porch, and she wasn't alone. She was with her husband, Thor, and an older man she introduced as Adam Harrison.

Christina knew who he was from her Internet research. He was the head of Harrison Investigations, specialists in the paranormal, though he never actually claimed when speaking to the press that he believed in the supernatural or the occult. He seemed an expert at double-talk, at sounding forthcoming without actually saying anything at all.

He was an impressive-looking man. He was obviously in his seventies — or more — but he stood ramrod straight and had a full head of snow-white hair. His eyes were both warm and sharp, the kind of eyes that seemed to see far beneath what was obvious on the surface.

She led them all into her parlor together, where the conversation was casual at first. Then, as if they'd simply run out of script, everyone stopped speaking and they all just stared at one another.

"I have a ghost," she said into the silence.

"So you told Gen," Thor said, and she had to smile. His tone was so soft and reassuring, though the man himself was pretty much a giant, and very blond. No one, she was certain, had ever fit the name better. She had met him for the first time when she had attended Gen's wedding, but she had liked him right away.

Christina looked at him. "So you . . . you believe I have a ghost?"

He glanced at Adam with a trace of amusement. "I'm fairly open to the possibility," he said.

"You told me you think Beau Kidd is

haunting your house," Genevieve offered encouragingly.

"Yes."

"Why?" Genevieve asked.

"Why?" Christina echoed. "Because I've seen him."

"No," Genevieve said, a small smile curving her lips.

"Why would he be haunting this house?" Thor explained.

"Did he ever live here?" Adam asked.

She shook her head. "No."

"Has he . . . threatened you in any way?" Genevieve asked.

Christina shook her head. "No. Though he had me thinking I was going crazy, moving things around in the house, putting coffee on," she admitted. "I thought maybe my cousins were playing tricks on me."

Genevieve frowned, hands clasped before her, leaning forward. "Christina, you don't think Dan or Mike would . . . would try to scare you out of here, do you?"

"Or worse?" Thor added.

"Worse?" she demanded. She felt as if she were bristling, just like Killer when his hackles rose.

The dog, in fact, seemed to know intuitively that she was upset. He barked, then walked over to stand next to her, glaring at the others.

"Dan had quite a sense of humor when you were kids," Genevieve reminded her. "Once, down in the Keys, he threw a bunch of fish he'd bought into the water and they died, remember? And they thought they had a real problem on their hands. The park service wound up getting involved."

"Dan has grown up," Christina said. "And my cousins aren't playing tricks on me," she added firmly, then turned to stare at Adam, as if daring him to disagree.

"I believe you," he assured her.

He was such an interesting combination, she thought. So dignified and authoritative in looks, but when he spoke, his words were quiet, and his smile made you feel you'd known him forever.

"Gen . . ." she said, then took a deep breath. "Look, I know you all kept a low profile over the events in the Keys . . . The treasure you found, how you found it. The fact that you were nearly killed. But there was something else going on there, wasn't there?" She stared hard at her friend. "Ghosts."

Gen smiled, meeting Christina's eyes. "Ghosts can be good, you know," she said.

"So, can you see Beau Kidd?" Christina asked.

"No. Do you see him right now?"

Christina shook her head. "He's . . . not here right now."

"But he visits you because he wants his name cleared, right?" Adam suggested.

"Yes. But . . . I hoped you could talk to him. He should really be haunting someone else, someone who can help him. Can you . . . can you at least feel him?"

Adam smiled gently. "I rarely have any direct connection with the supernatural, but I know those who do," he told her.

"He talks to you? He actually carries on conversations with you?" Thor asked.

She nodded.

"When did he first appear?" Adam asked.

"He first appeared at the foot of my bed a few days ago. I thought he was a dream — or that *I* was dreaming, I should say — but he . . . he seemed so real that he scared me half to death. I ran out of the house, and then he came up behind me. He tapped me on the shoulder, and I ended up passed out on the lawn."

"You passed out — outside?" Thor asked, then turned to Adam in concern.

"Yes, I know. I should stay inside, because the killer — the Interstate Killer or the copycat, whoever — isn't snatching women who are safely locked in their houses. But anyway, later . . . later I had to accept that Beau was here, that he does exist."

Genevieve was watching her. "Don't you remember, Christie?" she asked softly.

"Remember what?"

"When we were kids. We'd go places, and you would rattle off all kinds of history, stuff you had no way of knowing. Christie, you saw things back then. And then, when your grandfather died . . . when I talked to you after, when I told you how sorry I was, you said that you knew he was okay, that he told you he was fine. Christie, you've always had . . . a connection to the other world."

Christina shook her head. "No. I . . . I don't have a connection or a gift or whatever you want to call it. If I did, I'd be able to see my parents. And if ghosts are so real, why doesn't Granda, the nicest man in the world, haunt this place instead of Beau Kidd?"

Thor cleared his throat. "Maybe because your grandfather doesn't have anything to prove and Beau does?"

Christina looked pointedly at him. "You talk to him, then."

"He's chosen to talk to you, and he'll either let the rest of us in or he won't," Adam said.

Christina groaned softly. "*He* doesn't even

know why he's connected to me. It might be something as simple as a flower I put on his coffin — he was buried on the same day as my grandfather, right nearby, and I went over and left a flower. I don't even know why."

"It is a connection, however tangential," Adam mused.

"Then again, it might have been the Ouija board," Christina said.

"Ouija board?" Adam repeated, frowning.

"Yes . . . it's from when I was a kid," Christina said defensively. "A bunch of us pulled it out the other night, and he . . . talked to us. To me."

"Ouija board . . ." Adam said thoughtfully.

"Should we get it out?" Genevieve suggested.

Adam shook his head. "No, not at this point. I think we'd be better off trying . . ."

"I agree," Thor said, looking at Adam.

"With what?" Christie demanded.

"A séance. A full-scale séance," Adam told her, his tone serious.

Dead serious.

Silence filled the room after he spoke. Then Killer suddenly jumped up and began to bark, followed by a thunderous pounding on the door.

He didn't like it. He didn't like it one bit. There was too damn much activity.

He took a deep breath. Time to take a break. Time to lay low. He could do it; he'd done it before. Of course, he could also go away for a while, get a change of scenery.

No.

He was good. They'd never been able to catch him, so he could play it out the same way again and let someone else take the fall. It was easy to arrange. So easy.

He had to stay calm, confident. He couldn't let the little things tear down the brick bastions of his own talent. He was good, and this was all a challenge.

He started; his name was being called.

With a smile, he answered.


"You look great tonight."

Dan McDuff turned. Marcie McDonnagh was standing there, just outside the women's locker room.

"You look pretty damned good yourself," he told her.

"Aw, shucks," she said, and smiled. Her hair was hidden beneath the black-and-gray wig she wore, but the exaggerated female vampire makeup just made her look wickedly, sensually attractive, he thought.

She ran up and hugged him suddenly, then pulled away self-consciously. "We made it, Dan! We both made it. Our pay goes up. Our prestige goes up. Hera and Zeus, here we come."

He had to smile in return. "I wanted it so badly, I'm still not sure I believe it's real," he told her.

"Me, too." She let out a happy sigh.

"We should celebrate," he said.

She nodded.

"My cousin and some friends are coming tonight. Maybe we can all go out after the show and celebrate."

"I'd love to celebrate, but I've got an early class tomorrow. I'm going to have to ask you for a rain check."

Was that the brush-off? he wondered. He wasn't sure, and he didn't really care. It wasn't as if he'd been trying to pick her up. He had just wanted to celebrate their victory.

"Sure," he said.

Suddenly they both started. Above them, from the main park, a scream had echoed so loudly that it had penetrated to the catacomb of hallways and workrooms below.

Dan laughed. "They're doing a good job

up there," he said.

Marcie shuddered. "Yeah? Strange, isn't it? People, tourists, are paying to be scared, but all we have to do is live in the area, walk into a dark parking lot alone, to be afraid."

"I'm here if you need me," he told her gravely.

He could have killed her. Grabbed her right then and there, and shaken her.

She'd scared the hell out of him.

There was an unknown SUV in her front yard, a late-model Volvo, nice. Just the type of car for a boy-next-door serial killer to drive, he had tormented himself, his heart in his throat, when he reached her house. He'd heard the dog barking, but she'd never come back to the phone, and now there was a strange car in her driveway.

But Christina was evidently just fine. She opened the door and stared at him, her eyes wide with dismay as the realization of what she had done dawned on her. "Oh, my God, Jed!"

"Yeah, Jed," he said dryly.

She winced. "I'm sorry." She swallowed hard, and Killer barked. Jed absently patted the dog to quiet him. "Come in, please. My old friend Genevieve arrived with Thor, her husband, and I forgot all about the phone.

Did you ever meet Gen? She came up here with me a few times when we were kids. She grew up in Key West, but we've been friends for years. I thought she was so lucky, growing up, actually living in Key West." She was babbling, and she knew it. She forced herself to stop, then stared at him, looking stricken. "Jed, I am honestly so sorry."

"It's okay. There's only a serial killer running around with a penchant for gorgeous redheads, and then you — a redhead, I might mention — drop the phone and don't come back to it. No problem."

She flushed. "Jed . . ."

He sighed in a combination of resignation and relief. "It's all right."

"Come on in. I have people for you to meet."

He decided that he hadn't met Genevieve before, because he would certainly have remembered someone so beautiful. She was tall, tanned and attractive, and she and Christie must have made a pretty sight, walking along the water's edge together. To his surprise, he did know the very tall, very blond man who was Genevieve's husband. "Thor Thompson!" he said.

"Jed Braden," Thor returned, grinning.

The others stared at them blankly. "I was

297

in underwater retrieval and recovery for a while," Jed explained.

"He was a cop," Thor said to his wife.

"Jed Braden — the author," the older man said, offering his hand. "Adam Harrison."

"Uncle Adam," Christie supplied.

"Uncle Adam?" Jed said dubiously, staring at her. He knew Christina's family and knew she had no one left but her cousins. He would have known if there was an Uncle Adam.

"My uncle Adam," Genevieve supplied quickly.

It was a lie. Jed knew it instinctively. But why were they lying?

"You're right. I am the author, Mr. Harrison," he said.

"Adam. Just Adam will be fine. And congratulations. You've created a couple of real page-turners, including one on the Interstate Killer, if I remember correctly."

"Yeah. Fictionalized, but . . . yeah," Jed said flatly.

"Um . . . well," Christina said, glancing at her watch. "It's a bit early, but how about lunch? Do you guys want to stay here? There's plenty of room. Why don't you all bring your things in, and then we can go out and grab a bite? Later tonight a bunch of us are going to go over to the new theme park and see my cousin Dan. He's the Grim Reader in their Halloween extravaganza."

She looked anxious, Jed thought. As if she didn't quite know what was going on herself.

"Lunch sounds wonderful," Genevieve admitted.

"We don't want to impose, though," Adam said.

"You wouldn't be imposing," Christina told him.

"I'll give you a hand. Let me help you get your things," Jed offered.

They all went outside, Killer jumping up and down happily as he followed. As he was reaching into the back of the SUV, Jed saw Ilona, in her minivan, pull into the drive next door. She waved as she got out of her car.

"Are we still on for tonight?" she called.

"Yes, come meet my friends," Christina called back.

Ilona walked over and shook hands as she met Genevieve, Thor and Adam.

"We're going to head out for lunch," Genevieve said.

"Tony's down overseeing a new menu at the Mainstay." She flashed them a smile. "You know where it is, Christina — right down the street from that place where your family hangs out all the time. O'Reilly's. Why don't you go there? Tony would be thrilled. He's added a new line of low-carb, low-fat entrées, really good stuff."

"Sounds good to me," she said, and looked at the others for confirmation.

"Why not?" Adam said.

Jed hadn't exactly been invited to lunch, but he didn't care. It suddenly seemed important that he go along.

Christina felt nervous all through lunch.

It wasn't difficult to explain Gen and Thor to Jed. Gen was a very old friend, and Thor was like a Christmas present, since he and Jed knew each other. But Jed was suspicious of Adam, and she knew it. She could see in the way his dark eyes measured the older man that he had strong doubts about the uncle story.

Tony greeted them at the restaurant door, and they were given a great, circular table that made conversation easy. Christina was glad they had listened to Ilona, except that Tony insisted lunch was on the house.

"As long as I get a real evaluation when you're done," he told them.

"Of course we'll be totally honest," Christina promised. "But you really don't have to buy us lunch."

"It's my pleasure. Hey, how many times have I mooched off your family over the years?" Christina could tell that his feelings would have been hurt if they refused, so she gave in with good grace and they ordered.

"I gather you're not from Florida," Jed said to Adam. He was leaning back comfortably, casually, in his chair, but Christina could tell that there was nothing casual about him at all as he studied the older man, waiting for his response.

"Nope. I'm a Virginian, by birth, choice and the grace of God," Adam said, grinning. He lifted his beer to Jed. "But I do admire your great state, as well. There's a lot of history here — and some great ghost stories."

"It's true," Jed said. "We're not far from Ocklawaha, where Ma Barker and her son Fred had their massive shoot-out with the feds back in 1935. The place was shot to pieces, more rounds fired than you could ever imagine, but one chandelier went untouched. The place is supposed to be haunted to this day."

"My favorite Florida ghost is up in Tallahassee," Genevieve said. "In Tallahassee Old City Cemetery."

Christina chimed in then. "I know that place. It's a beautiful old cemetery, very haunting, with lots of old trees dripping with Spanish moss."

"And Elizabeth Budd Graham, right?" Jed asked politely.

Tony had come up while they were talking and overheard the last bit of their conversation. "Who's Elizabeth Budd Graham?" he asked curiously.

"A well-known ghost," Jed answered, looking intently at Christina.

"She was born sometime around 1886," Gen said. "She was supposed to be a witch, though not a mean one. In fact, she married, had a child and was apparently well loved, but she died young. Her grave faces west, and there's a beautiful epitaph on her stone. 'Doubly dead that she died so young.' Very sad. You've never heard about her or been to the cemetery, Tony?"

"Can't say I have. What does she do?" Tony asked.

"Nothing bad. People bring flowers to the grave. Supposedly, when you're there, you can feel a sense of peace and solve problems in your own heart."

"Florida is just full of ghosts, huh?" Jed said politely.

"Full of tourists, thank God," Tony breathed, then frowned and looked at Christina. "Christie, with everything going on . . . you know that Ilona and I are right next door if you need us, right?"

"I do. And thank you."

He nodded. "I'd better leave the ghosts to you guys and get back to the kitchen. Enjoy."

When they finished lunch, they drove back to Christina's house. Before they even went inside, Jed started to excuse himself, but Christina slipped around in front of him, trying to manage a little privacy.

"You're still coming tonight, right?" she asked him, annoyed that she sounded so anxious.

He nodded. "I'll be back in time. It's the late show, right?"

"Right. So . . . where are you going?" she asked him, then backpedaled. "Sorry. It's not really my . . . business."

She was surprised when he openly smiled at her. "I'm going out to see Larry Atkins again. Beau Kidd's partner. His place is huge."

She was startled. "You think Beau Kidd's old partner . . . you think he might be the killer?"

He shrugged. "Why would he have shot his own partner? He said Beau drew a bead on him, and that was why he shot, but it seems strange to me that Beau didn't just drop his own weapon when Atkins drew on him. Hell, why did Beau pull a weapon in the first place?"

"Beau drew his gun because he'd discovered the body when it was still warm, and he heard a noise and thought the killer was creeping around behind him," she said, then saw that he was staring at her and realized what she'd said, what she'd revealed. She inhaled quickly. "I mean, that's certainly one way it might have gone, right?"

"It's a possibility," he said, still looking at her skeptically.

"I take it you've developed an interest in the new killing spree," Thor said, his tone casual as he walked over to join them.

"Yeah, well, I kind of had to," Jed admitted.

"Do you have plans for the rest of the day?" Thor asked him.

Christina watched the way Jed studied Thor, then shrugged and looked down for a moment before meeting his old friend's eyes again and replying, "I'm off to see someone."

"Can you go where you need to without a badge?" Thor asked him.

"Right now, I'm glad I don't have a badge."

"Want some company?" Thor asked.

Jed weighed the question. "Sure," he said after a moment.

"What are you thinking?" Genevieve asked Christine a few minutes later, as they stood on the lawn and watched the two men drive away in Jed's car.

"I'm thinking he's never going to believe me when I try to tell him that the ghost of Beau Kidd has taken up residence in my house," Christina said. She looked anxiously at Genevieve and Adam. "He is in there, I swear it."

Killer started going crazy behind the front door, so she let him out. He ran to the front of the lawn, where he sniffed the air, then started running in circles.

"What on earth is the matter with him?" Christina wondered aloud.

"He's guarding you against a swarm of mosquitoes, obviously," Adam said with a smile.

She smiled, the tension broken.

"Well, we might as well unpack," Adam said. "We're going to a park tonight?"

"Yes. All the parks make a big spooky deal out of October," Christina said.

"October," Adam repeated. "A big spooky deal in a great many places. And," he added softly, "it ends with All Saints' Day."

A while later, their unpacking done, Christina entertained them with a few of her jingle ideas on the piano, then came to an abrupt halt.

"I was supposed to go into the studio to record that last piece on Monday." She inhaled deeply. "My singer was the third victim."

Adam, who had been sitting back with his eyes closed, appeared to have drifted off, but appearances were obviously deceiving, because he spoke up immediately. "Maybe there's more to Beau Kidd showing up here than you know," he suggested.

"What do you mean?" Christina asked.

"Maybe he's here to protect you," he said softly.

Chills shot down her spine.

"We will have a séance," he told her.

"Now?" she asked doubtfully.

He shook his head. "No. We need everyone here who was here the night you used the Ouija board. Saturday night?" he suggested.

She nodded, suddenly terrified.

There was no reason for her to be frightened, she told herself. She wasn't alone in the house any longer. Adam, Genevieve and Thor were all installed on the second floor, and that was reassuring, right?

And Jed? she asked herself.

She wasn't afraid at all when she was with Jed.

She stared at Genevieve. Her friend seemed so relaxed, so confident, despite the fact that they were talking about ghosts. And despite the fact that a serial killer was roaming the state.

Christina realized that Adam was watching her.

"It is a gift, talking to the dead," he said softly. "If you can just learn to accept it."

A gift? she thought. Maybe so.

A very dangerous gift.

# 13

"I told you, Jed. You need a horse. You need to quit going over old history, quit trying to make a monster out of a good man, and buy a horse."

Larry Atkins had been sitting in the rocker on his front porch, as if waiting for Jed. He barely seemed to notice Thor getting out of the car with him, not that it was easy to ignore Thor.

"Hello, Larry," Jed called.

Larry Atkins stood up. "I know what you're thinking, Jed. You're a little ahead of the guys wearing the badges, but go ahead. Search the place. Sure, now I'm a suspect. Hell, I shot my partner."

"Nice place you have here," Thor commented.

"Right. Nice place. Off the beaten track. Means I must have been a sick killer, right? I even shot my partner so he'd take the blame. I might be at it again. Hell, I have room, I have privacy. I must be bringing women here, tormenting them, their screams going unheard. . . . Search the place if you want, Jed."

"I don't have a warrant, Larry," Jed said.

"I know you don't. Damn it, Jed, I'm not guilty of anything. Come with me, and I'll show you."

"Larry, no one is accusing you of anything," Jed said.

"You're here, aren't you? With that Scandinavian bruiser over there."

Jed glanced quickly at Thor, who grinned with amusement, unoffended.

"Come in," Larry insisted.

There was little help for it, and hell, they had driven all the way out there. Larry led the way, and he did a thorough job of it. They went through all the rooms, then down to the small basement, which was really more of a glorified crawl space, and then out to the stables. He took them through the tack room and every single stall.

"Are you happy?" Larry demanded when they were finished

"I have a question for you," Jed countered.

"Yeah?" Larry said.

"Today, looking back, do you think Beau meant to draw on you? Do you think there's any possibility he thought you might have been someone else?"

Larry stared at him blankly; then he swallowed hard. "He drew on me," he said at last.

"But it was dark, right?"

"The killing stopped," Larry said.

"Right. But you're not answering my question."

"I had to draw my gun. I was cleared," Larry told him.

"Right. Thanks, Larry."

They left, and Jed found himself staring at Thor when they got back in the car. "Well?"

"I think it was dark, and Beau Kidd did draw his weapon. I suspect that Larry Atkins didn't identify himself. But other than that . . ."

"What?"

Thor shook his head. "I don't know. Underwater mysteries are more my thing. But I don't think this guy is guilty of killing those women."

"No, he's not the killer," Jed agreed. "The thing is . . ."

"What?" Thor asked him.

Jed shook his head. "There's something I should be seeing. Something I need to see. The connection . . ."

"The connection to what?"

"I don't know. And that's it. I can't even

figure out why I'm so certain that there is a connection, but I know it's there." He hesitated for a moment, then stared at Thor as he finally turned the key in the ignition. "So just what the hell are you really doing here? What's your connection to all this?"

There was mist everywhere, so much artificial mist that it was almost impossible to see.

But then, this was October in a theme park, Christina thought, and the customers were paying extra for the privilege of being scared right down to their Nikes.

"Christie?" Ana called softly.

"Right here."

Ana giggled. "I think they got a bit carried away with the fog. Did you see the monster in the lagoon? Incredible."

"Did you do any of the makeup?" Christina asked her.

"I gave a workshop for most of the vampires. There — if you can see it." She pointed. "That one is my design."

"Good look," Christina complimented her.

"Thank you. And the zombies over there . . . my design, as well," Ana said proudly.

"Nice and gruesome," Christina told her.

And it was true. They were walking down what was referred to as the Hallway of Horror, heading toward the giant chair where the Grim Reader was about to tell a heart-stopping tale. The mist was not just ample, it swirled around them. The makeup on the "creatures" who strolled alongside them was excellent, and the effects along the way were done extremely well. It should have been delightfully spooky.

Except that Christina felt as if nothing could spook her anymore.

She had a ghost living in her house.

"Where are the others?" Christina asked, finding Ana in the mist.

"Behind us, I think." Ana laughed softly. "I think Thor is scaring all the creatures away."

"He's not spooky. He's just very good-looking."

"He's just so tall, looming out of the mist and all." Ana linked her arm through Christina's and shivered, lowering her voice. "It seems so strange, doesn't it? One of the victims worked here. And everyone is still . . . still trying to creep out the audience."

"I'm sure that this place is chock full of security," Christina said.

"I guess."

Suddenly they heard a scream, and Christina felt genuine panic rush through her for the first time all night.

But then the scream was followed by laughter, and Ilona and Tony broke through the mist to join them.

"Ilona was shrieking like a girl," Tony announced.

"I am a girl," Ilona reminded him. "And when that huge tree thing just appeared out of the mist, it scared me."

A moment later, the others caught up with them, as well. Mike was deep in some kind of philosophical debate with Adam, and Genevieve was walking between her husband and Jed.

"There's way too much mist," Jed said.

"Well, it's a new park. They're probably trying to get a handle on it," Tony said with a shrug.

"Dan should be just ahead, up in a big chair where those freaky lights are," Mike told them.

"Almost there," Ana said cheerfully. "Oh, look at the ghouls over there. Those are mine. I'm especially proud of them."

The mist swirled around Christina again as she stopped to stare at Ana's ghouls. Then, when she turned back around . . . mist. Nothing but mist.

"Hey," she called uncertainly.

No one answered.

She felt . . . something. Someone touching her. Fingers stroking her hair . . .

"Hey!" she protested, then spun around. No one was anywhere near her, and she felt panicked again.

Don't be ridiculous, she told herself. She was in a theme park. She might not be able to see them, but there were lots of people — undoubtedly including plenty of security personnel — around.

She turned, forcing herself not to panic, to look up toward the lights. Dan would be in that direction. She started to move, but her foot lodged against something hard. She cried out as she lost her balance and went crashing down to the ground. Into the swirling mist.

She lashed out and struck someone, then heard what sounded like someone sucking in their breath. She reached out, fumbling around, trying to find something to grab for balance so she could rise, and touched . . .

A body.

The mist began to clear, and she blinked, peering more closely at the woman on the ground next to her. The woman's eyes were closed, her face deathly white. Christina swallowed the scream that rose in her throat

314

when she realized it was white makeup, and that the other woman had on a long wig, black and gray and white. She was one of the vampires, Christina realized quickly.

"Are you all right?" she asked anxiously, when she noticed that the woman wasn't moving. "Hey," Christina said, reaching for her.

She was cold.

And there was a thin line of blood seeping from her lips. . . .

"And there, my children, you have it. Another tale from the ghastly, ghoulish pen of our renowned literary giant, Edgar Allan Poe. Come back tomorrow for a story straight from the pages of another American literary great — along with a few suggestions of the Grim Reader's favorite places, where the mist and the graves and the hauntings are real."

God, he loved applause, Dan thought as he listened to it. He relished the sound; he lived to perform.

As he stepped down from his chair, his smile brightened, though he wasn't at all sure anyone would realize that it was a smile. Not with his makeup, which was one of Ana's designs.

And there she was, he realized. Tiny, adorable, standing at the front of the audience. While the others began to break away, she just stood there, rapt.

"Hiya, kid," he said, striding toward her. He was on such a high from performing that he grabbed her, dipped her and planted a kiss on her lips.

A park-goer passing by looked at him, startled.

"That was great," Ana cried, struggling up.

"I agree," Michael said, coming up and patting him on the back. "Congratulations, that was terrific. And I hear you got your part. Congratulations."

"Thanks," Dan said, grinning.

Mike rolled his eyes. "All we need is you walking around thinking you're a god. Hey, do you remember Christie's friend Genevieve?"

"Sure do," Dan said, reaching out to give Genevieve a quick hug.

"This is my husband, Thor," Genevieve said.

Dan looked up. He was tall himself. This guy was taller.

"And this is Adam Harrison," Michael finished.

"And you know us," Ilona said, waving to him.

"Terrific show," Tony told him.

Dan frowned. "Where's Christie?"

They all stared at him, then looked around.

"Shit," Michael said.

"Where the hell is she?" Jed, who'd been silent until then, demanded. Then he turned and disappeared into the mist. As he did, a bloodcurdling scream tore through the night.

"What the hell?" Ana gasped.

A teenage girl burst through the fog, screaming, then giggled.

Mike looked at her in disgust, then turned to the others and asked, "Where the hell is Christie?"

"Help! Help me!" Christina shouted.

She had found the other woman's wrist and checked her pulse. She was alive but unconscious, and she wasn't responding to Christina's anxious attempts to revive her.

Around her, Christina heard screams and laughter. "I need help here!" she shouted, trying to make herself heard above the general revelry.

A moment later, she heard footsteps and someone calling her name.

Jed.

"I'm over here, Jed. Help me!"

A dark shadow moved through the silver mist, and seconds later, she saw his face. "She's hurt!" Christina cried out.

"What?" he asked, looking puzzled.

"One of the vampires. Help me. She's hurt."

He got down on his knees beside her, his police training evident as he moved efficiently to determine the woman's condition.

She heard her name called again. Ana's voice, followed by Tony's, then Mike's and Genevieve's . . .

"Over here!" Jed yelled. "Call an ambulance and park security!"

A floodlight suddenly cut through the mist. A park employee who introduced himself as Dr. Saryn knelt down to help, and while the others crowded around, Christina saw two nurses hurrying over with a rolling stretcher.

Suddenly she had a terrifying thought. Half the people here tonight were in costume. What if they weren't real medical personnel? What if they were going to take the woman away and . . . She told herself not to be ridiculous and returned her attention to what was going on.

"Oh, my God!" Dan said, his eyes on the girl being lifted onto the stretcher. "What the hell happened?" he asked anxiously.

"Who knows, in this fog," one of the nurses said irritably.

"I know her," Dan said, upset. "Her name's Marcie . . . Marcie McDonnagh. She's my friend, she's my . . . Hera."

"As of now, she's my patient," Dr. Saryn said. "I've sent for an ambulance. Her pulse is strong, and she doesn't seem to have any broken bones. It looks as if she tripped. There's a good-size hematoma on the back of her head." Saryn turned to Christina. "You found her?" he asked.

"Yes."

"Well, she owes you her thanks. She could have gone unnoticed for a long time in all this." He waved to indicate the mist, which seemed even more surreal as it swirled in the beam of the floodlight.

Arms slipped around Christina from behind. Jed's. She was amazed to realize that she wasn't feeling afraid anymore; instead, she was angry. But she didn't mind the support.

"Someone needs to report this," she said firmly. "She didn't trip, she was pushed. Someone attacked her."

Everyone stared at her blankly.

"Look," Saryn said, "I have to get this woman to a hospital. If you want to report a crime, call the police."

He left, the nurses following with Marcie on the stretcher. Dan cast Christina a worried glance, then ran after them.

"Quite a night," Adam Harrison murmured.

"What did you mean?" Jed asked Christina, eyes narrowed. "What did you mean when you said someone attacked her?"

"I . . . I don't know," she admitted. "It just seemed like someone in the crowd was getting rowdy or something. I felt as if . . . as if I was being pushed."

"Teenagers!" Ilona exploded.

And why not? Christina asked herself. Even if someone had pushed her, why was she so sure there had been any malice behind it? Ilona was right; it had probably just been some rowdy teenager. "Let's go get some dinner," she said. "Seeing as the Grim Reader is done for the night."

Jed hadn't intended to stay at Christina's house, but wasn't at all sure about "Uncle" Adam. Not that Christina would be alone with him. Genevieve and Thor would also be there — and Killer, of course.

But there was just something bugging him. About the house? Or about Christina?

She had almost certainly been right about

320

whatever had occurred between Beau Kidd and Larry Atkins on that day twelve years ago when Larry had killed his partner. Larry didn't act like a man who was coming unglued because he had committed murder. He did act like a man with a serious guilt complex, a man who was afraid that he had killed his partner over a mistake. There was really only one explanation for why Beau Kidd had pulled his weapon: because he hadn't seen his partner and was afraid of who was out there in the dark.

But how the hell had Christina figured that out?

Ilona and Tony had opted to stay at the park when the rest of them went to dinner. While they were eating, Christina's cell phone rang. It was Dan, reporting that Marcie was going to be all right, though she didn't know what had happened. She only remembered waking up in the hospital. Despite the good news, Christina looked distraught when she hung up.

"What is it?" Mike asked her.

She shrugged. "He's worried — any more problems and the park might wind up closing."

"More problems?" Adam asked. "What else happened?"

"One of the women who was killed, the

second victim, worked at the park," Christina explained. "And I hate to say it, but that mist tonight was a pretty major mistake on someone's part, a lawsuit waiting to happen."

"They have insurance up the wazoo, I'm sure," Mike said.

Dinner broke up and people started heading their separate ways at that point. Back at Christina's, Jed found himself striding in without waiting for an invitation. If his presence seemed unusual to anyone, it wasn't mentioned.

Christina immediately went into the kitchen to make tea, despite the fact that they had just eaten, and Jed realized that was simply the way things had always been done in that house when Christina's grandmother had been alive. You came over and you had tea. It was a nice tradition, he realized.

As they drank tea and munched shortbread, the conversation turned to diving for treasure, which was the way Gen and Thor made their living. Jed talked about some nearby underwater caverns Thor had never been to, and they decided to take a group dive trip.

"Better do it before it gets much later in

the year," Christina said. "That water gets chilly."

"How far are they from here?" Thor asked.

"I'd say an hour and a half," Jed said, and as he spoke, he realized he was seeing a map of the state in his mind's eye.

A map with all the highways.

And an *X* where each body had been found.

Twelve years ago, the first and last had been found alongside I-4, off International Drive, right where the tourists went. Another was found off the turnpike, two more off the Beeline Expressway.

This time . . .

The first body had been found just off I-4, off International Drive, the next two by the turnpike.

The killer was even choosing the same highways as the dumpsites for the bodies.

He surfaced from his thoughts when Christina said, "I'm going to have a get-together on Saturday night."

"A big party?" Jed asked

"No, just Tony and Ilona, Mike and Dan, you and Ana, Adam, Thor and Genevieve. And myself, of course."

She was testing the idea out on him, he realized. Why? "That sounds nice," he said. "Will Dan be off?"

"Yes, he can put in for the early shift. He's not the only Grim Reader, of course, plus he's got his role as Zeus now, and they'll be starting rehearsals soon. In another couple of weekends, the whole Halloween thing will be over, anyway."

It seemed like a long explanation, he thought. Was she nervous? "Any special reason for this get-together?" he asked her.

"Sure . . . to get together," she said.

Genevieve yawned then, and everyone started excusing themselves to go up to bed. Jed had just reached the upstairs landing with Christina when his cell phone rang.

It was Jerry Dwyer.

He dreaded learning that another body had been found, but Jerry hadn't called to report another murder.

"There's going to be a wake tomorrow night for Allison Chesney. Seven to nine. You coming?"

"Thanks. I'll definitely be there."

"Yeah. You never know who might show."

He hung up. Christina was staring at him. "Allison Chesney's wake is tomorrow," he told her.

"I know," she said.

"I was thinking it would be a good idea to go."

"You were? Me, too."

"I was thinking I should go."

"Jed, I actually knew her."

He hesitated. "Sometimes a killer will go to a funeral or a wake. Depending on what makes a monster tick, sometimes he takes pleasure from seeing his victim's loved ones mourning her. I don't think you should go."

"But I do."

"Christina . . . I don't want the killer to get a good look at another gorgeous redhead," he said.

Once again, she stared at him before turning away. "These killings have to stop!" she said passionately.

He walked over to her, taking her hands. "Christina, I know that. Is there something I don't know? Something I should know?"

She seemed to be looking past him. And she looked irritated. "No," she finally said.

"Then . . . ?"

She shook her head.

"Do you mind that I'm here?"

"No. But I'm exhausted."

"I see." Was that like, Not tonight, dear. I have a headache? They hadn't really been together long enough for that, he thought. But the only thing he said was "All right."

He walked across the room, stripped off his shirt and jeans, and slid beneath the sheets. When he turned back to look at her, she was staring across the room, toward the door.

"Go away," she whispered.

He started to rise. "What?"

She spun around. "What?" she echoed.

"Do you want me to leave?"

"No!"

"Didn't you just say, 'go away'?"

"No, not to you. Really."

She stripped with an admirable and arousing speed, sliding next to him beneath the sheets, far too naked to be ignored, so he pushed aside the question of who she had been talking to and simply took her into his arms.

She pressed closer and closer to him, as if she were trying to become one with him.

Her flesh rubbed against his, her nipples hard against his chest. She slid her arms around his waist, and her hands moved, fingers teasing, so light at first. When he didn't allow himself to react, her touch became more insistent, more erotic. There was no way in hell that what she intended could be misinterpreted — or resisted.

He drew her more tightly into his arms, his mouth fusing to hers. Her body seemed to melt against him, insinuate itself with explicit intimacy against his hollows. He broke the kiss and stared at her. Her eyes were brilliant, and he could hear the rampant thunder of her heart.

Her lips were wet, parted . . .

She rose against him, meeting his eyes again. "Just hold me," she said. "I'm not feeling tired after all."

Evidently not, he thought, wondering what had changed.

Her lips skittered across his flesh like liquid fire. Her mouth closed around him.

He made love to her until they were both panting and exhausted, and then he held her through the night.

Still, he was puzzled. She kept staring at the door, as if she were afraid that someone was going to enter. Someone she didn't want to see.

She was dreaming. She knew it, but she couldn't stop it.

She was in a room, but there was a blindfold over her eyes, so she couldn't see,

And everything ached. Everything. No matter how hard she tried, she couldn't move, because there were ropes binding her wrists and ankles to a chair. She couldn't even scream, because she was gagged.

Suddenly she heard footsteps. Leisurely footsteps, coming closer . . .

Her terror was overwhelming, because she

knew what was going to happen. Knew . . .

She wanted to escape. She had to escape. Christina.

Beau Kidd was calling to her. She recognized his voice.

Help me. Get me out of here, she pleaded. My hand, take my hand . . .

"Christina?"

She woke up to find Jed at her side, staring at her with concern in his eyes.

Her night-light was on, as always, and she could see his face. Feel the vitality and heat of his body, the power of his slightest movement. The life in him.

"Hey," he said, and softly touched her face. "Nightmare?"

It was fading already. She could barely remember anything at all.

Not that there was anything to remember, anyway. She hadn't seen anything, hadn't seen anyone. All she had was an impression, a trick of the mind.

She moved closer to him, secure in the clasp of his strong arms. "I guess," she murmured.

"We all have them sometimes," he told her.

"You have nightmares?"

He hesitated, then said, "Sometimes we live our nightmares."

She exhaled, watching the shadows play across his face. "And sometimes we have to let them go," she told him softly.

He smiled slowly, smoothed back her hair. "You all right?"

She nodded. And she was all right, of course. It had just been a nightmare. It meant nothing.

So why did she suddenly feel such a sense of fear? Of danger awaiting her somewhere in the darkness?

# 14

Christina awoke and found herself relieved that Jed had gotten up early and, according to the note he'd left her, gone downtown to meet Jerry. She quickly showered and dressed, reflecting on how amazing it was to find herself feeling that way, given that she had been at least a little in love with Jed Braden most of her life. And she was grateful that he'd been there, but there were some dangers even he couldn't help her fight.

Like those in her mind.

Or the fact that she was seeing a ghost.

And now . . . what? Was she feeling what the victims had felt?

Downstairs, Adam Harrison had already made coffee. He was sitting in the wing chair in the parlor, her box of newspaper clippings at his side. "Morning," he said.

She looked around. The parlor was quiet. "Have you seen . . . Beau?" she asked.

He shook his head. "Sorry. Genevieve may see him, but sometimes . . . well, it's really up to him. That's why we need to have a séance," he told her. "Sometimes ghosts only appear to specific people, and for specific reasons. Other ghosts will appear to several people, or just to anyone." He offered her a rueful grin. "It's not an exact science. Beau may be feeling uncomfortable now, with the house suddenly so full," he told her.

He hadn't had any difficulty showing up last night to remind her that he needed her help, she thought. He'd sat in the chair in her room, insisting that she tell Jed all the information that he gave her. But when she had given him an imploring look and begged him softly . . . he'd left.

In the daylight, her anger was asserting itself. He showed up to haunt her, to confuse her and make her talk to the air, so Jed would think she was genuinely crazy. To give her horrible nightmares . . . and then leave without telling her anything useful.

Thor and Genevieve came in then. "Good morning," Thor said.

"Beautiful day, isn't it?" Genevieve said cheerfully.

"Coffee on?" Thor asked.

It might have been an ordinary visit.

Except that when Thor left to get coffee for himself and his wife, Genevieve walked into the center of the parlor and stood very still.

"Anything?" Christina heard herself ask hopefully.

Genevieve let out a sigh. "Yes . . . and no. I can feel something, but . . ." She smiled. "Let's take a trip to the cemetery, shall we?"

"Sure."

"What's wrong?" Genevieve asked her.

Christina shook her head, then tried to explain. "I had a nightmare last night. I was tied up, gagged and blindfolded."

"Does the killer bind, gag and blindfold his victims?" Genevieve asked.

"I . . . don't know."

"Okay, what then?" Genevieve prodded.

"Then I woke up."

Genevieve watched her thoughtfully. Adam Harrison stepped closer and looked into her eyes. "It's possible that . . ."

"That . . . ?" Christina asked, not entirely sure she wanted to hear the answer.

"We know Beau Kidd has made a connection with you," Adam said, "so maybe, because of Beau, one of the victims is managing to speak to you, as well."

"Oh, God. So I was feeling what she felt. Before . . ." Christina stared at him, fighting a wave of debilitating fear.

"It's all right. You woke up. But no one ever really knows how far the mind can go. A dream like that is all right, Christina," Adam said reassuringly. "A dream could end up providing the clue that cracks the case. The dead do tell tales."

Jed waited in Jerry's office until his friend came back and tossed a file on the desk. "It's all copies — you can have everything there," he said.

Jed arched a brow to him. "What did you find?"

Jerry had taken the chair behind his desk. "Amazingly little. I suspect their private work stays private, but there are a few articles in there about several cities, even a few states, hiring Harrison Investigations in . . . abnormal circumstances."

"Like UFOs?" Jed asked.

"No, more like things that go bump in the night." Jerry leaned forward, opening the folder. "Here's one . . . a Florida story, even, about Old Dixie Highway, outside St. Augustine. There was a rash of abductions of teenagers. The locals were claiming there were lights in the trees by the highway, that the kids were being abducted by the ghosts of three women who'd been hanged there by a lynch mob soon after Florida became a state. The city brought in the state, and the state brought in Harrison Investigations."

Jed looked skeptically at Jerry. "Let me guess. Harrison Investigations performed some sort of a voodoo rite and the abductions stopped?"

Jerry leaned back, shaking his head. "Harrison Investigations found the kids being held in a shack in the woods. One kid's dad was head of an oil corporation. The kidnapper, an ex-employee with a grudge, intended to ask for ransom eventually, but first he wanted his old boss to suffer."

"The police couldn't find this shack, but Harrison Investigations did? Was there ever an explanation?"

"Adam Harrison found the shack himself," Jerry said. "He claimed he heard noises when he was walking through the woods."

Jed shook his head, clearly still doubtful.

"Our own fed, Gil, told me that Adam Harrison is totally legit. He hasn't worked with him personally, but he knows people who have, and they swear by the guy."

Jed stared at Jerry, feeling irritated. He didn't know why, but he'd wanted to find a reason to mistrust the man, especially once he'd discovered the Harrison Investigations angle. The guy had to be some kind of charlatan. Didn't he?

"What I want to know," Jerry told him, "is why this man just appeared on your girl-friend's doorstep."

Jed shook his head, not bothering to dispute Jerry's use of "girlfriend." In fact, he realized to his own amazement, he kind of liked it. "Nothing to do with the case," he said. Which he knew was a lie, but since no one was letting him in on the truth . . .

"He just arrived?"

"Yesterday. He came with a couple of her friends. Christie's known the wife, Gene-vieve, forever," Jed explained. "She's mar-ried to some guy named Thor."

"Genevieve Wallace and Thor Thomp-son?" Jerry asked.

Jed frowned, staring at him. "Yeah. How did you know?"

Jerry offered him a wry grimace. "Thor's not exactly a common name. And there's a story there. They were involved in a dive down in the Keys and somehow unearthed a centuries-old mystery — and a killer. I read about it. It was in all the papers. How the hell did you miss it?"

Jed stood without answering, picking up the file Jerry had put together for him. "Thanks."

"Hey," Jerry called as he started out of

the office. "I'd love to meet Adam Harrison."

"I'll see if he can do lunch next week."

"Cool. Let me know."

Jed gritted his teeth. Jerry was serious.

But as he walked out onto the sidewalk, Jed realized that he was glad of one thing. Adam Harrison might be nuts for believing in the supernatural, but at least he was a legitimate nut.

And he did feel better knowing there were more people in the house with Christina, because there was no escaping one crucial fact: she was a beautiful redhead.

He was still searching for a deeper connection between the victims. Or was it entirely random and based on looks? But where was the killer first seeing his prey? How did he know who to snatch, and how to snatch her so she disappeared into thin air? Why did no one ever scream when she was being taken? What trick was the killer using?

They bought bouquets. Lots of them.

"I still don't understand what we're doing," Christina told Genevieve as they walked along a path through the cemetery. "I don't believe — I can't believe — that the souls of the people I loved are still here beneath the ground or in a coffin, or . . . or that they stay behind at all."

Genevieve was quiet for a minute. "Sometimes souls do remain behind."

"So how come I can't say hi to my mom, and tell her that I love her and miss her? Why do I have to see a man I never knew when he was alive?"

"No one really knows, but I'm guessing your mom knows you loved her very much. Same with your dad," Genevieve said. "They were good people, and they lived good lives. Whatever heaven really is, I'm sure that's where they are. But some people . . . some people stay behind, and other people can see them. Think of a dog whistle. The dog hears it just fine. We don't."

"Speaking of which . . ." Christina dropped down to pick up Killer. No need taking a chance on him running off and getting into trouble.

"Your parents and grandparents first?" Genevieve suggested.

Christina saw that Adam and Thor had gone ahead and were already waiting at her family grave site. She and Genevieve joined them, and she arranged some of the flowers, then stepped back and pointed to a nearby grave. She closed her eyes, feeling the breeze waft across her skin and through her hair, and pictured the scene as it had been twelve years ago.

The priest, reading the service.

Beau Kidd's mother, crying her eyes out.

When she opened her eyes, the others had moved closer. "Genevieve?" Adam said softly. She nodded, then walked over to Beau Kidd's grave, knelt down, placed a bouquet of flowers and laid a hand against his stone.

The world had to know her brother was innocent, Katherine Kidd thought, walking along the sidewalk that surrounded the cemetery and feeling an overwhelming sense of sadness. Beau's name had to be cleared. She felt a moment's anger as she wondered if the powers-that-be would eventually wind up shooting some other innocent man and claiming the killer had only been a copycat after all.

That couldn't happen.

The truth had to come out.

Beau's death and the widely accepted accusations had ruined their lives. Her mother was no more than a shell of her former self. They'd only been able to stay in the area because they'd had some genuinely good friends, people who knew that Beau couldn't have been guilty, no matter what everyone else said.

But she'd had some very bad times, growing up. Very bad. Teenagers were often cruel by nature, and so many of them had pointed at her, whispered about her. She had learned in high school to stay away from boys, to keep her distance from the popular crowd. If she kept a low profile, she wouldn't hear the whispers.

She hadn't gone far away for college, but somehow, in Gainesville — which she had chosen so she could be near her parents if her mother fell into one of her depressions — she had found that there were people willing to let the past stay buried.

Like her brother.

She'd majored in theater arts, with an emphasis on scenery design. She had a perfect job in her field now, and she was gaining a reputation. She was doing well.

Yeah, right. She was twenty-five, lived with her parents and didn't date.

She stopped walking for a moment, looking through the wrought-iron fence. The cemetery was really quite beautiful, she thought. So many of the old oaks flourished here, but then, it was a very old cemetery. She smiled, thinking of the transplants she worked with. So many New Yorkers, a lot of Midwesterners. They thought of Florida as new and raw. They didn't realize just how old some of the little towns and cities were. The path she was on led her under the trailing moss draping from the old oaks like dripping tears.

Most of the funerary art was old, a lot of it broken, some covered with lichen, giving the cemetery a forlorn and haunting feel. Even the sidewalk that rimmed it was broken in places, tree roots cracking the concrete and breaking through. Too often the city looked to the new when it came to repairing things, seldom to the old.

She was just about to head into the cemetery itself when she felt the wave of cold rush over her, followed by the sensation of being followed. She turned around to look, but the sun was in her eyes, blinding her.

Suddenly she heard a car engine rev, and a vehicle went rushing by her, sending adrenaline jetting through her.

Had someone been planning to run her down? Or was she getting paranoid now, afraid of threats that existed only in her own mind?

She turned around again and saw a woman approaching her, a tall redhead, with stunning blue eyes, carrying a Jack Russell terrier. She was followed by another woman, and two men, one older and the other blond and extremely tall.

Maybe these people had been following her. They could have tracked her from inside the cemetery. Or had she been stalked by whoever was driving that car, and then they had hurriedly driven past because . . .

Because these people would have been witnesses if something had happened to her.

"Hello," the redhead said. "Katherine? Katherine Kidd?"

"Yes. Who are you?" Katherine demanded.

"I'm Christina Hardy. I . . . well, I know this will sound very strange, but my grandfather was buried the same day as your brother. I . . . brought him some flowers."

"How did you know who I was?" Katherine asked.

"You look like your brother," Christina said.

"I look like my brother?"

"I've seen pictures," Christina said quickly. "And these are friends of mine," she said as the others caught up, then introduced them.

"How do you do?" Katherine said politely.

Should she be afraid? she wondered. There were four of them and only one of her.

But she no longer had that unnerving sense of being followed, the sense of danger that had tormented her before, and she realized that she had decided they meant her no harm, unlike the driver of the car, who . . . well, she wasn't going to think about that right now.

"My brother was innocent," she said without thinking. She should have recorded the words years ago, she thought. She could never stop herself from saying them.

"We know," Christina Hardy told her. "Are you here to visit his grave? We'll walk you back."

Kathleen realized she must have looked spooked, because Christina spoke up again right away.

"I'm a . . . friend of Jed Braden's, and I know you talked to him about looking into your brother's case."

"Yes," Kathleen answered. She indicated the flowers in her arms. "Yes, I spoke to him about my brother, and yes, I'm here to visit Beau's grave."

"We'll go with you," Christina said. "And then we'll see you back to your car."

Kathleen felt a sudden fierce chill and wondered why she hadn't felt it before. She *was* in danger. Grave danger. No pun intended, she thought, trying not to show her fear.

■ ■ ■ ■

"Come in," Michael McDuff said absently. He was busy planning a St. Patrick's Day show for one of the parks. He thought if they worked on it, they could probably start right after Valentine's Day and stretch St. Patrick's Day out for an entire month.

Like Halloween.

"Hello, Mike."

He should have sensed her coming; should have felt her. But he hadn't. He'd been too absorbed in his project. He looked up.

Angela was back. He'd seen more of her in the past few days than he had in the past two years, he thought. And part of that time, they'd been married.

"Hello, Angela."

She walked in and perched on the edge of his desk. He leaned back and asked, "What do you want?"

"Just checking in to see how you're doing," she said.

"No, you're not."

She crossed her arms over her chest and looked sullen for a moment, then apparently decided to be forthright for once. "I heard that the lead for Hera was hurt the other night."

"And?"

"Dan and I always got along pretty well, and I know he's been cast as Zeus, so if they need another Hera . . ."

He shook his head, amazed at her gall. "I'm not the casting director. You know that. If I were, I certainly wouldn't have put my own brother through the torture of waiting to hear if he got cast. And Marcie McDonnagh is going to be fine, not to mention that they cast her understudy, as well."

Angela slid off his desk. "I just thought you should know that if, and I mean if, you discover that they need someone to cover until she's ready to go back to work, I'm available."

He shrugged. "Okay. You're available."

She smiled and, apparently thinking better of pushing further, left, swinging her hips as she went.

Once she was gone, he realized he had clenched his hands into fists in his lap. "I know where I'd like to have my hands," he said out loud as he forcibly relaxed his fingers.

He stood, grabbed his jacket and started out of his office. No sense trying to work anymore today.

When they returned to the grave with Katherine Kidd, Beau was there. Christina saw his eyes as they lit on his sister. Saw the tears that welled in them.

"She's beautiful, huh?" he asked Christina.

"Yes," Christina replied without thinking.

"Yes?" Katherine Kidd looked at her, frowning.

"Is he here?" Adam asked Christina softly, but Katherine overheard.

Katherine's eyes grew shielded, and she stared at Christina. "You're not one of those kooks, are you?" she asked harshly.

"Tell her how much I love her," Beau said. "Tell her how sorry I am that she had to suffer for what everyone said I did."

Christina stood silent, swallowing.

Beau was nearly in tears, clearly wanting so badly to communicate with his sister in some way.

"Tell her that . . . that I had friends over my first year in college and we were drinking, and that's why that stuffed dog she called Calliope wound up drenched in booze and had to be thrown away. I should have confessed to that sin a long time ago."

Katherine started to turn away in disgust. The others were standing silent, waiting.

"Tell her. For the love of God, tell her!" Beau pleaded.

"Beau says . . . Beau wants me to tell you that you had a stuffed dog you called Calliope," Christina said in desperation. "Beau had some friends over, and they spilled liquor on it, so you had to throw it away." In her arms, Killer barked, as if for emphasis.

Katherine spun on her in sudden fury. "You're horrible! A horrible person. I don't know where you heard about that, but . . . you're cruel. Stay away from me. Stay away from me, and stay away from my family!"

She walked away, her stride long and determined.

Silence followed her exit, except for Beau, who began to cry. But only Christina heard him.

Suddenly he stopped crying and said emphatically, "She shouldn't be alone. Not right now."

"Beau thinks we should follow her," Christina said tensely.

"Follow her?" Genevieve said in disbelief. "She'd probably call the cops on us."

"Call Jed," Thor suggested. "Tell him to call her and ask her to meet him . . . where?"

"At O'Reilly's," Genevieve offered.

"Perfect," Christina said. "We can follow discreetly and make sure she's not in any trouble without scaring her even worse," she said, already dialing.

Jed sounded both surprised and wary when she explained as much as she could. He was clearly hesitant to do as she asked. "Jed, I'm afraid for her," Christina finally said, and that was all it took. He promised to call Katherine right away, and she hung up.

"He'll protect my sister?" Beau asked anxiously.

"Yes," Christina said, and Beau let out a sigh of relief. "What don't you follow her? Why don't you let someone else see you?" she demanded.

He stared at her. "Don't you think I would if I could?"

Killer whined. Christina let him hop out of her arms, and he ran right over to Beau and lowered his head to nudge the man affectionately.

"Killer can see him," Genevieve said.

"Great. Me, and my little dog, too," Christina said. "Come on. Let's go catch up to Katherine and follow her to O'Reilly's. At least we can get lunch."

Jed didn't know why he felt such a sense of urgency, but he drove faster than he should have and arrived at O'Reilly's within minutes of Christina's call, grateful that Katherine had agreed to a meeting at the pub.

He entered and immediately saw her at one of the high tables near the bar. He was relieved to see that she seemed to be okay.

"Have you learned anything that can help Beau?" she asked him eagerly as soon as he sat down.

"Anything I tell you is my own opinion, and nothing official, you know that."

"Of course. I know you're not a cop."

"I'm sure there's a connection between the victims, but I'm not sure what it is yet."

"Great," she muttered.

"I think I know a few things that may get us closer to the truth, though."

"Like?"

"Larry Atkins pulled his weapon too quickly, but I don't think he's a murderer."

Her features hardened. "He is a murderer. He murdered my brother."

"He shot him," Jed said quietly. "It's not the same thing."

She waved a hand dismissively. "Beau is still dead. And despite the rising body count, most people still believe he was a psychotic killer. Larry Atkins received a nice pension, and he's living out in the hills with his horses. Excuse me for being just a little bit bitter."

"Look, I'm all for vindicating your

brother," he said. "And I'm all for stopping the murderer at work now. But there isn't room for vengeance in the mix."

She wasn't looking at him, he realized. She was staring past him, in the direction of the tables outside, and she looked upset. He turned around to see what was upsetting her and saw that Christina was there with Genevieve, Thor and Adam. And Killer. She had been coming to O'Reilly's her whole life and undoubtedly knew she could keep the dog with her if they ate outside.

But why was Katherine so upset to see them?

Katherine stared at Jed. "Did someone tell you to call me? To meet me here?"

He didn't try to lie. "Yes."

"Christina Hardy?"

"Yes."

"Your girlfriend is crazy."

He didn't know how to respond, because he wasn't sure he could deny it.

Big tears welled in her eyes. "You know, people tell me to get over it, that I was just a kid when it happened. They say my brother has been dead for twelve years. Like that's supposed to make it hurt less? Well, that's bull. And you tell her . . . you tell that woman that . . . just tell her to leave me alone!"

"Katherine, she isn't trying to hurt you," Jed assured her, then let out a sigh of exasperation. "I don't know what happened at the cemetery, but I do know this. The two of you — as in you and Christina — should be scared to death. You're both fools if you don't see your own resemblance to the victims. You need to be really careful. Yes, she called me. She was worried about you. She's out with a group of people she knows and trusts. You were hanging in a deserted cemetery by yourself."

She sat back in her chair, staring at him "What am I supposed to do? Stop visiting my brother's grave? Stop going to work?" she asked.

"Do you have to work this afternoon?" he asked.

She shook her head. "No," she admitted. "Not till Monday."

"I'll see you home from here, then," he said. "And I want you stay in this weekend, unless you're out with both your parents. Or the Fifth Army Brigade," he added with a smile.

She actually smiled back. "All right."

"Have you ordered?"

"Not yet. You don't have to have lunch with me," she told him. "I can eat at home."

"I'm hungry. Lunch is a good idea."

He waved the waitress over, and they ordered. Then she leaned toward him. "Just keep her away from me, okay? I can see the attraction, but . . ."

Jed looked out the window. Christina caught his eye, blushed and turned away.

Jed looked more closely and frowned. The dog was seated several feet away from her on the bench, as if leaving room for someone to sit between them. Killer suddenly moved his head, as if he were having his ears scratched — except no one was scratching them.

Jed turned away quickly, gritting his teeth. He was not getting sucked into whatever delusion Adam Harrison was there to investigate. A real killer was on the loose, and they needed logic and sanity to catch him.

"Hey, McDuff!" Mr. Smith shouted.

Dan had been just about to head out. He wondered why Smith was stopping him now, when the man knew the Grim Reader had an audience waiting for him. He got his answer right away.

"Dan, I just got word. They've canceled the shows for tonight."

"What? You're kidding!"

He frowned, his heart thundering quickly. This wasn't anything to do with him, was it? Did they think they knew something about him?

"Sorry, Dan. They should have told us sooner, so you could have been called," Smith told him. "They're keeping the rides and some of the special attractions at the front of the park open, but they're closing everything down back here until they get a handle on the fog situation and why it went crazy last night. It's just for tonight. I hope."

"I'm early shift tomorrow."

"Then your last show finishes just before dark and you'll get paid."

"Okay. Thanks."

"Hey, congratulations on Zeus. I think the show is going to be huge."

"Thanks. I hope so. Hey, have you heard anything more about Marcie?"

"She's doing fine."

"She's still going to play Hera, right?"

Smith nodded. "Yeah. They kept her in the hospital overnight, but the doctors say she just tripped and banged the back of her head. It was a mild concussion, nothing more." He hesitated. "Thank God. We don't want another Patti Jo."

"No, we don't. Anyway, I'm glad to hear she's doing well," Dan said, and forced a smile. "Well, good night, then. Guess I'll take off this makeup and head out."

"Got a Halloween party to go to, huh?"

"I'm sure I can find something to do with an unexpected night off," Dan replied.

It was dark.

Angela McDuff noticed just how dark the minute she left the salon. The bright forest-green neon lights over at O'Reilly's had gone on, deepening the shadows and rendering them even more mysterious. She shouldn't have made an appointment for so late, she supposed, but she'd needed to have her hair done. After all, appearances were everything in her business. And she meant to offer a damn good appearance wherever she went. Because she sure as hell didn't intend to stay here.

Not that Orlando could be considered a hick town. Not these days. It had too much going on, thanks to the multiple tourist attractions that drove the area. But it had been a one-horse hick town once, and it was still surrounded by hick towns full of old Florida crackers, and she absolutely was not going to stay here forever.

There was only one place for a woman of her talents and abilities. Hollywood. And she didn't mean Hollywood, Florida.

She swore softly, not sure why she was quite so worried, except that she had seen him today, and the absolute hatred in his eyes when he looked at her now, well, that was scary.

And then there were the murders. Women were just so damn vulnerable.

With long strides, she headed for the parking lot, noticing along the way that shadows seemed to be everywhere. She cursed the fact that the mall had planted so many trees, because in her overactive imagination, it seemed as if someone was hiding behind every one of them.

It was just because she was alone, she told herself. Because it was so dark. And it had to be the darkness that made the air feel cooler, and the breeze that made the trees sound as if they were whispering.

There was someone behind her, she realized. A man. She risked a quick glance, and even in the darkness she could tell that he had on a dark sweatshirt and a baseball cap. His shoulders were hunched over, and he was gaining on her.

The cap must be to conceal his identity. And his clothing was dark so he could move unnoticed through the night.

She told herself not to be ridiculous, that she was all right. She reached into her purse and pulled out her keys. She would reach her own car in a minute and set off the alarm.

She forced herself to quicken her pace, but not to run.

Just then she was blinded by headlights.

"Hey, are you all right?" someone called out to her.

She let out a sigh of relief and looked quickly over her shoulder. Whoever had been following her was gone. She felt giddy inside and walked past the car, waving to thank her savior. She smiled, catching a glimpse of the interior of the vehicle.

A moment later, she was inside it.

And she knew everything she shouldn't know. Mainly . . .

That she was going to die.

# 15

Jerry Dwyer and Mal O'Donnell were attending Allison Chesney's wake, taking a shift and representing the city's finest. They stayed to the rear of the room, where Jed and Christina joined them.

Jed spoke quietly with Jerry while they scoped out the attendees. There wasn't much in the way of family. No parents, just an aunt and a number of cousins. The aunt was a dignified woman with blazing red hair who had thanked them for coming when they entered.

Christina stepped over to speak with her, and Jed could see that the aunt was grateful for her words. After a while, when the pew in front of the coffin was empty, Christina walked over to it, knelt down and lowered her head in prayer.

Watching her, he couldn't help feeling uneasy. What did she think she was doing? Talking to the dead? Did she think Allison

Chesney would sit up and begin to chat?

He stayed away from the coffin himself. He'd been to the autopsy, and that was more than enough for him.

While Christina did . . . whatever she was doing, he thought about the pressure the police were under to solve this case. Though he couldn't see them, he knew that several hundreds of people were lined up outside the funeral home. They were quiet and orderly, out of respect for the family, but they all bore placards demanding that the police find the killer.

At last Jed walked over to Christina, ready to get her attention and lead her away. He couldn't help but look down at the body of Allison Chesney.

The undertaker had done a good job, but it didn't matter. No matter what anyone did, there was no escaping the fact that she looked like exactly what she was: dead.

He'd seen people look deader, he thought. Was there even such a thing as deader?

This poor woman did look almost as if she could sit up and talk.

Margaritte had never looked that way.

He closed his eyes, and in his mind he saw his wife lying in the coffin, her features gray and skeletal. What if Margaritte could suddenly sit up and . . .

He took Christina's elbow to get her attention. "We need to go," he said stiffly.

She nodded.

They were silent as they walked out.

He had scanned the guests in the funeral parlor and searched through the crowd outside, hoping to trigger something in his mind, some memory. He knew Jerry and Mal had done the same, hoping the killer would show up.

And he probably had. He was most likely one of the people ringing the mortuary carrying a placard demanding his own capture.

When they reached her house, he turned off the engine and sat in the drive. She didn't seem to notice at first.

Being at the wake had been hard for her, he knew, but he couldn't change the way he was feeling right then, and he just didn't have any sympathy to give — especially when he knew she was lying to him about what she thought she was seeing and what Adam Harrison was doing there. Finally he said, "I'll walk you in."

She stared at him with a slightly puzzled expression on her face. Then her expression changed, resigned at first, followed by full-scale angry.

"Don't worry. I can find my door from here," she told him. He caught her arm with a groan when she started to exit the car, and she turned and glared at him angrily. "I'm sorry. I apologize for embarrassing you with Katherine Kidd," she said politely.

"Look, I just don't believe in ghosts. I'm sure you've got your reasons for thinking you see the dead rising, but I just don't believe in the possibility myself."

"Excuse me?"

"You are seeing ghosts, right?" he demanded.

"Singular, sorry," she snapped.

"Beau Kidd."

"Look, I'm not trying to hurt Katherine or anyone else," she said. "I don't want to see Beau Kidd. And I'm sorry you got involved with someone you think is a fruitcake. But don't worry. You can walk away. Ana and I will still be friends, but you don't have to have anything to do with me." She stared at him, her eyes cobalt with indignation. "Now let me go."

He had no choice but to do so, and the minute he did, she slammed her way out of the car.

"Christina!" he said, following, catching her arm again.

Just then Tony Lowell's minivan, with Tony at the wheel and Ilona beside him, pulled into their drive next door. Jed groaned inwardly at the thought that they could see what was going on, and who the hell knew what they would think. It looked like trouble in paradise over here for sure, and they were both looking at him with disapproval.

"Hey, guys!" Christina called to them, and forced a smile.

They drove on toward their garage, but they didn't look convinced.

"Look, Christina —"

"Please, just let me go. I'm safe. I have friends staying with me. Go keep an eye on Katherine Kidd, why don't you? I'm sure she could use your help."

He couldn't tell whether she sincerely meant that he should be looking after another potential victim, or if there was a touch of jealousy in her words.

Maybe he wanted her to be a little bit jealous, he thought.

"What does that mean?" he asked her.

She shook her head, staring at him. "I don't know. I don't know what anything means at the moment. Good night."

As she started toward the house, the door opened. Genevieve was standing there, another witness to the whole thing, he suspected.

Killer came rushing out to meet his mistress. He jumped up and down, happy to see Christina, then made a beeline for Jed, who bent down to pet the dog.

"Killer, come on in now," Christina called, and the little dog ran back over to her. From the doorway, Genevieve said something to her, and she turned and stared at Jed. "You are coming tomorrow night, aren't you?" she asked.

"Why? What's the big deal with tomorrow night?" he asked, pushing, hoping for the truth at last.

"Adam thinks . . ." Her voice trailed off, and she looked away.

"What?" he asked harshly. "What does Adam think?"

She looked at him again, and said in a rush, "Adam thinks we should have a séance. He thinks it might help catch the killer." Her eyes met his pleadingly. "Will you come? Please?"

"I don't know."

"Whatever," she said lightly, then walked inside.

He didn't have to tell her to lock the door. He heard the bolt snap into place.

"Do you think he was there?" Adam asked.

She jumped, having lost total track of the conversation. She had tried not to appear upset about Jed, since no one there knew about the details of their relationship. Actually, she didn't really know the details of it herself, she realized in mocking silence. Still, there was no reason to let anyone else know she was upset, so when she'd come in, she had started talking about the wake.

"It's very possible that the killer was there," Adam said, answering his own question.

"I think half the state was there," she told him.

"What about Beau?" Adam asked. "Is he here?"

Genevieve had made tea, which they were all sipping now in the parlor. She hadn't seen Beau Kidd since she'd come in, though. Great. No Jed, and now no Beau.

She shook her head. "Beau isn't here. But the problem is, he doesn't know anything. He thinks the real killer was somewhere behind Larry Atkins, his partner, and that's why he pulled his weapon. But Larry thought Beau was aiming at him, so he shot him. And since he died and never got the chance to explain, everyone decided he was the Interstate Killer and they stopped looking for anyone else. So he's haunting me, haunting this house . . . but he can't help."

Adam was quiet, thoughtful. "What about

the funeral?" he finally asked her.

"It was sad."

"I mean . . ."

"He wants to know if the victim haunted her own services," Genevieve explained.

Christina shook her head. "No," she said softly. "Or if she did, she didn't show herself to me."

"I still say that tomorrow's séance will change things," Adam said.

"How?" Christina asked. "Will other people be able to see Beau?"

"Maybe, maybe not," Adam told her.

"Then what . . . ?"

Thor came over and sat on the couch next to her, taking her hands. "Hey, look at me. You can't imagine a bigger doubter than me."

She smiled, thinking, Oh, yes, I can. He just left a few minutes ago.

"We will discover something tomorrow night," Thor promised her.

"I'm not sure Jed will be here, though," Christina said.

"He'll show. I guarantee you," Adam said. "He'll show."

Life could be a real bitch sometimes, she thought. She'd slept alone most of her life. Jed Braden had slept with her for only two days, yet she felt the loss as if she were bereft of a limb. What an idiot she was. She should have known better than to fall so quickly. Hell, hadn't she known her whole life not to fall for him at all?

"Hey, you okay?"

She had been brushing her hair in front of the old full-length mirror by her bureau. She could see Beau in the mirror, making himself comfortable in the overstuffed chair.

"I'm fine."

"I didn't mean to . . . chase Jed away."

"Don't worry. I did that all on my own."

He smiled sympathetically, then moved on to what was really concerning him. "I wish Kitty would believe you . . . believe in me."

Christina wasn't feeling all that generous toward Katherine Kidd at that particular moment, but she refrained from saying so to Beau. "She does believe in you, Beau. She's believed in your innocence all these years. And I'm sure there were many times when it wasn't easy."

"Yeah, I guess," he said. "I just wish she believed I was here now."

She turned to face him. "You're a ghost — that's pretty hard for most people to believe. But you're here for a reason. We have to figure out this case, Beau. I went to

Allison's wake tonight. It's so unfair. There has to be a reason why you're here. Can't you tell me anything?"

"I've told you everything I know," he said irritably.

She walked over to the foot of the bed, sat across from him and set a hand on his knee. It felt real, as if she really were touching something. Someone.

"We're having a séance tomorrow night. Adam thinks it will help."

"I hope so," he said, though he didn't sound entirely convinced. "Where is Jed, anyway?" he asked her.

"Looking after your sister, I hope," she said lightly.

"Yeah, I hope so, too. Oh, sorry. I hope that I'm not ruining your relationship. I do take off whenever it seems that . . . well, let's just say I'm not a voyeur."

"I don't think it matters anymore, anyway," she murmured, rising. "I'm going to brush my teeth, wash my face, turn in." As she walked toward the bathroom, she heard Killer barking at her bedroom door. "Hey, let him in, will you?" she asked.

The door opened, and Killer bounded in. It wasn't until she had a mouthful of toothpaste that she realized she had asked a ghost to open a door, and he had done so.

She walked back out. "You opened the door."

"Yeah. I make coffee, too, remember?" Beau said.

She smiled. "I just . . . well, you know. Ghosts are supposed to be insubstantial, able to walk through walls, stuff like that."

He shrugged. "Sometimes I know where you are, and I can just . . . be there. Sometimes I can't. Sometimes I can move things, and other times I can't. I didn't get instructions on how to be a ghost, you know."

"I guess not."

He smiled at her. "Go to bed. I guess I cost you the guy of your dreams tonight, but I'll be watching over you. I guess that doesn't mean much, huh?"

She walked around and kissed his cheek. He really did feel solid, and even warm.

"Thank you, Beau," she said. "Good night."

Killer curled up at the bottom of the bed. She missed Jed with a longing that was both emotional and physical, but it was still good to have the dog at her feet.

And the ghost of Beau Kidd standing watch.

The dream began just as it had the first time.

There was the feeling of being confined. Tied up. The awful darkness.

She was trying so hard to make a sound, to scream, but she was bound and gagged, and the worst was that she knew what was coming next. There was terror in the darkness, because soon her tormentor would come back.

She listened for the telltale footsteps, and every cell in her body seemed to scream. She would die. Eventually, she would die. The time would come when she was no longer entertaining, and then . . .

She started to fight the terror, clawing her way to consciousness. She was in her own bed; her Jack Russell was lying with her. She had to wake up, had to wake up. . . .

With a cry, she finally found her way back, and she gasped in relief. The night-light was on, as always, and Killer was standing by her side, staring at her, whining.

"Beau?" she whispered.

She saw him. He was in the chair, his head between his hands, and he looked up at her in absolute misery. "I'm so sorry," he told her.

"No," she said to him. "Don't be sorry. None of this is your fault. My grandmother warned me once that it was dangerous to see the dead, to talk to them. But now . . .

Beau, I am not going to be so afraid any-more. We have to find the truth."

Beau shook his head. "I don't know . . ."

"If I just stay in my dream . . ."

"No!"

"But —"

"Maybe you can't really be hurt in a dream," he said. "But then again, what if a dream can kill . . . ?"

It was irritating but true.

There was no way Jed intended to stay away from Christina's get-together. As much as he might mock and actually be angry that they seriously meant to hold a séance, he didn't intend to stay away. He was too worried about Christina. And he couldn't help it, but he was worried about Katherine Kidd, as well.

Hell, he was worried about any attractive young woman right now, but especially redheads. He wondered if the smartest thing for women to be doing right now was stock up on black hair dye. But that wasn't the solution, or not the whole solution, anyway. The red hair was a factor, yes, but he was convinced it wasn't everything.

When he arrived at the house, he could hear music. There were great aromas ema-nating from the house, as well. Something was being barbecued, and a lot of baking had been going on.

The door was unlocked, an oversight he decided to forgive, since there was such a crowd. Even so, he made sure to lock it behind himself. He stood unnoticed in the front hall for a moment, just observing. Mike and Thor were engaged in conversation in the hall, Mike expressing himself with his hands and somehow not spilling the beer he held. Jed waved hello and headed into the living room, where Dan was hunkered down by the CD player, apparently having put himself in charge of the music.

Adam was seated in a comfortable chair, leaning back and listening to the music, and he seemed to be pleasantly relaxed. Tony was carrying on a conversation with Genevieve about the perfect way to dress a turkey.

Ana and Christina seemed to be doing the most work. He found them in the kitchen, setting out trays and plates.

"Olives?" Ana asked.

"Here." Christina held out the jar.

"I already put out the celery, carrots and cukes," Ana said.

"Great. Hey, just grab the potato salad, will you? Hey, Mike!" she shouted. "Go check the barbecue, would you?"

"I'm here," Jed said. "Want me to do it?"

She looked up at him, eyes a very cool blue. "Sure, but hurry. I don't want it to burn."

"I'm on it," he said lightly.

He went out back, where steps led down from the wraparound porch to a covered patio. Beyond that was a pool. It was a small pool, kidney-shaped, but they'd had a great time in it, growing up. The McDuffs had always welcomed kids.

He went over to the big grill and discovered that the meat was safe. He quickly flipped the burgers, then the ribs and chicken. A minute later, he felt Christina come out.

Felt her.

He knew the scent of her cologne, but that didn't matter. He knew the way the air moved when she was near. He just knew that she was there.

"I have a plate for the burgers," she said.

"Great."

"Need help out here?" Thor asked, walking over behind Christina.

"I'll go back in and help Ana get stuff out on the table," Christina said. "You can give Jed a hand, Thor."

Jed looked down at the grill, trying to hide a dry smile. Great. Send out the Incredible

Hulk. If a man like that believed in ghosts . . .

"Have you been keeping an eye on Katherine Kidd?" Thor asked.

Jed shrugged. "I followed her to the store, I followed her home," he said. "I thought about asking her over here, but . . ."

Thor frowned. "Maybe you should have."

"This isn't my house. Not my place."

"Call her now and see if she wants to come."

Jed turned to him, arching a brow. "She's even less amused by this than I am."

"It's not meant to be amusing," Thor said. "How do they want them cooked?"

"Go for half medium and half well, I guess," Thor said. "Seriously, why don't you give Katherine a call? Two good things about that. One, she'll be here."

"And number two?"

"She won't be home alone on a Saturday night, tempted to go out."

The first batch of hamburgers was done. Jed slid them on to a plate and asked Thor, "You want to be in charge of ribs and chicken?"

Thor grinned and nodded. At that moment, Christina and Ana came outside. Ana had plates, cups, napkins and silverware. Christina was balancing two large platters, one holding buns and bread, the other divided into sections and containing baked beans, potato salad and coleslaw.

Thor walked over to join them at the picnic table, carrying the burgers. "I told Jed he should try to convince Katherine Kidd to come over."

"What?" Christina asked, blindsided.

"I said —"

"I heard you." She gazed over at Jed for a moment, then turned back to Thor. "You heard what she said at the cemetery. She thinks we're all nuts, you know. And cruel. She won't come."

"I think she will," Thor said.

Genevieve had walked over while they were talking and picked up the gist of the conversation. "Jed, let's just go over there. She'll be much more likely to accept if you ask her in person. Come on. I'll go with you."

Christina couldn't have been more surprised when Jed and Genevieve returned — with Katherine Kidd.

Whatever Jed had said to her had led to a complete change of attitude. She mingled cheerfully and had actually worked with Mike, so they had that to talk about.

When she approached Christina, it was

ruefully. "Thank you so much for inviting me," she said.

"We're glad you're here," Christina said, trying to sound as if she meant it. At her feet, Killer barked happily, then looked up, wagging his tail hopefully as he eyed the plate of leftovers she was carrying. "No more, Killer, you're going to explode," she told the dog.

Katherine was still there, smiling awkwardly, as if unsure what to say next.

Christina cleared her throat. "We're having a séance tonight."

"I know."

"But I thought . . ."

"The thing is," Katherine said, "I was awake all last night trying to figure out how you could have known about Calliope, and Beau and his friends getting drunk. I don't know what I think. I don't believe in ghosts, but maybe . . . I don't quite disbelieve as much as I used to."

Christina didn't quite know what to say to that, but luckily she was saved from having to figure it out by Ana's announcement that the desserts were laid out in the kitchen.

"Every man for himself," Christina said. "We'll regroup in the parlor."

That morning, Adam and Thor had brought an oblong table into the parlor and set enough chairs around it for all of them. All they had to do now was add one more for Katherine.

"We're really having a séance?" Dan asked, looking around the room. "Do you honestly want to make Gran come back so she can yell at us?"

"She did not yell at us," Christina protested.

"Constantly," Mike said.

"You two are horrible. I hope she does come back and yell at you," Christina said.

"Why are we having a séance?" Ana asked. "Are we trying to contact someone special?"

"It's October, and it sounded like fun," Genevieve said.

"What, no candles?" Ilona asked when she walked into the parlor, nibbling on a piece of cake.

"Candles! Good idea," Genevieve said, then left in search of some.

"If this is good, we should do it again and charge admission," Dan said. "I wonder if any of the parks have tried this yet. Hey, Mike, you're the idea man. You should suggest it."

"Not a bad idea," Mike said thoughtfully.

Christina watched as Genevieve returned and lit a few tall candles. Everyone seemed to be into the idea of the séance. Even Jed wasn't complaining.

Dan bent down to look under the table. "No tricks here that I can find," he said.

"Get out of there, Dan. No one's rigged the table," Christina said.

"I take it we're trying to contact my brother," Katherine said as they all took their seats. She looked at Christina and gave a slight smile. "I thought that he had a connection with you already?"

"Okay, lights off," Genevieve said.

"Is it going to be really dark?" Ilona asked, wide-eyed.

"I'm right next to you, babe," Tony told her.

Dan began to hum the theme song to *The Twilight Zone.*

"Do we need some incense or anything?" Mike suggested.

"I think we're just fine the way we are," Adam Harrison said, then started considering the seating arrangements. "Let's see, the house belongs to Christina, and Dan and Mike spent a lot of time here, too. Christina, you're good where you are. Dan, Mike, either side. Then, let's see . . . Ana next to Dan, Katherine next to Mike. Jed, you sit next to Katherine. Tony and Ilona . . . next to Ana. Who am I forgetting? Ah, Genevieve, you go at the end of the table, with

Thor next to you, and I'll be on the other side."

"What are we listening for?" Katherine asked. "Knock three times or something?"

"You never know, at a séance," Adam said.

The music had been turned off. The few candles that Genevieve had lit were burning, but even without them, the room wouldn't have been totally dark, because light was still filtering in from the hallway.

Christina clenched her teeth, already feeling a sense of dread. When she and Ana had played with the Ouija board Beau had appeared. Now here they were again. With any luck, Beau would appear to someone else tonight.

"Join hands," Adam advised the group. As soon as everyone did, he began to speak. "Life is crisscrossed with lines connecting the dimensions. Death is perhaps only another line, a different dimension. We know that sometimes lines can be crossed, and we know that sometimes those who should move on, should cross a line, cannot, because their business in one dimension was not complete, or because someone must be helped."

His voice had a deep, resonant quality. It was almost hypnotic, Christina thought.

"Sometimes," Adam went on softly, "there

are those with very special powers who depart this life and should find eternal peace, finished with the woes of this earth, but they stay because they have found a calling. Sometimes, they help us when we need to speak to the dead."

He had never once suggested that they close their eyes, never asked them to do anything except hold hands. But as Christina stared down the length of the table at him, the world seemed to change.

The room filled with mist, gently swirling, almost gentle. Now when she looked at Adam, there was something different about him. And when he spoke again, his voice had changed.

"I am Josh, and I am here to help you," he said.

"Josh?" Christina murmured.

The only things she could see were Josh and the mist, though she could still feel pressure on her hands from Dan on one side and Mike on the other.

Strangely, she wasn't afraid, even though she couldn't see them anymore.

"Beau Kidd, will you show yourself?" Josh asked.

"I'm here," Beau Kidd said, and he was, Christina realized. He was standing behind Josh.

"Why can't you rest, Beau?" Josh asked.

"Because I'm innocent," Beau said. "And also . . ."

"Also?" Josh echoed questioningly.

"I feel a sense of danger surrounding this house."

"Why?" Josh asked.

"I don't know, but there's a connection, and someone has to find it."

Suddenly a horrific, painful keening tore through the night and Beau simply . . . shattered.

The mist faded as everyone at the table leapt to their feet, staring at Katherine, who was backing away from the table, still moaning. "I saw him," she sobbed. "Oh, my God . . . I saw my brother."

# 16

There was silence.

Dead silence.

Adam Harrison turned on the lights and returned the parlor to its former self.

This was a family of performers, Jed reminded himself. And yet . . . Katherine Kidd had been the one to scream.

Sucked in by the show? Even he had to admit that it had been a good one. Adam Harrison had done an excellent job of speaking in a different voice, every bit as convincing as Christina carrying on conversations with dead people.

Katherine still looked simultaneously ecstatic and sorrowful.

"I saw him," she repeated. "I saw Beau." When no one else spoke, she turned to Adam and asked, "I ruined it, didn't I?"

"No . . . no," Adam said.

"It was so . . . real."

Mike cleared his throat. "Maybe for you. I

didn't see a damn thing."

"Then you weren't looking," Katherine insisted.

"I thought it was creepy," Ilona said.

"There was fog," Mike said, sounding genuinely unnerved. "There was fog."

"I saw it, too," Ana breathed.

Jed noticed that Adam was looking pale, exhausted. "Adam," he said softly, "you should sit down before you fall down." Jed might think the man was nothing but a clever fake, but he looked ill, and he was no spring chicken. "In fact, you should probably go lie down. Let me help you upstairs."

Adam nodded.

Christina sprang into action then. "I'll get you some water, Adam. And put on more tea." She hurried out of the room.

"Adam?" Thor said with a frown, watching as Adam accepted support from Jed.

Adam lifted a hand. "I'm fine."

They made it up the stairs, and Christina arrived a moment later with a glass of water.

"Thank you, my dear," Adam said.

She smiled. "The tea is on."

After she left, Jed said, smiling to take the sting out of the words, "The Irish think you can fix anything with tea. Frequently laced with whiskey."

"They're not really so far off, are they?"

Adam asked.

"About the tea or the whiskey?"

"Both," Adam said, and sat down at the foot of his bed.

Jed sat across from him in a wicker chair and asked, "So . . . what are you really?"

"What did you see tonight?" Adam asked instead of answering.

"Mist. And I'll be damned if I can figure out where it came from, unless it was just a mass hallucination."

Adam smiled. "Think I hypnotized a whole roomful of people?"

"And your voice . . . Your voice was entirely different," Jed said.

"And Katherine Kidd saw her brother." Adam sighed. "Too bad. We were on the way."

"On the way where? Where would we have wound up?" Jed asked, well aware of the skepticism in his voice.

"With a link, perhaps. Although . . . perhaps we found a link after all," Adam said.

"Adam, do you really think the ghost of Beau Kidd haunts this house?"

Adam smiled. "I seldom tell anyone exactly what I think, unless they happen to be very good friends or in my employ."

"Mr. Harrison, I've heard nothing but

good about you. Still . . ."

"You don't believe in ghosts."

Jed shrugged but didn't say anything.

Adam went on. "You, of all people, should believe in ghosts."

"Oh?"

"Ghosts can haunt us in many ways. And you are haunted every day of your life."

Jed stiffened. "What are you talking about?" he demanded harshly.

"You can't let go. You feel guilt for your wife's death. You can't understand how someone so young and beautiful, with everything to live for, should die — and you should still be alive. You see your wife every day of your life. You need the guilt to keep going. And now you've transferred that guilt to everything that happened with Beau Kidd. So maybe Beau is really haunting you?" Adam suggested.

Jed drew back, feeling anger — and a strange creeping sensation. "Don't be ridiculous. I wasn't even here when they pulled out the stupid Ouija board."

Adam didn't reply to that. Instead he said, "I understand they've uncovered similar murders in other places."

Jed stared at him, frowning. "How do you know that?"

Adam smiled. "I have my contacts in the

FBI, Mr. Braden."

"All right. Let's say you're right and the killer was very busy here twelve years ago. Then Beau Kidd was killed, and the killer knew he had an out for the murders here, so he started to travel, committing his crimes wherever he found himself. But finally he came back here — back home — and started killing again."

"Nature of the beast," Adam said softly.

"Meaning?"

"This is what I think, and I believe you and I are pretty much in agreement on this. The killer started here, and now he's back, after using Beau Kidd to buy some breathing time. He is intelligent, and criminally clever. He knew when not to kill in his own backyard. But it's in his nature. He managed to satisfy his blood lust undetected while he was away, and now he's convinced he can get away with his crimes again here, maybe even find a way to trick someone else into taking the fall for him again."

Jed nodded. "But what's going on with Beau Kidd and Christina and this house?" he asked.

"A connection," Adam said.

"But what kind of connection? And how does it relate to the connection between the victims, a connection I still can't figure out?

383

I feel as if we're just going in circles."

"I don't think so," Adam said.

"And why not?" Jed asked.

Adam shrugged. "I'm not sure I should share my thoughts with you, Mr. Braden. You're far too skeptical."

"Why? Because I still can't embrace the idea that ghosts walk the streets at their leisure?"

Before Adam had a chance to answer, Christina came in bearing tea. She stared daggers at Jed as she poured.

Jed stood. "I guess I'll take Katherine home now."

"You do that," Christina said. "Adam, how do you like your tea?"

"One sugar and milk, thank you."

Jed hesitated by the door, but Christina wouldn't even look at him. He wanted to tell her that he would be back, that he hated leaving her alone in the house with a group of people who were seriously misguided at best, completely loony at worst — even if she apparently shared their delusion.

He was surprised when Adam looked at him with a pleasant smile. "Come back again, Mr. Braden. I enjoy our conversations."

"Thanks. I will."

Christina still didn't even glance his way.

Jed walked down the stairs, furious with himself. Dammit, he was getting sucked in. There were no such things as ghosts, he told himself. There were only memories. Memories that plagued and haunted and hurt. But somewhere inside he was beginning to believe he was wrong, had been wrong his whole life, and there were ghosts after all.

And maybe someday, when this was all in the past, he could even learn to let his own ghosts go.

"Thank God you're all right. You really scared me," Christina told Adam once Jed was gone.

A moment later, before Adam had a chance to say anything in response, Genevieve arrived at the doorway, Ana right behind her.

Adam looked over at them and grinned. "Wow. All these beautiful young women. I should feel a little woozy more often."

"Are you okay?" Ana asked, coming in and sitting on the foot of the bed.

"I am absolutely fine," Adam assured her.

Ana looked at him for a moment before she spoke again. "I hope you don't mind my asking, but Josh . . . Josh was your son, right?" she said softly.

Christina started; you could have heard a

pin drop in the room, it had gone so silent.

"Yes," Adam said.

"And he's been . . . gone a long time," Ana went on.

Adam smiled reminiscently. "Yes."

"It was like you were him, you know?" Ana said, simultaneously certain and questioning.

Again everyone else stayed silent, watching her as she kept speaking.

"I didn't see Beau Kidd, but I could have sworn I saw your son. That . . . that he was real."

Adam reached out and touched her face. "He is very real, thank you. He had the gift. And he died young. I never had the gift, but I do believe in it, and I've been able to gather people around me who have the gift and the courage to use it."

"Do you think I have a gift?" Ana asked.

Christina grimaced. "If you don't, you're welcome to mine," she said dryly, breaking the tension in the room. Everyone laughed.

"Perhaps," Adam said gently to Ana.

"Let's let Adam get some rest," Genevieve said firmly.

They went downstairs. Katherine and Jed had gone, and Christina suspected he would be going home after he'd dropped her off. It was obvious that the night was over.

"I'm going to head on out," Ana said.

"We'll walk you to your house," Tony said.

"I'm okay. I've walked from here to my house a thousand times," Ana assured them, smiling.

"Yeah, but not tonight," Dan said. "I'll walk you over."

"We live right next door," Ilona reminded him. "It's easy for us to do it."

"And deprive me of the pleasure of the midget's company?" Dan teased.

Ana groaned.

"I can walk you home if my brother is being a jerk," Mike told her.

"Oh, let the jerk do it," Ana said. "Good night, Christina. Thanks for the barbecue. And the séance. That was . . . cool."

Dan gave Christina a kiss good-night, waved to the others and headed out with Ana. Ilona and Tony left next, and Mike was right behind them. Christina was left standing in the doorway with Genevieve and Thor.

She was disturbed by the sense of loneliness that swept over her. She didn't remember feeling quite so forlorn in a very long time. "You know," she said softly, "I really thought . . . I thought Gran or Granda, even my mom or dad, might show up. If only for a minute," she said.

She felt Thor's hand on her shoulder, gentle, reassuring. "They didn't need to stay behind," he said. "They loved and were loved. Their lives were full."

"But my parents were so young," Christina said, all the remembered pain in her voice.

"They still lived their lives as they were meant to be lived," he offered.

Christina nodded. "Well . . . I'm going to bed, I guess," she murmured. "Thank you, both. Though I'm not sure we really got anywhere tonight."

She was startled when Adam suddenly called down the stairs, "We're all in and the house is locked up for the night, yes?"

"Yes. Unless Jed thinks you meant for him to come back tonight," Christina replied.

"He will or he won't," Adam said, sounding unworried either way. "Just make sure this place is locked up tight, okay?"

"Will do," Thor promised, suiting his action to his words, then said he was going to go watch TV for a while. The women decided to go up to bed. A minute later, Christina closed the door to her room and slipped into a thin flannel nightgown, washed her face, brushed her teeth and started brushing her hair, waiting.

She felt Beau's presence as soon as he

entered her room.

"The guy is a jerk," he told her.

She grinned. "Jed?"

"Yeah, Jed. You know the type. Hell, I know the type. I used to be the type. All macho bravado. But you need to cut him some slack. He's afraid, only he doesn't know how to be afraid. He knows what it's like to lose someone he loves, and he doesn't want to go through that again, so . . . he's afraid."

"Thanks, Beau."

"I'm here, though. I'll watch over you."

"Thanks again." He looked troubled, so she frowned and asked, "What is it?"

He hesitated. "I think I'm starting to understand why I'm here," he said quietly. "I think I showed up because . . . because the real killer was in this house," he told her.

What do to? Jed wondered.

He dropped Katherine off at her house, watching her until she was safely inside. She waved from the doorway, then closed — and, he assumed, locked — the door behind her.

During the ride, he had once again stressed to her that she was an attractive redhead and needed to watch out. She had only smiled and said, "Now, there would be an irony. Beau Kidd's sister killed — by the real Interstate Killer."

"How about just being careful, and avoiding all irony?" he'd suggested.

A part of him wanted to rush right back to Christina's, but another part of him wanted to go home and look at his files again. The second part won out, so he put the car in gear and drove to his town house.

The minute he entered, he realized how barren his home was. Of course it was. He had made a point of it. He hadn't been able to stand looking at the pictures, the knick-knacks, the souvenirs of laughter shared, of . . . life.

There was no personality here, while already the house Christina now claimed as her own was full of individuality.

He smiled to himself.

Hell. If he were a ghost, that was definitely where he would go if he had to pick a place to haunt, he had to admit. The house was steeped in personality. It held a whisper of the music that had been her grandfather, and the homey atmosphere that had always surrounded her grandmother. There were pictures everywhere. . . . Christina's mother as a child, as a teenager, posing with her date for the prom, her wedding . . .

He gave himself a shake, walked over to his desk and impatiently spread out the files. He found the notes Larry Atkins had made after interviewing Beau about Janet Major. According to Officer Kidd, they were not heavily involved. The officer said they had met at O'Reilly's, off International Drive. He kept reading, but the words began to jumble on him.

He picked up another file, the one on Grace Garcia. Again Larry Atkins had written the notes.

"Miss Garcia worked part-time at O'Reilly's," Atkins had written. "Her manager, Peter Hicoty, was in tears when I spoke with him. 'We all loved her,' he said. 'We all loved her here.' "

Jed set down the file. He glanced quickly through the rest of them. He'd read them all before, but he hadn't realized what he was looking for then. O'Reilly's.

He couldn't find a connection in every file, but given where the dead women had lived or worked, it seemed likely that, at the very least, they had all stopped in at O'Reilly's to eat or grab a drink.

How had everyone missed the possibility?

He immediately called Jerry, even though it was late.

Jerry immediately asked, "You got something?"

"Maybe. O'Reilly's."

"O'Reilly's?"

"Yeah, it's a pub down near International Drive."

"I know it," Jerry said.

"Check it out. I'm not suggesting that anyone at O'Reilly's is the guilty party. But I think it's where the killer chooses his victims," Jed said.

"It's something," Jerry told him. "I'll get a car out there."

They rang off. Jed looked around his town house. The emptiness, the coldness, weighed on him. He glanced at his watch. It wasn't really that late, he told himself. He went out, got in his car and drove back to Christina's.

He parked out front, then sat in his car and looked around. Only two cars remained in the driveway: Christina's, and the SUV Thor, Genevieve and Adam had driven up in.

The house looked quiet. He told himself that he should just drive away, but he hesitated. He had said that he would come back, even if he hadn't said when.

He exited his car and started up the walk. Before he could knock, Thor opened the door. "I thought I heard a car." He smiled. "I see you decided to come back tonight after all."

"Yeah."

"Well, come on in."

Together they walked into the living room, where Thor had been watching a movie.

"So what did you think about tonight?" Thor asked.

Jed shook his head. "I'm not sure. When Adam and I were talking earlier, he was about to say something, but then we were interrupted. I suspect he's sleeping now, though."

"Why don't you go up and check? He might still be awake."

"You think?"

"He's not the type to leave anything unsaid," Thor told him. "At least go up and take a look. He won't mind."

"All right. Thanks."

Jed headed for the stairs.

Christina tossed and turned.

It was happening again.

She was in agony from the things that had been done to her, and she swallowed, choking down her tears. The monster would come again, she knew, but that wasn't as bad as knowing that her time was ticking away. She read the papers. She knew. Once they were taken, the victims had only a few days left. And then . . .

She tried to scream. It was a silent sound behind the gag.

And then it wasn't.

Jed never made it to Adam's room. He heard Christina scream, and he turned, tearing down the hallway, throwing open her door.

She was sitting up in the bed, but she didn't seem to be seeing anything.

He rushed to her side. Shook her. Sat beside her and drew her against him. "Christina? It's me. Jed. Christina!"

By then Thor, Genevieve and Adam had rushed into her room and were standing around the bed, looking concerned.

"Christina?" Jed said again.

She shuddered, cried out, then buried her face against his chest.

"What is it?" Jed asked.

"He . . . he has someone right now," she whispered. "I'm sure of it. When I dream, I'm . . . her. I know it sounds crazy, but it's true. He has a woman, and she's terrified. She knows she's going to die."

Adam walked closer, taking her hands. "What does she see?" he asked gently.

"Nothing. It's dark. She's blindfolded. And she can't cry out, because she's gagged."

Jed inhaled and held his breath. What she was claiming was . . . impossible.

And yet, it sounded so convincing. Christina wasn't lying. He would stake his life on that. Whether what she had seen was a dream or something more didn't really matter. To her, it had been real.

"And they were all here tonight . . ." Adam murmured.

"What?" Jed demanded.

"Adam thinks Beau appeared because someone in the house is the killer," Thor explained.

"That's ridiculous!" Christina exclaimed. "You're talking about Ana, and Mike and Dan. Or my next-door neighbor and his girlfriend. It's impossible. There has to be another explanation."

"There could be, of course," Adam said.

O'Reilly's. The name filled Jed's mind like a giant neon sign.

"Dan," he murmured consideringly. He hated to think it, but Dan was an actor, used to pretending to be someone he wasn't, and he'd known one of the recent victims, as well as the woman who'd supposedly fallen in the fog.

"What?" Christina demanded indignantly.

She was furious, and he knew it. He should have seen it coming, in fact. Christina was fiercely and understandably loyal to her only living relatives.

She leapt out of bed. "That's the most ridiculous thing I've ever heard. We're going to go see him right now and he can tell you so himself."

A few minutes later, all five of them went downstairs and headed for Jed's sedan. Killer followed, barking and running around their feet.

"I'll lock him in the house," Christina said. She picked up her dog, hugged him and talked to him on the way back to the house, but she was firm. He was locked inside.

When she rejoined the group she turned to Jed and said challengingly, "Are you sure you don't want to knock on my next-door neighbor's door and accuse him of being a murderer, too, huh?"

"All right, why not?" Jed said equably, and together they walked over to Tony's door. He could almost feel the waves of anger emanating from her. He had attacked her family. That was a sin for which there might be no such thing as forgiveness.

She knocked at the door of Tony's sprawling ranch. All the windows were dark, but in a few seconds they heard a sleepy voice asking what was going on, and Tony opened the door. He was wearing a robe, which he had apparently thrown on quickly, since it was inside out, and his hair was tousled.

"Sorry, Tony, you were sleeping, I take it?" Christina said.

"Um . . . yeah." He was only half awake, but he still tried to offer a smile.

Ilona appeared behind him, asking, "What is it, Tony?" She, too, was wearing a robe, and she was yawning.

Jed thought he could hear a television from somewhere deep in the house. They must have fallen asleep in front of the bedroom TV.

"I don't know," Tony told her, then turned to Jed and Christina. "What's up?"

"We're just checking to make sure you guys got home safely," Christina lied.

"Um, Christina," Tony said as if he were talking to someone who wasn't quite there mentally, "I live next door."

"I know."

"Did you guys make sure Ana got into her house okay?" Jed asked.

"Dan walked her home," Tony said.

Christina could be as angry as she wanted, Jed thought, but he wasn't taking any chances. He turned, leaving her to say good-night, and he was running by the time he reached Ana's property.

He banged the door hard.

He heard what sounded like a scream inside and got ready to break down the door, but in the end he didn't need to. There was a flurry of footsteps and the door was flung open, revealing Ana, in pajamas and a robe. She stared at him as Christina came loping up behind him.

"What are you two doing here?" Ana asked.

"You're okay?" Jed asked anxiously.

"Of course I'm okay," Ana said, puzzled.

"Dan walked you home, right?" Christina said.

"Yes. So why are you . . . ?" She paused, staring at them.

"What is it?" Christina asked.

"Haven't you heard?" Ana said. "There's an alert out. Another woman is missing."

Christina let out a moaning sound.

"And . . . we know her," Ana went on.

"Who is it?" Jed demanded.

"Angela McDuff," Ana said. "Mike's ex-wife."

## 17

The cop who interviewed Mike was named Jerry Dwyer, who, it turned out, knew Jed well.

As soon as Mike heard about Angie he had expected to be called in and questioned. After all, wasn't the ex always the first one to be suspected? He'd expected to be stuck in a bare-bones interrogation room and questioned harshly.

You were married to her, but she twisted you around her little finger and used you to get ahead. Then she left you and tried to take you for everything you had. A real redheaded bitch, huh?

Then they would start trying to tie him to the earlier murders. Of course, he would point out that he'd been a kid back then, only eighteen, to which they would respond that lots of sickos started killing by eighteen.

But apparently he'd been watching too much TV. Dwyer hadn't been anything like what he'd expected. The man had asked him questions, of course, but sitting in Mike's own living room and perfectly pleasantly.

"When did you last see your wife?" Dwyer asked.

"Ex-wife."

"Ex-wife."

"I was at work. She stopped by my office almost a week ago."

"Did she want more money or anything like that?" Jerry smiled to show it was nothing personal. "Sorry, I have to ask."

"No. She didn't want more money. She keeps thinking I can do more to advance her career," Mike said.

"Can you?"

"Yes and no. I suggest names. But the producers and sometimes the directors have the last say on any casting decisions." He'd dragged on a pair of jeans when he'd heard the pounding on his door, but for some reason Mike felt as if he were wearing a tie and it was getting too tight. He inhaled, exhaled. "Look, if I'd been going to kill Angie, it would have been a long time ago, back when she took me for a ride until I couldn't help her anymore, then dumped me. I'm not that patient."

The cop almost smiled. "She like to get

her hair done?"

"You name it, she likes to get it done. She likes being perfect."

"Sounds like you still know her pretty well."

Mike smiled. "Hey . . . if you knew Angie once, you know her forever. She's not what you'd call deep."

Jerry watched him, nodding gravely. They were sitting on the sofas in the living room, two modern light-toned leather pieces perpendicular to the gas fireplace. Mike couldn't help thinking that the cop was going to get up at any minute and start going through the place room by room, taking it — and him — apart.

Instead Dwyer simply stood and said, "Thanks."

"Thanks?"

"That's it, at least for now."

Mike stood, as well, and stared at Dwyer. Swallowed hard. "You'll call me if . . . you find her?"

Dwyer stared back at him. "Of course. And keep thinking. You never know . . . you might be able to tell us something that can help us."

"Of course."

Mike walked Dwyer to the door. He could feel his heart hammering, and all he could

think of was the old Edgar A. Poe story —
"The Telltale Heart."

He was sweating bullets.

He couldn't breathe.

And his heart was beating so loudly they
ought to be able to hear it on Mars.

"Good night, and thank you again, Mr.
McDuff."

"Absolutely, Detective Dwyer."

As he closed the door behind the policeman, Mike thought he might have to dial
911; he was practically gasping for breath.

"Hey, don't break it down!" Dan called out
irritably. A second later, he opened the door.
His red hair was tousled, he was clad in gray
sweats, and his feet were bare. He stared in
confusion at the group on his doorstep — a
group that now included Ana, who'd de-
clared herself too spooked to stay home
alone.

"Is it trick-or-treat already? Did someone
drop a bomb? What the hell is going on?"
he demanded.

"Can we come in?" Christina said.

He backed away from the door, running
his fingers through his hair. "Sure, why not?
You guys do know it's late, right?"

"Dan," Christina said, leading the way in,
"Angie is missing."

He stared at her blankly for a moment, then said, "Angie is . . . missing?"

"Yes."

Dan looked genuinely shocked and confused, Jed thought. And why not? He was an actor.

Still sounding at sea, Dan asked, "Didn't she divorce Mike a long time ago? Drag him through an emotional wringer and hang him out to dry?"

"That's the point, Dan," Jed said.

Dan looked more confused than ever. "I should be concerned because the woman is a total bitch who did her best to destroy my brother?"

"Yes, a totally bitchy redhead who's missing!" Ana exploded.

"Dan," Adam Harrison explained quietly, "the police have probably questioned your brother about her disappearance already. She was supposed to meet friends for dinner the other night, but she didn't show up. The friends called the police, and since she's an attractive redhead, the police are taking her disappearance seriously."

Dan's jaw dropped, as if he'd suddenly figured out the reality of the situation. "Omigod!" he said in one breath. "I'll call Mike right now."

He went to get the phone, and Christina

stared at Jed. She looked disdainful, but he realized as she turned away that she was going to search Dan's house.

"Mike?" Dan, who either hadn't noticed or didn't care what Christina was up to, said anxiously into the phone.

While Mike was talking on the other end, Jed's cell phone began to ring. He knew it was going to be Jerry Dwyer, and it gave him no satisfaction to be right.

"Can you meet me?" Dwyer asked.

"Yes, sure. Where?"

"Where else?" Jerry demanded dryly. "O'Reilly's."

"I'll need a little time."

"Just be as quick as you can. I'm wondering how much more time she's got," Jerry said morosely.

Christina sat next to Dan on his couch, her fingers entwined with his. Ana was on his other side. Everyone else was dispersed around the room, and everything seemed fine.

Meanwhile, Jed had taken off without a word about where he was going. She had a feeling it had something to do with Angie's disappearance, though, and she was furious with him for not sharing whatever he knew, or even what he thought he knew.

Not to mention that he didn't believe in ghosts and clearly thought she was nuts because she did. And on top of everything . . .

How dare he suspect her cousin of being the killer? Just to satisfy his curiosity, she'd searched Dan's place, and she'd found nothing to indicate that he could possibly be holding anyone captive.

Just then the doorbell rang, and Dan went to answer before sitting back down next to her.

It was Mike. He paced the room, trying to remember every word he had said to Angie, every word she had said to him, in hopes of remembering something that might help the police. Then he threw up his hands. "I can't think of anything at all, damn it."

"Are you sure she's not doing this herself as some kind of a publicity stunt?" Dan asked. "God knows, she's ambitious enough to try damn near anything," he argued.

Mike let out a long sigh. "You want to know the really sad thing?" he asked.

"What?" Christina asked him.

"I should be worried about being questioned by the police, about being a suspect. But you know what gets me the most?" His words were almost a whisper.

"What?" Adam said.

"I'm half insane because I'm worried about her. Is that pathetic or what?"

"Actually, it's just human," Adam told him. "So don't give up hope. They may find her yet."

"I don't know. You think we made a mistake, putting her name and picture out there?" Jerry asked Jed. "Think the killer will panic and kill her? I mean . . . sooner than he would, anyway?"

"I don't know," Jed told him.

"I questioned Michael McDuff. I wanted to tell you, since I know you know the family," Jerry said, motioning to the woman behind the bar. "Another Scotch, neat, please," he said, then looked at Jed and scowled slightly. "I'm off duty."

"Did I say anything?"

"Yeah, well, you were a by-the-book kind of guy, but I'm almost as legit," Jerry told him.

"I just came from Daniel McDuff's place," Jed said.

"Figured it might have been something like that. Word has it you've been seeing a redhead yourself — Christina Hardy. Come to think of it, you're connected to Christina Hardy, who's connected to several of the victims, and Katherine Kidd. You're starting to look pretty interesting yourself."

"You've got to be kidding."

Jerry shrugged and grinned. "Hell, I can't get a decent date, and there you go . . . seeing two gorgeous redheads."

"I'm not seeing Katherine Kidd. I'm working for her."

"She's paying you?"

"I'm working for her because I feel like a piece of crap where her brother is concerned. Jerry, you know that, so why the third degree?"

"Exasperation, frustration," Jerry admitted.

Mal O'Donnell came in and took the bar stool to Jed's left. "Black and tan, sweetheart, thanks," he said to the bartender.

When the woman had moved away, O'Donnell stared at Jed. "You're on to something." It was a statement, not a question.

"I wish I was," Jed said tensely.

"Want to know what I think?" O'Donnell asked.

"Clue me in," Jed told him, taking a long swallow of his own beer.

"Beau Kidd did kill the first set of girls," Mal said.

"I think you're wrong."

"No. This is a copycat. Beau killed the first

girls. Then he was shot, and the killings ended," Mal said.

"They ended because Beau made a good scapegoat, and because you've got a damned smart perp, one who moved on to other places to feed his sick fantasy," Jed told him.

"How come you're so sure?" Jerry asked him.

"Because he's got a thing for the guy's sister," Mal said, nodding knowingly.

Jed shook his head. "I really don't think Beau did it."

"You helped with one thing, anyway," Jerry said to Jed.

"Yeah?"

"We reinterviewed everyone in hell today, and you were right about one thing," Jerry told him.

"And that was?"

"This place." Jerry lowered his voice. "Each victim — then and now — frequented O'Reilly's."

"So you've interviewed everyone who works here, then?" Jed said.

"Of course."

"And?"

Jerry shrugged.

"Whoever's taking the women has seen them here, then followed them from here at some point to figure out the pattern of their movements," Jed murmured.

Jerry leaned closer to Jed. "Angela McDuff was last seen leaving the Straight-N-Hair-O Salon, right across the parking lot over there."

Jed looked out the large plate-glass window. The parking lot was huge. There were plenty of lights, but also plenty of areas in deep shadow.

Jerry pointed. "Her car was found right over there. She left the salon with a big smile on her face. And then she was gone. No one saw anything."

"There must have been a fair amount of people in the mall and in the parking lot," Jed mused aloud, studying the layout.

"Maybe," Mal said. "But no one saw anything. She disappeared, and it had to be with someone she either trusted or knew, because she didn't scream or someone would have noticed. She knew there was a serial killer out there targeting women just like her, and she still got into a car and didn't even scream."

"What the hell does that give you that we haven't had from the beginning?" Jed demanded. "The women are being taken by someone they trust."

"Or someone they know," Jerry added.

"Either way, someone they see as nonthreatening," Jed said.

What the hell was his own reasoning? Jed asked himself. Adam Harrison claimed — based on the appearance of a ghost, for God's sake — that the killer had been in Christina's house. The first night . . . the night of the Ouija board. And at the séance, too? That meant Mike, Dan or Tony Lowell. Or himself. Or one of the women.

"What am I doing here tonight? Why did you call me out?" he asked the two cops.

"Fair warning," Mal O'Donnell told him gravely. "We feel we have a real suspect."

"Mike McDuff," Jerry said.

"You interviewed him tonight, right?" Jed inquired.

"I chatted with him at his home," Jerry admitted.

"Why didn't you just drag him in?"

"Because his ex-wife is out there somewhere. Hopefully, at this moment, still alive. We're going to be watching him. So if you know anything . . ."

Jed swore with disgust and slid off his bar stool. "You really think I wouldn't tell you if I knew who a killer was?"

"Good night, Jed," Jerry said.

"Yeah. Good night." Assholes! he added silently as he left.

And yet . . . hadn't he been thinking in

nearly the same direction? And he hadn't said a word.

And as for Beau Kidd . . . Did he just want the man to be proven innocent simply because the family deserved some peace?

Adam, Genevieve and Thor had gone to bed. The house was quiet. Christina stood at her bedroom window, looking out at the lawn.

She felt numb. She believed in Adam Harrison, and in Genevieve, her good friend, and in Thor. She had even come to believe in the ghost of Beau Kidd. And now . . .

And now she was exhausted, but she waited, thinking — hoping — that Beau would certainly make an appearance.

But he didn't.

As she stood there, she saw Jed drive up and park. He didn't get out of the car, though, just sat in it and stared up at the house.

Had she been waiting for Beau? Or Jed?

She left the window, walked downstairs, opened the front door and waved him in.

"I thought you might be sleeping," he said when he got to the door.

A logical assumption, given that it was . . . what? Three or four in the morning?

"I'm awake."

"So I see."

"Are you coming in?"

He hesitated. "Yes. I wanted to . . ."

"To what?" There was a hard tone in her voice.

"I wanted to make sure you were all right," he said.

She nodded. "I was with both my cousins, your cousin, Adam, Genevieve and Thor. Just being with Thor, I should have been okay."

"Yeah," he acknowledged with a smile.

He followed her inside, and she hesitated for a long moment, then started up the stairs. She heard him lock the door, then heard his footsteps on the stairs behind her.

In her bedroom, she closed the door, hoping Beau wouldn't suddenly decide to make an appearance. Then she turned and stared at Jed. "Are you working for the cops now?" she asked him.

"No."

"But you left because a cop paged you, right? The one who interrogated Mike?"

"Mike wasn't actually interrogated." He told himself he wasn't lying, exactly. Mike hadn't been interrogated — yet. And he certainly couldn't break what he knew was a confidence and tell her that Mike was considered the chief suspect right now.

"But that cop went to his house —"

"Jerry — that cop — went to his house and asked him a few questions. That's all."

He spoke quietly, but the whole conversation still scared her. "Just because he was married to a missing woman, that does not make him guilty," she said.

"You're right. And they don't have anything on Mike. Anything at all."

"Because there's nothing to have on him."

"Christina, I don't know what to say to you. I don't believe in ghosts, including Beau Kidd's, but I also can't help but believe that I — like most of the rest of the world — made a mistake by believing he was guilty. But if I'm wrong and your house is haunted, if the ghost of Beau Kidd keeps visiting you, why the hell can't he help in his own defense?"

She stared at him. "He saw Grace Garcia. He hoped she might still be alive. He went to her, and she was dead but still warm, so he figured the killer had to be close. He drew his weapon because he heard noise from the shadows. He thought it was the killer. He never meant to shoot his partner. The evidence against Beau was just as ridiculous as anything the cops could trump up now against either of my cousins. It's grasping at straws. It's circumstantial. No court in America would convict a man because he was once married to one of the victims."

He turned away from her. "We should get some sleep," he said softly.

"You're staying?"

"Unless you're asking me to leave," he said, turning around to meet her eyes again.

Christina stood very still, staring back at him. "I never want you to leave. I guess you don't know, but when we were kids, I had such a thing for you. You were a hunk on the football field, and then you were a hunk in uniform. But you were also my friend's cousin, and then you got married. I knew some of what you were going through when Margaritte got sick, when she died. I guess we both knew what it's like to lose the people closest to us, to feel as if we're facing the world alone. Even to feel guilty, like why are we still here when they're not?"

"Christina . . ." he murmured uncomfortably.

"No, listen to me. What I'm trying to say is that I've always been crazy about you and I still am, but the thing is . . . I don't want you if you think I'm really crazy. I just wonder if maybe you don't want to believe in me. You don't want to believe in ghosts for the same reason I didn't want to myself.

It made me angry. If ghosts were real, why didn't my mom come see me? Why can't I tell my father one last time that I adored him, and I'm sorry about all those times I was a wise-ass and tried to sneak around! Why can't I say thanks to Gran for believing in me, or my grandfather, who I swear visited me when I was a kid, but I'll be damned if I've seen him anywhere since. You would want to believe in ghosts if you could see Margaritte one more time. But you'll probably never see her. Because she was good and loving, and she doesn't have anything to prove, to solve, by coming back. Beau is here because he wasn't guilty. He wasn't guilty then, and he isn't guilty now. And he needs people to know that."

He was staring at her, and she realized she'd said a hell of a lot more than she had intended to.

"Well," he murmured.

"Well?" She tried to make the word a challenge, tried not to let her voice falter, tried not to show that she was terrified she had scared him off by proving herself desperate and far crazier than even he had ever believed.

"That's a lot to think about," he said huskily.

"Yes, I know."

"Do I have to . . . respond to all of it tonight?"

She shook her head.

He walked on over to her and pulled her into his arms. "I . . ."

"Yes?"

"Um . . ."

"Oh, come on. You must have something to say."

"Maybe we all see and believe whatever we need to so we can get by, so we can go on," he told her.

She frowned, and he spoke quickly again. "But when I see you, I see life. I see the promise and hope of the future. I see someone who bounced back from every wicked curve thrown her way. I see someone beautiful, strong, full of character, talent . . . and sexy. Did I say sexy?" he murmured, his lips teasing her earlobe.

It wasn't exactly a declaration of undying loyalty.

"I see life," he whispered again. "I see the prayer that I might find a life again myself."

It was definitely enough.

She slipped her arms around his neck, returned his kiss and savored the pressure of his body against her own. She should have been exhausted, but adrenaline was racing through her.

It was like the first time. . . .

Clothes ended up strewn everywhere. Kisses were openmouthed, wet, hot, awkward, sweet and flaring with hunger. Hands were everywhere.

Each touch of his naked flesh was more erotic than the last. She couldn't believe it was possibly to love so hotly, burn so brightly. Ecstasy tore through her when his lips teased her navel, then tasted the flesh between her thighs, when his legs parted hers and he became like one with her, throbbing inside her. . . .

She knew it couldn't always be so hot, so frenzied. Sometimes it would be the way it was later, when they were both half asleep. When a slight touch stirred something in one of them, and a second touch stirred something in return . . .

Lazy, drowsy, they began to make love again, and for a while it was sweet and slow, before gaining momentum, becoming cataclysmic.

Darkness, she decided, was good.

Darkness meant not having to face the truth, but darkness meant trust, as well. Because in the darkness she did trust him. For the first time in her life, she was sorry when the first light of morning came to drive away the shadows.

But finally she slipped back into sleep, and in sleep there were dreams. Dreams of someone else, dreams in which *she* was someone else. Dreams that were far too real.

Tears streamed down her face.

She had been close, so close, to salvation.

Or maybe she hadn't been. Maybe she was just hallucinating before dying. Maybe, until the very second that the life was snuffed from her body, she would believe, would hope . . .

Her agony was growing. Wrists, ankles, back . . . the pain was constant.

She needed to stop crying. Even her tears hurt.

And they brought an ever greater pleasure to the fiend who savored her degradation and humiliation.

Actors, actresses, performers . . . they thought they were so great, according to her killer, so much better than everyone else.

But he . . . he knew better.

# 18

Christina was more than half asleep — mostly asleep, she decided somewhere deep in the recesses of her mind — when she heard a phone ringing. Then she heard Jed answer, heard him say that he would be along in a bit.

She opened one eye and looked at him questioningly as he flipped his cell closed.

"Katherine Kidd," he told her.

"Oh?"

"She just heard about Angela McDuff being missing. She called to say that she's sorry, that she wants me to come by. She wants me to bring Adam."

"Good idea," she said, trying to sound unconcerned.

"We can all go," he said.

"No, she only asked for you and Adam."

"Actually, I think she'd be happy if you came."

"Why?"

"I think she feels that she owes you some kind of apology."

"She doesn't."

At her side, he was silent for a minute. "She really thinks she saw her brother last night."

Christina rolled over on her back. "I've got it! Here's a theory for you. Beau really was a killer twelve years ago. Now he's back, and even though he's a ghost, he's killing again. He has Katherine doing all the dirty work for him. She lures the victims, then he holds them prisoner down in his grave. Later on, she dumps the bodies."

Jed didn't look at her. He rose and headed for the bathroom. A minute later she heard the shower come on.

He didn't seem to appreciate her sense of humor, she thought, or understand that it seemed every bit as ridiculous to her to think that her cousins could be involved.

He came out, dressed, and drying his hair with a towel. "You should come with me," he told her.

"No, thanks."

"I'll go see if Adam will join me."

"Maybe Thor will go, too. Then Genevieve and I can talk about old times, and dish about you and Thor," she said lightly, forcing a smile.

He paused by the bed and lifted her face. He kissed her lips. "Can a ghost kill?" he asked in all seriousness.

Was he mocking her? She couldn't tell. She hesitated, then said, "He . . . uh . . . makes a decent cup of coffee," she said.

"All right. I'll see you later." He started for the door, then turned back. "Wait for me?"

"All right."

"I'm serious. I mean —"

"You mean I shouldn't go anywhere — especially with my cousins — right?"

"There's no real evidence," he said.

"There's no evidence at all," she snapped in return. "Don't worry about me. I want to decorate the house for Halloween, so I think I'll get started on that. I'm a bit late, but, hey . . . there are still ten days left. And I can hunt up all the Thanksgiving stuff while I'm at it," she said. "Ana wanted to go out for Halloween," she said softly. "She wanted all of us to get dressed up like characters from the Wizard of Oz. She was going to be Toto."

"Sounds . . ."

"Sounds lame when you're talking about a serial killer in the same breath, huh?"

He didn't know what to say to that, so he just said goodbye and left.

She sat there in her bed and listened to his footsteps on the stairs, followed by voices. Adam's, Genevieve's, Thor's . . . Jed's. Even Killer woofed his two cents. Finally the front door opened and closed, and then she heard a car start up, drive away. And still she stayed in bed, listening to the sound of silence.

"Adam, do you think you can help Katherine in any way? Do you think maybe she knows something that can help clear Beau but doesn't realize it?" Jed asked, meeting the older man's eyes in the rearview mirror. Thor was next to him, too tall to fit comfortably in the back seat. Jed wasn't sure he was ever going to believe in ghosts, but he was intrigued by the efficacy of the power of suggestion and hypnosis. He was sure Adam knew that he didn't believe in the supernatural, but then again, from everything he'd gathered, Adam Harrison never actively tried to convince anyone that the spirit world existed.

"I don't know. I'm not sure how much she could know. She couldn't have been more than twelve or thirteen when the first set of murders took place. She believes in her brother, blindly, because she loved him. That doesn't mean she actually knows anything, even subconsciously."

When they arrived at the Kidd house, Katherine had obviously been waiting. She walked out to greet them, looking thin and tense, despite her jaunty earrings and her gypsy-style skirt.

"I've been watching the news. Lieutenant Tiggs is being interviewed. He just told the reporter that authorities think they're looking for a copycat killer!" She shook her head in dismay. "How can they say that?"

"They haven't found any reason to fault Larry Atkins for shooting your brother, Katherine," Jed explained. "I'm sure there's a lot of departmental pressure to keep the story as-is until they know something different. It's also smart. If you and I are right and we're still looking for the same killer, he's more likely to make a mistake if he doesn't realize they're on to him."

She nodded, but her attention was already focused on Adam. Her lips trembled suddenly. "I saw my brother last night," she said. "I really saw him."

"I believe you," Adam said quietly.

She hesitated. "Can you hypnotize me?"

"Probably."

"I can't help thinking . . . if I could only remember the night he died, I might think of something we don't know, something that would help."

"You can't bring your brother back, you know," Adam said gently.

"Nothing can bring my brother back. I know that. But I still think there's something from back then I need to remember."

"All right," Adam said after a minute. "Let's go in, shall we?"

"Here's one of the boxes of Thanksgiving decorations," Christina said, pleased. She and Genevieve were down in the basement, where it was cool and pleasant. Her grandmother had always marked boxes clearly, so it was easy enough to find what she was looking for.

Genevieve laughed. "What was your first clue? That great drawing of a turkey, maybe?" she said.

"Mike did that. Mike could always draw," Christina said.

"Okay . . . what else?" Gen asked.

"Why don't you grab that box over there, past the pool table? I think it has seasonal serving trays and things."

"I envy you your basement," Gen said as she was getting the box in question. "I wish I had one, but with the water table down in the Keys . . . no way."

Upstairs, as they set the boxes down,

Christina looked at Genevieve and burst into laughter.

"What?"

"You're covered in spiderwebs. I think I have to get down there and really sweep the place out."

"Spiderwebs?" Genevieve said, horrified.

"Not so jealous of my basement now, huh?"

"Maybe not," Gen laughed. "I don't want a bunch of spider bites. I'm going to run up and take a shower. I'll be back down in a few minutes."

"I think I'll run over and get Ana, see if she wants to help decorate."

Christina cut across Tony's lawn to reach Ana's house. At the door, she rang the bell and waited. No one answered, and she started to walk away. Ana often worked weekends, so there was nothing strange about her being gone. But then she thought she heard movement within.

"Ana?" she called.

Nothing.

She walked around the house. Ana must be home, she thought, because she could hear the television; it was on somewhere in the back of the house.

"Ana?" she shouted, walking toward the back, where she noticed Ana's car parked.

Her friend was clearly home, so why wasn't she answering the door or responding to her name?

Christina's heart suddenly started to pound too swiftly, but she gave herself a mental shake.

There was no reason to be afraid for Ana. She had dark hair, not red. Other than being a woman, she didn't resemble any of the murder victims in the least.

Heart racing, temples pounding, Christina raced to the back door. It wasn't exactly wide open, but it was ajar.

She was tempted to go in, then realized that if someone was in there, she had no way to fight, no way to save her friend, who had to be alive. Had to. She needed to get back to her own house as quickly as possible and call the police.

She raced back across Tony's lawn to her own house, wondering if she was being watched by a killer. She looked around, searching for signs, then stopped stock still, too stunned to keep moving.

Dan's car was there. Not parked in front of Ana's, but down the street, partially hidden by a large oak tree.

She felt ill.

Horrified.

No. It couldn't be.

She turned to run back to her own house. To reach a phone.

But as she stood there, the front door of Ana's house opened and Dan stepped out. He had a piece of paper in his hand, but he didn't look at it. He just stood there, then crumpled the paper in his fist.

Even from a distance, she could see the veins stand out in his arm.

She waited, momentarily frozen, as a chilly October breeze gusted past, drawing her hair across her throat.

As if in warning.

She realized that she was partially shielded from Dan's sight by a large bush, but if she wasn't careful, he would see her.

She looked around desperately and tried to figure out where to run for safety.

Ana's house?

Tony's?

Her own?

She made up her mind and ran.

Adam Harrison didn't dangle a pendant in front of Katherine's face and tell her she was getting sleepy. Instead he had her sit in a comfortable chair and close her eyes. Then, in a soothing voice, he described a scene so calm and peaceful that Jed nearly fell asleep himself.

At last Adam told Katherine that she was a child again, living at home, and though her brother was a cop, with a place of his own, he still came to the house a lot. Sometimes he took her and her friends to a movie or one of the local water parks.

"Beau is dating a girl named Grace Garcia, Katherine. Do you remember her?"

"Yes. She's from Ybor City. Her family are cigar makers. They came over from Cuba."

Katherine's voice had changed, Jed realized. She actually sounded as if she were thirteen, not the twenty-five he knew she was.

"So you knew Grace."

"Yes."

"And what did Beau say about her?"

"He liked her. But he was scared when he met her."

"Do you know where he met her?" Adam asked.

Katherine smiled. "I know. I know, because I was with him."

"And where was that?"

"The pub."

Jed felt his muscles go tense.

"What pub?"

"O'Reilly's pub. Lots of people went there. Beau said anybody who was really Irish always went there."

Anybody who was really Irish.

"I can see Beau now," she whispered.

Jed went still. He could have sworn he saw the man himself. Standing by his sister — staring straight at Jed.

And then the ghost began to speak, and Jed knew he must be losing his mind.

"That's it," Beau said. "It all makes sense. O'Reilly's. It's in the middle of everything."

"Oh, hell," Jed said. The damn ghost had seen what they all should have seen.

Still staring at Beau, Jed pulled out his phone and punched in Christina's number.

No answer.

He turned and, deserting the others without a thought, ran for the car.

"Jed!" Thor called after him.

"Call the police. Get Jerry Dwyer over to Christina's!" Jed shouted over his shoulder.

Then he was in his car and driving, a million thoughts filling his head.

O'Reilly's.

The one place all the victims had in common. All the Irish went there. Redheads.

It was between two highways. Two of the highways where the victims had been found. But before they were murdered, they were abducted and taken to a place where they were held until the killer was ready to strangle them.

They were lured into the killer's car. Lured . . . how? Suddenly it hit him.

A woman would trust another woman.

Christina had been close, so close. He remembered her mocking suggestion that Beau had come back to kill again and was using Katherine to lure his victims. It had been an intentionally ridiculous suggestion. Beau had never killed. And Katherine had never procured a victim.

The people had been the wrong part of the equation.

But the equation itself had been right on the money.

"You deserve so much more time than I can give you," her captor said.

Angie thought that she was going to vomit. She hadn't eaten, but the gag was choking her. Not to mention the terror that she was feeling.

She'd lost track of time.

Was this it? The end?

"Pretty, pretty, pretty," he said. "So pretty."

She could tell from the direction of his voice that he was standing above her, but he leaned down then, fingering her hair. She wanted to cry out. She wanted to protest.

He moved the blindfold, and finally she

could see his face. Her stomach lurched. Not because he was so ugly.

Because he was so fucking ordinary. Who would ever suspect . . . ?

And then . . . the woman! Who knew where she was now, but she was as bad as he was.

The light hurt her eyes, and she blinked. Everything hurt. She was lying on a cold linoleum floor after being tied to a chair.

And now . . .

Banging sounded from somewhere above, and he started suddenly. "What the hell was that?" he asked aloud, looking in the direction of the noise. He turned back to her and said, "Not a sound, you hear me? Not a sound."

Then he left her lying there and went to investigate.

Christina ducked onto the side porch. She knocked, but there was no answer, and she thought about calling out, hoping that Tony and Ilona were home and just hadn't heard the door, but she didn't want Dan to hear her.

She still couldn't believe she was sneaking around her neighbors' house, hiding from her own cousin. It was ridiculous; there had to be a logical explanation for what she'd seen, but meanwhile, she wasn't taking any chances.

The door was locked, so she went over to a window. It was open, and she breathed a sigh of relief. She pushed the screen in and crawled into the house.

It was almost dark inside. Tony had kept most of his hurricane shutters up, and where there weren't shutters on the windows, there were drapes.

It took her eyes a minute to grow accustomed to the dimness. Dust motes seemed to ride the air.

She started looking for a phone. She seemed to be in the dining room. A quick look around and then into the living room didn't turn up a phone.

Maybe in the kitchen.

She started to turn away, but something on the coffee table caught her attention. A newspaper clipping from the front page of today's paper reporting on the murders. The article was accompanied by a picture of Beau Kidd and a smaller shot of Angie McDuff.

As she stared at it, wondering why her neighbors would have decided to save something so unpleasant, she heard Killer barking madly, followed by a loud knocking on the front door and then footsteps moving toward it. She wasn't sure why she panicked, but she hurried to hide herself behind the couch.

She saw Tony, wrapped in a bathrobe, stride toward the front door and open it impatiently.

She couldn't see who was standing there, but then she heard his voice.

Dan's voice.

"Hey, Tony, I'm a little concerned. Have you seen my cousin? I went to her place, and her car's there, but she's not."

"No, sorry. Haven't seen her. I worked late last night, and I was just getting some sleep."

To Christina's dismay, Dan stepped into the house.

"You're a liar, Tony. Her dog is outside going insane. That dog knows where she is."

"She's not here, and I don't give a damn about a dog."

They were moving closer to her location.

"Tony . . ." Dan began.

Christina almost screamed. Almost gave herself away. She could see them so clearly now. Could see her cousin produce a wicked-looking knife.

"I want my cousin now, Tony," Dan snapped.

■ ■ ■ ■

Christina's house had never seemed so far away, even though Jed was driving as fast as he could.

Fast enough, as old Seamus McDuff would have said, to run over small children, ducks and nuns. He'd never really understood the point of that particular combination, Jed thought, but it was still a great old expression.

Where were the sirens? He should be hearing police sirens, dammit.

He tried Jerry's number. "What the hell is going on?" he demanded when Jerry picked up.

"Hell! I can't go busting into someone's house just on your say-so."

"There's just cause for a warrant."

"And I'm getting one! I've got cops almost there, and more ready to bring the warrant, okay?"

Jed hung up in frustration. The light in front of him was yellow. Then red.

He stepped on the gas.

Small children, ducks and nuns.

Christina turned, considering her options. There was a hall that led to the bedrooms, and there were stairs that led to the basement.

She heard Tony cry out hoarsely.

She stared at Dan's knife.

Then two men moved down the hall toward the bedrooms. She realized they had a clear line of sight toward the door, and the decision was made for her. She held dead still for a minute, then slipped from hiding and raced down to the basement. At the foot of the stairs, she was stunned to see a naked bulb swinging above a big service sink, illuminating a scene that made her blood run cold.

The basement was all one big room, the walls half hidden by piles of junk. Old boxes to the left. Golf bags. Racks that held old coats. Rain boots. The buildup of a lifetime. Everything more or less as it should have been. Except . . .

She clapped her hand over her mouth to keep from screaming. There was an old mattress in the middle of the floor, and a naked woman lying next to it, staring at her. She was gagged and hog-tied, a blindfold pulled down just below her eyes.

It was Angie McDuff.

Christina raced over to her and dropped to her knees. Angie was bound with scarves, not rope, but the bindings were tight and

Christina's fingers were as numb as her mind. She kept looking fearfully toward the stairs. What the hell was going on?

Dan had pulled out a knife, but Angie was being held captive in Tony's house.

And where was Ilona?

She couldn't untie the knots, but she saw a pair of garden shears hanging from a hook on the wall and ran over to grab them. In seconds she was back. Angie's eyes had gone huge, but she kept still while Christina sawed at the knots binding her wrists and ankles, then cut the gag from behind.

Angie tried to croak out words.

"No." Christina laid her fingers across the other woman's lips and shook her head wildly. She could hear someone on the stairs. They had to get out.

She stood and pulled Angie up. After being tied up, Angie couldn't stand and started to sag, so Christina practically dragged her over to the single window at the back of the basement, where the land outside sloped away.

She couldn't get it open.

She grabbed a golf club and smashed the glass completely out of the frame, then heaved Angie up to it and shoved her halfway through. "Get out," she commanded breathlessly. "Now."

Seemingly impervious to the shards of glass, Angie crawled through. Christina was pulling herself up to follow when she felt fingers grab her hair, and she was wrenched away from the window.

"Bitch!"

She spun around. Tony was there. He was still in his robe, but it was open, and he was naked beneath it. "Bitch!" he repeated as he drew his hand back. A second later his palm landed across her face with such force that she staggered back, seeing stars. She staggered and fell, landing on the mattress.

"Tony!" she gasped as he walked over to stand looking down at her.

"You guys always thought you were so talented, but who's the best actor now, huh?"

She couldn't believe it. He sounded cheerful, friendly.

"Tony, what did you do to Dan?"

He smiled. "Not half of what I'm going to do to you, sweetie."

"Don't be an idiot!" she cried, fighting the wave of sheer terror sweeping over her. "Someone will be here any minute. Genevieve is going to get out of the shower and realize I'm not there. She'll call the police, and they'll find you here."

He smiled, totally complacent.

"Someone always comes along, but I always win. Beau Kidd came along at just at the right time. I thought I was going to get caught dumping the body, but he got caught instead."

"But this time —"

"This time you're dead, Dan's dead, and I'm here to tell 'em how I tried to save you from your cousin."

Christina caught her breath. Someone coming up almost silently behind Tony.

Ilona. Thank God.

"Ilona, help! Help me, please. He can't hurt both of us at the same time. Run away and get help!"

Ilona just stood there.

And Tony started to laugh.

"I gotta tell you, it really helps to have a babe when you're not an adorable seventeen-year-old with his arm in a sling anymore. And Ilona, well, she's my babe, right, gorgeous?" he said, turning to Ilona.

"I'll get the scarves," Ilona said.

Christina stared at them disbelievingly. This couldn't be happening. "You won't make it this time," she said harshly. "You've forgotten something."

"What?" Tony asked.

"The naked woman wandering around outside," Christina said.

■ ■ ■ ■

There were cop cars in front of the house, and cops in the cop cars. But they weren't doing anything. They were just waiting, unable to go bursting into Tony Lowell's house without either probable cause or a warrant.

"No warrant yet?" Jed demanded, hopping from his vehicle.

A uniformed officer climbed out of his car, shaking his head.

Killer was there, Jed realized. The little Jack Russell was at the front door, going insane and throwing himself against it again and again. "Killer!" he shouted, and the dog paused, hearing his voice. He ran forward and picked up the little animal. By that time Genevieve had run over to him, so he thrust the dog into her arms. "Take him."

"I —"

"Get away from here," he told her.

There were tears in Genevieve's eyes. "They say they can't break in."

"I can."

He wasn't a cop. And he didn't give a damn if anyone sued him from here to eternity. But before he could break in the door, he gasped.

A filthy naked woman was staggering

around the side of the house toward him.

"There's your probable fucking cause!" Jed shouted.

But he wasn't waiting. The door was locked, so he rammed it with his shoulder, then swore. That was one solid door.

He rammed it again. Out of the corner of his eye, he saw one of the officers going to help Angie McDuff. At the moment he didn't give a fig how she happened to be where she was. Alive . . . He only cared about getting inside and finding Christina.

He rammed the door one more time, and the wood finally shattered and gave. He burst into the house. The shadows within were almost smothering after the afternoon light outside. He moved forward, and nearly tripped over something lying on the floor.

He hunkered down.

A body.

Fuck.

He felt for a pulse. He found a face, a throat. An Adam's apple.

As his eyes grew accustomed to the darkness, he began to see more clearly. It was Dan. With a knife sticking out of his rib cage.

The man could be dying, but Jed had to find out what he knew. Trying to watch out for a sudden attack, he leaned low and placed his ear against Dan's lips as Dan tried to speak.

"Tony . . . and . . ."

There was a sudden, shrill cry of fury, and someone came racing at him, brandishing a butcher knife and shrieking like a banshee.

Jed turned just in time and ducked, letting her fly right over him. Then he straddled her, reaching for the knife. As he fought to subdue her, he was stunned to hear a woman's voice behind him.

Angie, with a policeman's jacket over her shoulders, was shouting, "Get down to the basement! Tony has Christina down there."

Jed leapt up, and with another shriek, Ilona started to rise.

She didn't make it, because Angie kicked her. Hard.

Jed didn't wait to see more. He was already searching for the stairs to the basement.

Tony screamed in rage and leapt, landing on her with all his weight. She struggled to move, but she was pinned by his body, although at least the mattress had helped cushion her when he landed.

He immediately reached for her throat, but she was able to bring up a knee and slam him hard. When she rolled to escape, though, he twisted his fingers into her hair again and stopped her, so she sent a fist flying backward and caught him in the nose.

She hoped she'd broken it.

But he was strong, and he knew how to use his weight to control her, all the while working to get his fingers around her neck. She desperately searched the mattress and as much of the floor as she could reach, seeking the garden shears she'd used to free Angie.

She found them at last, curled her fingers around them and lifted them to strike.

But he sensed her intention. He let go of her neck and grabbed for her hand, trying to wrest the shears from her. In a moment he had them, and he raised them over his head . . .

She screamed, shrinking as far back against the mattress as she could.

But he didn't strike.

She saw something . . . someone . . . move in the shadows behind him.

Beau Kidd was behind him.

Before Tony had a chance to strike, Beau wrested the shears away. Tony let out a disbelieving roar of rage as they seemed to fly away from him on their own. If he had any sanity left, it wasn't apparent as he snarled like an enraged cougar and attacked her again, fingers stretched and grasping, intent on her throat.

This time he was stopped by a very real and visible force.

Jed had arrived.

His face looked like thunder, and he hefted Tony off her as if Tony weighed no more than a two-week-old kitten, then slammed him against the brick wall of the basement.

With Tony out of commission, Jed dropped to her side, smoothing back her hair, looking at her anxiously. She smiled, unable to speak, and he stood, reaching for her hands, ready to help her to her feet.

There was thunder on the stairs as a trio of cops came down, two uniforms and, behind them, Jerry Dwyer.

"Where the hell is Lowell?" Jerry demanded.

"There," Jed said, indicating the fallen man with a nod of his head.

"Bastard," Jerry breathed. "He'd damn sure better not get off on some technicality."

Later, Christina was unable to remember exactly what happened next, certainly no more accurately than anyone else.

Tony Lowell started to laugh and staggered to his feet.

No one else moved, no one drew a weapon, but the garden shears just picked themselves up and flew right across the basement, embedding themselves in Tony Lowell's chest.

With a look of absolute shock, he fell back against the bricks, a massive bloodstain spreading across his chest.

# 19

Christina opened her eyes.

Everything was as it should be.

The small porcelain clock — Gran's favorite, brought over from Ireland — sat on the mantel, the seconds ticking away softly.

It was dark. True dark. She'd actually forgotten to turn on the night-light before going to bed. Of course, she'd been just a bit involved when day gave way to night, and she hadn't thought about a light. Quite frankly, she hadn't thought about anything at all, other than the fact that she was alive, and not just alive, but alive and in the arms of the man she'd adored all her life, who seemed to feel the same way about her.

She frowned slightly when she realized she was alone in the bed. Where had he gone?

She sat up and saw that morning was coming. Already the darkness was growing diffuse, so she hugged her knees and watched the day arrive. And as the light filtered in, she saw the man she loved at last.

He was seated in the overstuffed chair, bare-chested but wearing jeans, and he was just watching her.

"Hey," she said in greeting.

"Hey yourself."

"Are you . . . all right?" she asked.

He nodded. "I . . . went out for a bit."

"Oh?"

He rose and walked over to the bed. "I was at the cemetery."

"Oh?" she said again.

"I went to make my peace with Beau Kidd," he told her.

It had been a week since the events next door had nearly cost her her life. It had been a mind-numbing experience for her, and she left it to better-trained minds than her own to make sense of everything that had happened. They'd already pieced together some of the story.

Tony had started killing young, apparently luring his victims by pretending that he was hurt and needed help. They'd discovered that he had done a lot of traveling after Beau Kidd had been killed for his crimes. The time he had spent in various places coincided with a number of unsolved murders with similar signatures.

Then he had found Ilona. Someone, according to Angie, who was sicker and even more excited by cruelty than he was himself. Ilona — who at times seemed entirely rational and at others as insane as any Jill the Ripper — had filled in some of the pieces they were missing. Tony had never been a cop or a criminologist. He'd learned to wear gloves and how to hide his tracks because he'd watched television.

He'd looked like a normal guy, not a monster, Christina thought.

The guy next door.

Ilona had tried claiming to be battered, terrified, suffering from every syndrome out there, but Angie had quickly put the lie to that angle.

Mike had commented to Christina a few days after the horrors had come to an end, when they'd all gathered at O'Reilly's, that he had seen his ex-wife, and she'd been like a different person, grateful to be alive and certain that only Christina had saved her.

Dan, who had refused to stay in the hospital more than a night, had actually blushed when he'd explained to her why neither he nor Ana had opened the door. "We were . . . well, you know," he said, gulping his Guinness.

"I don't know," she said, puzzled.

447

"Oh, good God, are you all blind?" Ana exclaimed. "We were doing it, okay? We've had a thing for each other for years, and . . ."

She trailed off, and everyone stared at her for a long moment, then burst into laughter.

But that wasn't the only surprise that night. Apparently emboldened by Dan and Ana's confession, Mike spoke up and said, "I suppose that I ought to confess I have a date scheduled with a certain redhead," he told them.

"Who?" Dan demanded.

"Me," Katherine Kidd announced softly.

That led to more staring and more laughter, not to mention a lot of teasing, interrupted only by the arrival of their food.

Genevieve, Thor and Adam had left the next day. Christina had been sorry to see her friends go, but she was comforted by the knowledge that they'd made a date to go diving together the weekend after Halloween.

She doubted, however, that she would ever see Adam Harrison again, and she told him she was sorry about that when she slipped into his room to help him pack.

"You never know, Christina. You never know. Perhaps one day I'll call on you to help someone else."

"Gladly," she said as he smiled, and folded

his last shirt. "At least your time here wasn't wasted. I really did have a ghost."

"You've always had ghosts around you, Christie. You see them when you need to, and they find their way to you when they need you."

"But I haven't seen Beau since . . ."

"Since you were in Tony's basement."

"Right."

"Did you see the papers, though? He was vindicated. That was what he needed. I don't think he'll be back."

"Do you think that Katherine saw him, that she was able to say goodbye?"

"I do," he assured her.

After that she and Jed had been alone in the big old house, and now there he was, standing beside her bed, watching her.

"You went to Beau Kidd's grave?" she asked.

He smiled and sat down next to her. "I think he kept you alive until I got there, and I had to thank him."

She smiled and touched his face. "Did you see him?" she asked.

"I prayed for him," he said, and she didn't push it.

"Coffee's on," he told her, apparently eager to move away from a topic he still had trouble with.

"Thanks."

He left the room, and she showered, dressed and went downstairs to the kitchen, where she poured herself some coffee.

Suddenly she knew he was there, and she turned around. He was in his full dress uniform, looking very handsome. He felt so real when he took her into his arms, and so did the gentle kiss he planted on her forehead.

"Thank you," he told her.

"Thank you. You saved my life."

"You're welcome. But now it's time for you and Jed to make your own lives."

"I know. Does he?"

"I'm willing to bet he does. You should go to him now."

"I won't see you again, will I?"

"I don't think so. I think it's time for me to rest in peace, as they say."

She nodded and felt tears sting her eyes at the last touch of his hand. She fought them back and headed out to the porch, where she found Jed, his bare chest gleaming as he typed on his laptop beneath the rising sun. A large package lay on a glass-topped wrought-iron table next to him.

Definitely not an engagement ring, she thought, and smiled, arching her eyebrows in curiosity.

"It's for you," he said. "Open it."

She did, discovering a blue checkered dress and something furry. "What . . . ?"

He shrugged awkwardly. "Okay, I copped out on the lion, I admit, but Dan said he'd do it. You have to be Dorothy, though, because the only way Killer will stay in his basket is if you're the one carrying it."

"What?"

"We need to get together with friends, have fun . . . do normal things. Really live our lives. I thought we could start with Halloween."

"Oh," she breathed.

"How am I doing?" he asked her.

"Magnificently," she told him.

"Good. Then there's one more thing."

He pulled a small box out of his pocket.

Opened it.

Held it out to her.

It was a diamond ring. Beautiful. Marquis cut, in an antique setting.

She stared at him, unable to speak.

"May I?" he asked, his tone husky, a little unsure.

She nodded, offering him her left hand.

"I wish you'd say something," he murmured, dark eyes meeting hers.

She smiled, pushed the computer aside and sat on his lap, then found his lips.

At last, she broke away, breathless. "How am I doing?" she asked.

"Magnificently," he told her.

The employees of Thorndike Press hope you have enjoyed this Large Print book. All our Thorndike and Wheeler Large Print titles are designed for easy reading, and all our books are made to last. Other Thorndike Press Large Print books are available at your library, through selected bookstores, or directly from us.

For information about titles, please call:
(800) 223-1244

or visit our Web site at:
www.gale.com/thorndike
www.gale.com/wheeler

To share your comments, please write:
Publisher
Thorndike Press
295 Kennedy Memorial Drive
Waterville, ME 04901